ALSO BY BEN MARCUS

*The Age of Wire and String*

*Notable American Women*

*The Father Costume*

*The Anchor Book of New American Short Stories* (Editor)

*The Flame Alphabet*

# Leaving the Sea

# Leaving the Sea

Stories

Ben Marcus

 Alfred A. Knopf · New York · 2014

THIS IS A BORZOI BOOK
PUBLISHED BY ALFRED A. KNOPF

www.aaknopf.com

Knopf, Borzoi Books, and the colophon are registered trademarks of
Random House LLC.

Selected stories in this work were previously published in the following:
"On Not Growing Up" (Spring 2008) in *Conjunctions;* "Fear the Morning" as
"The Morning Tour" (Fall 2004) in *The Denver Quarterly;* "Watching Mysteries
with My Mother" (May 2012) in *Electric Literature;* "First Love" in *The Ex-File*
(Context Books, February 2000); "The Father Costume" as *The Father Costume*
(Artspace Books, May 2002); "Origins of the Family" as "Bones" (February
2001) in *Frieze;* "The Loyalty Protocol" (January 2013) in *Granta;* "I Can Say
Many Nice Things" (Summer 2013), "Against Attachment" as "Children Cover
Your Eyes" (February 2005) and "My Views on the Darkness" (June 2009) in
*Harper's;* "Rollingwood" (March 2011), "What Have You Done?" (August 2011),
and "The Dark Arts" as "Wouldn't You Like to Join Me?" (May 2013) in *The
New Yorker;* and "The Moors" (2009) and "Leaving the Sea" (September 2013)
in *Tin House.* "The Moors" subsequently published as *The Moors* (Madras Press,
December 2010).

Library of Congress Cataloging-in-Publication Data
Marcus, Ben, 1967–
[Short stories. Selections]
Leaving the sea : stories / Ben Marcus. —First edition.
pages ; cm.
"This is a Borzoi Book."
ISBN 978-0-307-37938-2
I. Title.
PS3563.A6375L43 2014    813'.54—dc23    2013004576

Jacket design by Peter Mendelsund

Manufactured in the United States of America

FIRST EDITION

For Heidi

# Contents

# Contents

# 6
## The Moors   

# What Have You Done?

When Paul's flight landed in Cleveland, they were waiting for him. They'd probably arrived early, set up camp right where passengers float off the escalators scanning for family. They must have huddled there watching the arrivals board, hoping in the backs of their minds, and the mushy front parts of their minds, too, *yearning with their entire minds,* that Paul would balk as he usually did and just not come home.

But this time he'd come, and he'd hoped to arrive alone, to be totally alone until the very last second. The plan was to wash up, to be one of those guys at the wall of sinks in the airport bathroom, soaping their underarms, changing shirts. Then he'd get a Starbucks, grab his bag, take a taxi out to the house. That way he could delay the face time with these people. Delay the body time, the time itself, *the time,* while he built up his nerve, or whatever strategy it was that you employed when bracing yourself for Cleveland. For the people of Cleveland. His people.

They had texted him, though, and now here they were in a lump, pressed so tightly together you could almost have buckshot the three of them down with a single pull. Not that he was a hunter. Dad, Alicia, and Rick. The whole sad gang, minus one. Paul considered walking up to them and holding out his wrists, as if they were going to cuff him and lead him away. *You have been sentenced to a week with your family!* But they wouldn't get the joke, and then, forever more, he'd be the one who had started it, after so many years away, the one who had triggered the difficulty yet again with his bullshit and games, and why did he need to queer

3

the thing before the thing had even begun, unless, gasp, he *wanted* to set fire to his whole life.

So he strode up as cheerfully as he could, but he must have overdone it, because his father looked stricken, as if Paul might be moving in for a hug. He could have gone ahead and hugged the man, to see if there was anything left between them, except that he was going to behave himself, or so he'd pledged, and his father seemed thin and old and scared. Scared of Paul, or scared of the airport and the crowds, where disturbingly beautiful people and flat-out genetically certified monsters swarmed together as if they belonged to the same species. Maybe that was what happened to a man's face after seventy: it grew helplessly honest, and today's honest feeling was shit-stoked fear, because someone's son had come home and his track record was, well, not the greatest. Paul understood, he understood, he understood, and he nodded and tried to smile, because they couldn't really nail him for that, and they followed him to the baggage claim.

In the car they didn't ask him about his trip and he didn't volunteer. His sister and Rick whispered and cuddled and seemed to try to inseminate each other facially in the backseat while his father steered the car onto the expressway. Alicia and Rick had their whole married lives to exchange fluids and language, but for some reason they'd needed to wait until Paul was there to demonstrate how clandestine and porno they were. They had big secrets—as securely employed adults very well might. Plus they wanted Paul to know that they were vibrantly glistening sexual human beings, even in their late thirties, when most people's genitals turn dark and small, like shrunken heads, and airport trip be damned, because they couldn't just turn off their desire at will.

Alone they probably hated each other, Paul thought. Masturbating in separate rooms, then reading in bed together on his-and-hers Kindles. Ignoring the middle-aged fumes steaming under the duvet. Just another marriage burning through its eleventh year.

What's the anniversary stone for eleven years of marriage? A pebble?

Paul sat and watched the outskirts of Cleveland bloom in his window, as if endlessly delayed construction projects held professional interest for him, a village of concrete foundations filled with sand, rebar poking through like the breathing tubes of men buried alive.

His father took the exit onto Monroe and the woozy hairpin up Cutler Road, which Paul had always loved, because of the way the light suddenly dumped down on you as you pulled above the tree line. The city stretched below them, the whole skyline changed since he'd last visited, ten years ago. The old stone banks—Sovereign, Shelby, Citizens—squatted in the shadow of new, bladelike towers that weren't half bad. They were tall and thin and black, hooked at their tops, and were either sheathed entirely in charcoal-tinted glass or simply windowless. Someone had actually hired real architects. Someone had decided not to rape the Cleveland skyline, and there must have been hell to pay.

It was still a good fifteen minutes to the house. The time for basic small talk had passed, so maybe it was okay to try big talk. Someone had to break the silence before they died of it, and Paul figured he might as well address the elephant in the room. Or the elephant in the car, or whatever.

"Mom couldn't come?"

"Oh, Paul, she wanted to," his father said, eyes dead on the road.

"She wanted to and you prevented her?" Paul said, laughing. "You held her down?"

"No, that's not it." His father frowned.

"Mom's resting, Paul," his sister said from the backseat.

"She's excited to see you," Rick added, in a voice too loud for the car. Big Rick the Righteous. The peacemaker. Telling folks what they want to hear. Making folks feel better since 1971.

"Thank you, Rick," Paul said, without turning around. "Now I know who to ask when I need to find out what my mother really feels."

Rick was right. Paul's mother was waiting in her robe when he came in the door, and she rushed up, hugged him, kissed him, smothering him with love while Paul stood there holding his bags.

"Oh, Paul!"

"Hi, Mom."

"Paul!" she cried again, grabbing his face, tilting back to see the whole huge mess of him.

She looked so small inside her robe.

"You shaved! You shaved it off!"

"I did," Paul said, stroking his chin, smirking.

He suddenly felt proud. This was his mother's great gift—to make him feel good about absurdly common things, like grooming.

"Oh, my goodness, you are so handsome."

His mother was crying a little. She couldn't hug him enough.

"Pauly!"

This was nice. This was really nice.

"Morton, do you see how handsome your son is? Do you see?"

She studied Paul again, and he found that he could meet his mother's eyes and it did not feel terrible. He smiled at her and meant it. He wanted to pick her up and run out in the street.

His mother would never, thank God, see him or his abused, overfed body for what it was. Even Andrea, at home, had to admit that Paul was not exactly handsome, per se, though when she was being affectionate she told him that he looked serious. He had a fair-minded face, she would say.

"Morton?" Paul's mother called again.

Concern flashed across her face as she realized that she'd been left alone with Paul. The panic of someone trapped in a cage with an animal. Zookeeper, let me out of here! Paul felt bad for her, his poor mom, stranded with him, when who knows what he might do?

Paul's father must have gone to the kitchen. Rick and Alicia had run upstairs to fuck, or whisper some more. Or whisper and fuck and hide while poor Mom dealt with Paul, as always. They'd done their time with Paul in the car, and now it was Mom's shift. This was how it would be for the whole visit, the three of them playing hot potato with fat Paul.

She fussed at Paul's coat zipper, then adjusted her robe, but there was nothing to fix and no one to groom and they'd already hugged. She was panicked. She wheeled and hurried into the kitchen, calling, "Come, come, you must be starving," then fled from sight.

Paul waited with his bags.

"Where do you want me?" he yelled. He needed a bathroom and he wanted to change his clothes. "Where am I, Mom? What room?"

His mother didn't answer; his father was gone—resting, probably. Everyone in his family was constantly needing to rest, but never from physical exertion. Always from the *other* kind of exertion. Resting from *him,* Paul the difficult, who latched on to your energy center with his little red mouth and sucked it dry. You'd think that, given how long he'd steered clear of Cleveland, they'd be rested by now.

Alicia appeared at the top of the staircase, wearing a long T-shirt. She was disheveled and flushed. That hadn't taken long.

"You're up here, Paul," she said, and he followed her, climbing the soft, carpeted stairs to his old bedroom.

.   .   .

His parents lacked Wi-Fi in the house, which figured, because old people hated the Internet. But they probably hated the Internet because they only had dial-up, and had to crawl through the *USA Today* Web site, which never fully loaded, with videos that never played, and click on e-mail attachments that took hours to download, so why even bother? The upshot was that Paul couldn't really get on to any of his sites. He had a few JPEGs buried deep on his hard drive in a folder called "old budgets." He brought the pictures up on the screen of his laptop. To be safe, he locked the door of his room, and then he settled in to try, sitting on the chair that his dad had painted red for him decades ago. He'd been back in his childhood house, what, all of ten minutes before his pants were at his ankles and his little person was out, lonely from the long flight, looking for friction. But the pictures on-screen reminded Paul, for no good reason, of people he knew. Civilians, instead of anonymous, Photoshopped nubiles. Civilians who had suddenly become naked, who were visibly uncomfortable in their poses, who seemed to want desperately to get dressed and head home to make pasta for someone. Paul's sad man was cold and small in his hand, and nothing was working.

He had tricks for situations like this, a way to will himself into something passing for readiness, at least enough to travel to the other side, because stopping halfway through was tough to live down. He could have used a splint, Popsicle-sticked the little fucker until it stood, but that was when Alicia knocked and he jumped up and pulled on his pants, figuring there was about a 32 percent chance she'd know what he'd been doing.

"So," she said, when he opened up, crossing her arms in the doorway. He guessed that this was the only cue he was going to get that they should have their little talk—brother and sister, adults now, believe it or not.

Alicia used to be forbidden to enter his room. In high school Paul had made a chart of those who couldn't come in: Mom, Dad, and Alicia, their names in large block letters, plus, in smaller letters, Nana and that whole crowd. Fucking Nana and her skeletal friends, geriatric narcs who kept wandering upstairs to spy. Posted on his door as if he hadn't also delivered the information verbally, numerous times, when admonitions were his preferred mode of rhetoric. What a man he'd once been, ordering everyone around. And they had obeyed! Never in his life would he command so much power again.

All signs of Paul were gone from the room now. Blush-colored paint reddened the walls, the punched-in holes spackled up and painted over. New floors—linoleum intended to look like wood—new furniture, sanitized air pumped in to cleanse the place of the errant son. It looked like a showroom for a home office dedicated to lace crafts and scrapbooking. It was hard not to realize what kind of kid his parents wished they'd had, and when he thought about that kind of kid it was tempting for Paul to want to track, hunt, and eat the little thing.

"How are you?" Alicia asked, and it seemed like she was really trying, for which bless her, because they had days to kill and might as well be friends.

They closed the door, sat on the bed. God, she looked old. Her face was slack and tired, and her eyes were muddy, as if she'd rubbed them all day and then poured red wine in them. But who was Paul to talk? He upsized his clothing almost every year and had moved on to the big-and-tall shop, which still carried some good brands. If his face remained smooth and babyish at forty, without the friendship-defeating beard he used to wear, with his shirt off he was shocking to behold, and he knew it. *Shocking* was maybe too strong a word. Actually, no, it was fitting. He had small, thin shoulders and from there his body spread hard and wide, into a belly that spilled around to his lower back. A second belly in the rear, which might be why he ate so much. Two mouths to feed.

Paul said that he was fine, and Alicia looked at him intently, asked if that was really true. Paul insisted that it was, it really was, but how was *she,* and how were things with Rick, and did they like Atlanta?

"We live in Charlotte," Alicia said, stiffening. "We moved three years ago."

Of course he knew that, had been told that, but it wasn't like Alicia's e-mail address had changed or anything, and you didn't send things to people by mail anymore.

Paul assessed his sister and couldn't really tell, because she wasn't exactly a slender woman. Maybe she was technically showing. Some women hide it well. So he asked. He knew they wanted one, and what harm was there in asking?

"No," she said, a bit too cheerfully, which was weird, given the thoroughly public way she and Rick had always demonstrated their urge for children of their own.

"It's getting late, though, right?" This he knew. This was information he was quite familiar with. The sun starts to set at forty.

"We're okay with it," Alicia said. "We really are."

Which was what you said when you weren't okay, so he would drop it. But to himself he couldn't quite drop it. Who was broken, his sister or Rick? Who was flawed and rotten on the inside? Or was it both of them, which was maybe what had attracted them to each other in the first place? Maybe there was a dating service for the barren. Sexually on fire, but fucking barren. Of course he knew how they'd met. He'd been there. In this very house. And Rick had been his friend. In high school they'd once almost gone camping together.

If Alicia's childlessness troubled her, he knew she wasn't going to show him. He was last on her list for candid disclosures, displays of vulnerability. *Human feeling.* Not for Paul. He was going to get a censored Alicia, and that was probably what he deserved.

"Can I ask," she said, "if you have someone?"

She seemed genuinely hopeful, so earnest that Paul overlooked the strangeness of the phrase "have someone." He admitted that there was someone, there was, and her name was Andrea, and we'll see, won't we? Isn't that all you can ever say, even thirty years into a marriage, not that he would know? We'll see how it goes?

"Oh, Paul!" Alicia cried. "Oh, that's wonderful!"

It was pretty wonderful, he admitted, really wonderful. It was hard not to smile and sit there feeling crazily lucky. Maybe this would be easier than he had thought.

But when Alicia pressed him for details, including the pre-cise occasion on which he had met this mysterious woman, the fucking GPS coordinates for this highly improbable event, not to mention a photo, a photo of the two of them together, it was clear that she didn't believe him, not even remotely.

Paul veered the conversation to their parents. The common, if chewed-up, ground they shared. How were they? et cetera.

"You know, Dad is Dad," Alicia said, shrugging. "He had me washing dishes the second we got to the house yesterday. I'm his little slave."

"You could say no, you know."

Alicia looked at him coldly. "No, Paul, *you* can say no."

"Yeah, I guess. But they don't even *ask* me. I don't *get* to say no."

"Ha-ha."

"And Mom?"

"She's doing *so* great. She's really amazing. She's such a fighter."

Paul squinted. What did this mean? Whom had she fought? Paul had never even seen his mom get mad. He tried to put the question in his face, because he felt odd asking—how could he not know if something had happened to his mother?—but Alicia moved on to the party, the stupid family reunion, which crouched like a nasty-faced animal on Paul's horizon.

The reunion was tomorrow night. Cousins and uncles and grandparents and all the people they had bribed to love them. The

whole family tree shaking its ass on the dance floor. A Berger family freak-out. Getting together to bury their faces in buffet pans
and lie about their achievements.

"What are you going to wear?" she asked.

Paul said that he might not go.

"What do you mean you might not go? Isn't that why you're
here? You can't not go—everyone's going to be there. What are
you going to do, stay home and beat off?"

So she knew.

"I don't know. We'll see."

"We'll see? Jesus, Paul, you are such an asshole."

There was a time when she'd have been afraid to say even
this, the obvious truth. Paul might have responded with heirloom
breakage, a dervish whirl through his sister's valuables. The truth
was he was too tired to break anything. You needed to be *in shape*.
So chalk that up to some improvement between them. By the
time they were eighty, there was no telling how evolved they'd be.

"I know," he admitted. "I'll probably go. I'll try to go."

"Goddamn. Don't do us any favors."


At dinner that night, the questions came, and Paul tried to suck
it up.

"How's business, Paul?" Rick boomed. Everyone else at the
table shrank, as if someone had thrown up and they didn't want
to get splashed. Probably Rick hadn't been at the family meeting
where they'd decided to go easy on Paul, lay off the hard stuff.
Like, uh, questions.

"Let's not set him off," his father had probably advised. "Let's
nobody get him going. It's not worth it."

His mom and Alicia must have nodded in agreement, and now
Rick had steered them off the plan, going for the jugular, the
crotch, the fat lower back.

"I don't know, Rick," Paul answered. "Business is fine. You mean world business? The stock market? Big question. I could talk all night, or we could gather around my calculator and do this thing numerically. Huddle up and go binary."

He wished for a moment that he belonged to the population of men who asked and answered questions like this, who securely knew that these questions were the gateway for nonsexual statistical intercourse between underachieving men.

Rick was confused, so Alicia jumped in.

"You know what he means, Paul. What do you do for work? What's your job?"

"I cash Dad's checks and spend the money on child sex laborers down at the shipyard."

His mother put her hand to her mouth.

Perhaps there was something about sitting at this table that had made him take the low road so hard and fast. The table, his room, that red chair, the house, the whole city of Cleveland. The blame could be shared.

"Paul," Alicia warned.

"Yeah, I know. Fine. I haven't taken Dad's money in years, Alicia, if you must know."

He stopped to eat and everyone else was quiet, looking at him. He'd promised himself that he'd try harder, and already he wasn't. He took a breath and looked at Rick, and Rick blinked, waiting.

"I work at a cabinet shop, Rick. We make custom kitchen cabinets. I operate the tenoning jig."

That wasn't so bad.

Rick, alone, burst out laughing, because cabinetmaking was one of the funniest things in the world, maybe, or because he was one retort behind and he wanted to be sure he got the joke this time. He looked around for company, but no one else was laughing.

"You do what?" he said.

Suddenly, Paul's father leaned in, intensely curious. Mr. Tuned Out had gotten his little button pushed. He stared at Paul, and Paul couldn't tell if he was excited or angry. "You're a carpenter?" he asked, in absolute wonder.

"Woodworker, actually, Dad, is what it's called. Fine joinery and that sort of thing. Huge difference. Carpenters, well, you know. I don't have to tell you."

Paul stopped himself. What a thing to say to a man who used to build houses, a carpenter before he became a big contractor. But fuck it. His dad had been retired forever. Didn't even work in his own shop anymore, probably. And there *was* a big difference between a woodworker and a carpenter. That wasn't his fault.

"Shit, though, Paul," Rick said. "Pretty good money in that, I bet, with so many people redoing their kitchens. Is it union?"

Paul admitted that it was, and Rick whistled with a show— slightly false, Paul felt—of admiration.

"Nice. Nice. Right? You could support a family with that, am I right? If you wanted to?"

Rick winked for everyone to see, and what a person to wink, with his failed seed. Why would he be turning the screws on Paul when he had nothing to show for himself?

"I do, actually, Rick," Paul whispered, looking down at his food. He couldn't believe he was telling them. "I do support a family."

He smiled and wanted to say more, to fill in the blanks, but they looked at him as if he were the strangest creature they'd ever seen. And maybe he was, but did that mean he couldn't have a family?

It was his mother, though, who did it. Such concern in her face, such pity, as if to say, Poor, poor Paul, who still needs to lie to us, and what did we ever do to create this man? He'd hardly begun to tell them, and yet she seemed so sorrowful looking at him like that. So he asked about dessert, and she brightened, jumped up, crowing from the kitchen about the best blackberry pie in the world. You had to try it. And who wanted ice cream, and, Alicia, could you help clear?

Paul's cell phone rang while they were watching television. He took the call outside, as if the reception were better in the yard. They were probably relieved that he'd left the house.

"Hey," Andrea said.

"Oh, my God, hey."

It was so good to hear her voice.

"So how is it?" she asked.

"It's okay. It's okay." He took some deep breaths. He just needed to talk to her and get grounded.

"You're lying." She laughed.

"No, no," Paul insisted. "It's fine, everyone's fine. I mean, it's weird to be here. The city is different."

"Yeah? Different how?"

She was so good. She really wanted to know. She wanted him to tell her everything, and he wanted to, and if he had more time he would, but who cared what was different about Cleveland? It didn't matter. He missed her is all and he told her that and she sounded happy.

"How's Jack?" he asked.

"I just put him down. He's such a sweetie. He actually *asked* to go to bed. He stood and waited by his crib for me to lift him in."

"Oh, my God," Paul said. "The little dude."

"I know."

"Give him a huge hug for me."

"Yeah, I will," Andrea said. "At five thirty in the morning when he wakes up I'll hug him and tell him Daddy misses him. Then I'll make coffee and wait for the sun to come up and wonder how the hell I'm going to get through the day."

"I'm so sorry. I'll make it up to you. I'll do the morning shift all next week."

"Oh, it doesn't matter, Paul."

They talked, but not about Cleveland, or the Berger psychosis, as he referred to it when he was home with her. They talked about little stuff that didn't matter, but soon Andrea's voice drifted off in a way that meant something was wrong, and of course he knew what it was, because it had been wrong for a while now, and it was his fault.

"And," he said, which is what he called her. When they were good, he called her "And How," which wasn't very funny, but as far as he could tell she liked it. Or at least she didn't seem to hate it.

"And, honey, I wish you were here with me."

She breathed into the phone, and Paul stood on his childhood lawn in Moreland Hills waiting for his wife to speak. Even when she wasn't speaking, even over the phone, he loved her desperately.

In cold tones she finally said, "I wish I were there, too, Paul. Me and Jack, to meet your family. Did you tell them?"

"I did," Paul said. "I mean I told my sister about you and then at dinner I did. I tried to."

"You tried to."

"I just got here. I landed a few hours ago. It's been intense. I'll tell them more. I want to. How could I not tell them about something so great?"

"Because maybe you don't think it's great? Because you're ashamed of us. Because you didn't tell them when you met me, and you didn't tell them when Jack was born, and now you still haven't told them."

"And."

"I'm sorry." She sighed. "I don't mean it. You know I don't."

They made up, saying the reparative things, but it went only so far. Andrea assured him that everything was forgiven, except when he hung up and went inside it didn't feel as if everything, or even anything, had been forgiven.

Inside, from the hallway, he watched his family watching TV, until his mother looked up and saw him. "Paul, come," she called. "Come sit." She opened her arms to him.


The Berger family reunion was being thrown in the conference room of the Holiday Inn downtown. Paul put on his nice shirt but left it untucked because his belly showed too much. There was a lot of grooming in the house, hectic and nervous, as if they were all going on dates.

When he couldn't stand it anymore, Paul went to wait in the car.

They parked downtown. The long black towers were lit up, so they did have windows after all. What amazed Paul was that the windows were round, like portholes on a ship. From a high floor in one of the towers, looking out your window, he imagined, would be like looking out from a cruise liner and seeing only air. Air and tiny buildings, tiny people below.

When they walked into the reunion, Billy Idol was on the stereo. The song "White Wedding."

"Seriously?" Paul said to Alicia, looking around at the few other Bergers who had also arrived on time. The very old Bergers, wearing woolen suits and standing in a circle, whom he wouldn't be talking to tonight. They held fishbowl-sized cocktails and soon it would be their bedtime.

"Seriously what, Paul?"

"Can we do something about the playlist?"

He tapped his foot, scanned the room. Would his cousin Carla be here? Not just a kissing cousin but a third-base cousin. Third base on more than a few occasions.

"Do whatever you want. There's the DJ. But please remember that people have been planning this party for months while you've been, what was it, down at the docks having sex with children. Right?"

It was so stupid to fight about it, and as the song thumped and shook the room with its black acoustics, hysterical and threatening, Paul had to admit that he'd really always liked it. Kind of totally loved the song, even though he had never admitted this to anyone. It was possibly a great song.

*It's a nice day for a . . . white wedding-uh.*

The Berger cousins arrived, and with them came their spit-polished children, ready to destroy the world and have someone clean up after them. Soon packs of kids ran wild, sweating and flushed in their fancy clothes, following some ancient order of clan logic that baffled Paul. Occasionally one of them would be yanked from the pack and forced to run a gauntlet of ogling older Bergers, who poked and kissed and hugged him until he broke free and returned to his friends, half-raped and traumatized.

The kids made the whole thing okay, Paul thought, because you could stand alone and watch them without being seen as a pathetic wallflower, unable to navigate a party and make conversation with your own miserable flesh and blood.

Paul set up shop at the drinks table, sucking down glass after glass of sparkling water. He was chewing on ice when he heard his name.

"No *way*," some enormous man was saying. "You are fucking *kidding* me! Paul, you bastard."

Through the fat and flesh and alcohol-swollen skin Paul saw Carl, his father's brother's son. Carla's brother, actually, which begged questions about naming strategy. Or, really, about basic mental competence.

"Dude!" Carl yelled. "I thought you'd written everyone off. What's *up*?" And he threw open his arms for a hug.

Paul leaned into Carl's heat and musk. He would hold his breath and do it, because maybe Carl had hugged Carla today and Paul could get a contact high.

A scrum of kids crashed into them, then tore off laughing. An intentional attack on the overweight forty-year-olds at the drinks table? Paul and Carl watched them go, hug deferred.

"You got some of those?" Paul asked.

"Oh, yeah," Carl said. "Afraid so."

They caught up, if that's what you called crunching twenty years into a reunion sound bite, and Paul found it easy to tell Carl about Andrea and little Jack. Carl blinked and maybe he was listening to Paul or maybe he didn't care. Soon Carl was scanning the room, looking behind Paul as he spoke, raising his chin now and then at someone going by. Little smirks of hello from Cousin Carl, working the room while standing still.

"It was hard going for a while there," Paul said, and Carl smiled and fist-pumped to someone across the room, doing a little bit of air guitar, then grabbed Paul by his shoulders.

"Dude, it was *amazing* to see you. I've got to go feed Louis or I'm going to catch serious hell." And then Carl was gone and Paul went to the back of the drinks line, which was now very long, to get himself another glass of water.

Paul danced. He danced with his mother, who was beautiful in an emerald-green dress. When his mother tired, halfway through the first song, he walked her to their table and grabbed Alicia, who looked okay, too, and they danced to Marvin Gaye and Def Leppard and Poison and then, with Rick joining them, to Blondie's "Heart of Glass."

It wasn't bad to dance. Dancing was better than not dancing. He was tired and sweaty and he felt good. Finally he collapsed at the family table, where his parents were already eating, along with some relatives he must have met before. They stared at Paul as if he were bleeding from the face.

"What do you say, Dad?" Paul shouted. "Are you going to dance?"

His father studied him. They all did.

"Paul here is doing quite well," his father said to everyone at the table. "He's become a professional woodworker, doing joinery at a high-end cabinet shop."

"It's not really a big deal," Paul mumbled.

"It is, though," his father said. "It takes years of training and a whole hell of a lot of skill to be a real woodworker."

"It's kind of automated now," Paul said quietly. "They have jigs."

"It's great that they hired you," some old man said, getting in his dig. Meaning *he'd* have never hired Paul.

"Used to be you had to cut twenty sets of dovetails to even get asked on a crew," his father said.

"Wow," Paul said.

"Twenty sets. By hand. Using a Jap saw."

"I could never do that," Paul admitted.

"No?" his father asked.

Was he leering at Paul? His own father?

"You're a mortise-and-tenon man. My word. Those are even harder, though, right? Makes dovetails look easy. Or do I have my information wrong?"

"I do those, but, like I said, there's a jig."

"So not by hand?"

"God, no, Dad. No way."

"I'd like to see one of these jugs sometime. You'll have to show me. Show me how the whole thing works now that everything's changed."

Paul looked at his father, and at his mother, who was chewing her dinner with the care of a professional taster, and he looked

at the other relatives around the table, who carried with them
a narrative of Paul that he could never, no matter what, revise.
A narrative that favored the outcome, a father with unexplained
bruises after an argument gone really wrong, rather than the supporting architecture that fucking deeply informs single events—
accidents!—that somehow get out of control. These people would
have to die for Paul to be free. Which was bullshit, he knew. It was
Paul who would have to die.

"I'd love to do that, Dad," Paul said.

His father regarded him across the dinner table with a face that
no longer showed any fear. *Who are you? Who are you, really?* his
father's face seemed to ask.

Paul excused himself to get another drink. He asked if he
could get anything for anyone while he was up, drinks or food, but
they were fine, they said, and waved him off.


From across the room, he saw his cousin Carla. She was circling a
table of kids like a waitress, and she was still utterly lovely. What a
girl she had been, and now she looked the same. Exactly the same.
He watched her, amazed, wondering which kids were hers, or if,
fuck, they all were, but he couldn't stand not saying hello right
away, so he ran up to her.

Carla beamed. Paul beamed. They said holy shit and hugged
tight. She was small in his arms, so little and warm against his
body, whereas Andrea was big, and taller than him, and incredible,
of course, in her own way. This wasn't knocking Andrea. He loved
her. But Carla was tiny! Oh, my God. It felt good to hold her.

Paul wanted to get her alone, but that was ridiculous. They
held hands down at their waists. Carla talked fast, smiling, radiant.
She said that things were great and she lived in the Twin Cities.
Just one of them! She assistant-nursed part-time at the children's
hospital and she had three kids and she'd finally gotten her mas-

ter's in something that Paul didn't make out. It was hard to hear. It was loud and horrible and dark in there, and it was so hot that everyone stank. Plus he wanted her to himself.

"Let's go have a cigarette," Paul suggested. "We can sit on the steps out front."

He didn't usually smoke, didn't even have cigarettes, but Carla followed.

Together they sat in front of the Holiday Inn, watching the valet wait for cars to pull up.

Carla laughed out of nowhere.

"What?" Paul said quietly. A voice inside him, very far away, was telling him, unpersuasively, not to seem so engrossed. It was unbecoming to fawn.

Carla covered her mouth, shook her head. A gesture of amused disbelief.

"I'll never forget something you said to me, Paul. I still remember it."

"What did I say?" He was proud in advance of this terribly clever thing he'd said as a kid. So clever that Carla had never forgotten it!

"You said, 'What is a cousin for if you can't put your finger in her vagina?'"

Paul closed his eyes. "I did not. Please tell me I didn't say that."

"Oh, you did." Carla laughed. "Several times."

He shook his head. "I am so sorry. What an asshole."

"You were bad!" she yelled, and she slapped his leg, laughing.

He nodded. "I was bad. I think I still am."

"Oh?"

Carla took this as flirtation rather than self-pity. Whatever Paul had once been—the rogue, troubled high schooler, doing stupid shit and justifying it with arcane philosophical arguments—he wasn't those things anymore. No way.

"You still coming to blows with Daddy Morton?"

"No."

Paul chuckled and shrugged it off. A real conversation was out of the question, and that was probably for the best.

"So," she said. "Wife, kids? Wait, no, let me guess. You're gay. You're gay! Is that what you mean by being bad? Oh, my God, you're not gay, are you? Jesus, Paul."

The old Paul, the Cleveland Paul, would have said, Should I finger you to disprove it? But tonight's Paul, new or old, disgusted with himself or just tired, tried to smile. He didn't have to uphold any principles in front of a shitty hotel with a woman he'd never see again. Though hand sex with a cousin occupied an unassailable place in the erotic universe—he'd stand and testify to that if he had to, and he felt sorry for anyone who hadn't tried it.

Paul looked up at the black tower with the shining portholes, the bright, glowing orbs rising into the sky like spotlights. He said how cool the tower was, how unusual. It was unlike any other building he'd seen.

Carla made a face and said, "Blech."

"What?"

"That's our hotel," she said.

"It's a *hotel*?"

"Yeah. We didn't want to stay there, but there were no rooms anywhere else. I guess they can't get any guests, so it's empty. I kind of hate it, to be honest. It's weird. But it's cheap, and that's good, because this trip cost us a fucking fortune. Holy smoke."

"Oh," Paul said.

They both looked at it again. If Andrea were here, she'd get it. Or maybe she wouldn't. How could he know?

"Well, I guess I should be heading inside," Carla said, and that was that, a big flameout.

"Yeah, back to the Bergers," Paul said.

The Bergers. His mother and father. Alicia. Rick, who wasn't a Berger in name but loved the Bergers more than the Bergers did. Paul's son, Jack, was a Berger, too, of course, one of the youngest, and so was Andrea, even though she hadn't changed her name. He could have been strolling through the reunion right now holding Jack and showing off Andrea to everyone. But the idea had been to test the waters. Even Andrea had agreed that Paul should visit Cleveland alone first. And when she'd said this he had been so relieved that he'd had to hide it from her. It wasn't that he didn't want his family to meet Andrea; it was that he didn't want her to see *him* here. Him with his family. That was the concern. The Paul of Cleveland, with his mean tone and low aims. She'd hate him forever.

Just then an ambulance pulled up and some paramedics tumbled out. They sprang the stretcher and pushed it right at Carla and Paul, stopping to hoist it over their heads and carry it up the steps, into the Holiday Inn.

Paul and Carla watched it go.

"You think that's for a Berger?" Paul cracked.

"It'd better not be," Carla said. "If Beaner choked I'm going to rip my husband's heart out."

She disappeared inside and Paul remained on the steps, thinking maybe he'd call home. Or maybe he'd cross the street to the black hotel and ride the elevator to the top so he could look through one of those portholes. Except what was so special about that building, anyway? He'd forgotten.

That night, before getting into bed, he set his alarm, packed his bags, scheduled a car service. It had been easy enough to change his flight, but all they'd had was one leaving at 4:00 a.m. It didn't really matter. He figured he'd sleep for two hours, then wait outside for the car, so that no one else would have to wake up. This way he'd skip the good-byes. With luck he'd be home by late morning. He could dismiss the sitter, take Jack to the park. He couldn't decide what would be better, leaving Andrea a voice mail or surprising her when she came home from work.

Rick walked into the bathroom while Paul was brushing his teeth, then backed out, apologizing. Through a foam of toothpaste Paul told him it was okay, waved him in. This would be their peaceful encounter, Rick sitting on the toilet lid waiting for Paul to spit and rinse.

"That was fun tonight," Paul said.

"It was so great." Rick shook his head. "And the toasts, oh my gosh. Amazing."

The toasts. Paul must have been outside.

"What your mom said. I mean, I choked up. That was just . . ."

Paul could only agree. What his mom said. Never in his life had he seen his mother make a toast.

"I love family," Rick said. "All of that family, together."

"Oh, hey, did someone get hurt tonight?" Paul asked.

Rick looked confused, as if this were one of Paul's trick questions.

"I saw a stretcher go into the hotel," Paul explained. "I thought maybe something happened."

"Hmm, no," Rick said. "I mean, not that I know of. But I was dancing it out pretty hard."

"Okay, that's good," Paul said. "Tell my sister good night."

"Will do, buddy. Good night yourself."


The two hours of sleep didn't happen. Paul lay awake and looked at the clock until eventually it was time to wait outside for the car. He crept downstairs with his bags, dropped them at the door.

He'd get a drink of water in the kitchen, maybe grab some fruit for the trip.

At the kitchen table, shuffling an amber colony of pill bottles, sat his mother. She didn't hear him come in, and he startled her.

She clutched her robe, looked past him into the dark hallway. Why was it that he still frightened her?

"Pauly, what are you doing?"

He mumbled, wishing he hadn't come in. His car would be here in a few minutes, and now he'd have to say good-bye.

His mother noticed his coat, figured it out, and he couldn't tell if she was disappointed or relieved. Why not both?

"I have to get back," he said. "I'm sorry."

"Paul, for what? Stay with us. Why do you have to go?"

She could not possibly want an answer. But maybe it was ugly of him to assume the worst. Maybe this was it. His sweet mother was sitting here asking. He would tell her.

"I'm a father, Mom. I'm married. We have a little boy. Jack. We call him Jackie. He's two, Mom. He's already two!"

His mother cried.

"Pauly, it's okay, honey. I don't know how else to tell you, but it's okay and we love you and we will always love you, and I wish you believed us. You are our little Paul, always."

She reached out to him across the table and he took her hands.

"But, Mom, it's true."

Had he really lied that much? Was his credibility gone forever?

"Sweetheart, I know it is. Of course it's true. I would love to meet him, I mean, to see him. What was his name, your boy?"

Oh, God, did he yell. He yelled the most awful things. He hit the table, stood up too fast. Something fell over, and now his mother truly wept, and she threw her arms up as if he were about to strike her. But why would he hit his own mother?

For years he would attempt to dismantle this moment. It was

among the most useless activities a mind could pursue, the revision of shit that had really fucking *happened,* yet somehow it became the activity his mind fell into the most.

He heard his name, barked by his father.

His dad was here now. Why not Alicia? Why not Rick? Get everyone together.

"Paul, you will not do this. Not to your mother."

His father trembled, ready for battle.

"I'm not, Dad. I'm not doing anything."

Paul backed away, giving his poor father courage.

"Go on now, Paul. Please go."

"Okay, I will. I'm sorry. I was telling Mom something. About my son."

"We believe you, Paul. We really do believe you. The wood-working, the family. We do."

Together they nodded up at him. *Tell him what he wants to hear and maybe he'll leave.* Were they even his family? Was this even his home? Or maybe they did believe him, and this was simply what it felt like to be believed. It felt wrong—it felt like nothing.

Paul determined that if anyone asked him, in the years to come, he'd say that if you've ever scared someone, even acciden-tally or as a joke, that person will flinch when he sees you. Even if you did it because you yourself were scared, because you were small-minded, or small-hearted, or because you had small aims and should never have been let out of your cage when your little life began. You might not notice it, but the people you have scared will flinch, on the inside. You will have to cross the street and give those people a wide berth. It is the most considerate thing to do. Just let them pass.

He left the house and rode the car service through the dark streets of Cleveland to the airport. He'd fly home, take the shuttle to his apartment. When he'd settled in, maybe he'd write his parents a letter. Put together a photo album, Xerox the marriage and the birth certificates. Would that suffice? He'd tie up a bundle and mail it to them. In their own time, they could examine the evidence of their son's new life. They could do it without him standing there. Paul would send proof and then he would wait. He'd be many miles away, where he could do no harm. At their leisure, they could examine the parts of their son that would not hurt them.

# I Can Say Many Nice Things

Fleming woke in the dark and his room felt loose, sloshing so badly he gripped the bed. From his window there was nothing but a hallway, and if he craned his neck, a blown lightbulb swung into view, dangling like a piece of spoiled fruit. The room pitched up and down and for a moment he thought he might be sick. The word *hallway* must have a nautical name. Why didn't they supply a glossary for this cruise? Probably they had, in the welcome packet he'd failed to read. A glossary. A history of the boat, which would be referred to as a ship. Sunny biographies of the captain and crew, who had always *dreamed* of this life. Lobotomized histories of the islands they'd visit. Who else had sailed this way. Famous suckwads from the past, slicing through this very water on wooden longships.

A welcome packet, the literary genre most likely to succeed in the new millennium. Why not read about a community you don't belong to, that doesn't actually exist, a captain and crew who are, in reality, if that isn't too much of a downer on your vacation, as indifferent to each other as the coworkers at an office or bank? Read doctored personal statements from underpaid crew members—because ocean life pays better than money!—who hate their lives but have been forced to buy into the mythology of working on a boat, not a goddamned ship, separated now from loved ones and friends, growing lonelier by the second, even while they wait on you and follow your every order.

And yet, when Fleming thought about it, this welcome packet, fucked up though it was, even though he hadn't read it, most certainly had more readers than he did. More people, for sure, read this welcome packet than had ever read any of his books or stories. This welcome packet commanded a bigger audience, had more draw, appealed to more people, and, the kicker, understood its cherished readers better than he ever would with his sober, sentimental inventions of domestic lives he'd never lived, unless that was too flattering a description of the literary product he willed onto the page with less and less conviction every time he sat down at his laptop.

Maybe he'd actually learn something about writing if he read the welcome packet. Maybe in his class he should instruct his students not to write short stories but to write welcome packets.

The room spun and he clutched the bed. It would be two straight weeks of this seesawing, punctuated by mind-raping workshop sessions in a conference room, and the occasional blitz of tropical sun if he could stand it. He had planned to get in shape for this trip, just to medicate a minor quadrant of his self-loathing apparatus, but when that hadn't happened, when instead he had fattened further, he bought new T-shirts, one size larger than last year. He looked okay in them. Not really that bad. He would just make sure not to take one off in public. Even in private, actually, he had cut down on the nudity. These days the shame had followed him indoors.

Would an oceanside room have made much difference? The brochure—which he *had* read, so he could fantasize in advance about where he would be sleeping—had called his room a gorgeous interior cabin, as if deep within a cruise ship was the fat, dripping heart you fought toward with your fork, where the treasure and sex and delicious food was hidden, and not just the exiled lodging for hired instructors on boats with a so-called educational component.

He was talking out loud in the darkness. He could do that because he had no wife with him in the bed, no baby in the next room. They stayed home, thank God, even though Erin wanted to come with him, wanted to bring the baby, made a case that it would be so *fun* for little Sylvie, even though little Sylvie had not shown an aptitude for fun, or, well, happiness in general. Don't blame the baby, though! Don't blame the baby, you monster! He wouldn't, if he could help it. The baby would be blameless. Cute little thing.

Anyway, if he'd brought them, and paid for them, because their passage was not included in the deal, they'd be going home in the hole, financially. *Don't let's go home in the hole,* he'd sung, trying to be funny. Erin didn't laugh, because that wasn't actually even the line from anything, and that wasn't how jokes worked. If he went on the cruise alone, he'd calmly argued, strictly to discharge the obligations of his employment, and not to have fun, absolutely not, they wouldn't be in the hole. Near it, maybe, clawing the surface of the world as their legs were sucked under, but not yet fully in the hole. Erin looked at him with her sharp face and her knife-chopped hair, bangs of razor perfection, chastising eyes and bones—the whole of Erin so fatally sharp that he was silently criticized by her appearance, criticized for more or less everything he'd ever done, even things from before he knew her, finally rebuked by the mere sight of her, and she didn't have to say a word. Now that was power. That was a serious wife. Somehow, or probably because of this, he was still stupidly, weakly in love with her, even if more and more it seemed that he wasn't fully sanctioned to touch her, a restriction instituted without any discussion he could remember. Perhaps in private she had feverishly quilted a force field around her body, stitching the damn thing by hand, and now it was finally complete. It didn't hurt to touch the force field, it just made him feel not wholly terrific. Erin seemed to know, anyway, that when they didn't have the fun she dreamed of it wouldn't be Sylvie's fault. You can't blame everything on a baby. Or maybe even anything.

Yet one day, he figured, years from now, sitting across from each other at a lawyer's office downtown, if that's even how these things worked, they would blame whatever came to mind. Babies, houses, jobs, each other, themselves. Or maybe not. Maybe they'd be fine. Hard to say.

So he was alone, with nothing much to account for except, of course, the morning's reading, the prep, the prep, the prep, and then the fucking horror of holding a class on this ship.

But he was so lucky! This was so great! How amazing to go on a *cruise*. His colleagues had stood around pretending to be jealous, and he'd held his ground pretending to deserve it, swallowing his dread. He had no choice in the matter. His student evaluations stank and he hadn't done much university service. *Service* being the word for sitting in rooms with profoundly powerless people exercising a kind of hypothetical problem-solving, as if anything they ever said, anywhere, would ever get implemented ever. Really ever. There was a Zen purity to the enterprise. Circular effort, in a vacuum, in outer space. He needed to engage in more of this, and somehow he needed to improve his student evaluations. Wouldn't this trip be a chance to collect a batch of raves from his little cruise-goers, who would surely be more susceptible to joy, with the sunbathing and cocktailing and theme dancing, and therefore be more likely to pass on that happiness to him?

Or are the happy even more protective of their mood, having finally arrived at bliss, clinging to it and in no way inclined to transfer such riches to the likes of him? Maybe so. But this time he had a strategy. Some old-fashioned hoo-ha from the school of please don't hate me. He would get his students to praise him by stroking their egos so hard, relentlessly stroking the shit out of every region of their egos, even the heretofore untouched areas of their egos they never knew they had, stroking them down sleek and smooth, that the students would curl up and mewl like stuffed animals with robotic voice boxes, purring and saying gaga and dada and yes, please, give me some more.

Not, you know, that he saw students as beasts or babies or stuffed animals or anything like that. These were real people! Like you and me! They fucking actually existed for real!

Up on deck nothing was happening. It was dark. The ocean, the sky, the ship. Sweet hell, the silence was nice. Whatever waves had gripped them earlier were gone. Everything was still. Not even the waiters were awake. Something was doing in the kitchen, though. A light burned under the door. Powdered eggs were getting mixed in water by a big, industrial paddle, maybe. The frozen planks of scored sausages, ridged like washboards, were getting knifed into singles.

He sat by the pool, leaning against the railing, because the deck chairs weren't out yet. The boat felt steadier now that he was outside. They'd left New York Harbor yesterday, so where were they now? He had no idea how fast they were going, or how you would begin to calculate their whereabouts, and it didn't really matter. They were on the Atlantic Ocean, which was nuts. They were fucking *at sea,* and in a few hours it would be time for the workshop. It was, actually, pretty great. Surrounded by dark space and dark water and nothing real. A fairly delicious portion of wind pumping off the sea at the perfect temperature. He wanted to thank someone for that and say, Nice going. You nailed it. Perfect use of wind in this setting. My compliments. Erin would, of course, really love it here, on her way to the islands, the occasional dirty coast threatening in the distance. Hot, salty air in the afternoon, stinging her sunburn. She'd be out on the deck early—not this early—swimming laps before the kids took over the pool with their savage games. The bashing, the mayhem, the vampire aggression. Even little Sylvie, if you could keep the fast-crawling gal on a leash so she wouldn't splash overboard and disappear forever, even Sylvie, his daughter, wrapped in so much flotation she'd look like a life raft, would very certainly, if he had only let her come, have had lots and lots and lots of fun on this boat.

He was supposed to have ten students but he only counted nine. Nine of them leaning forward on the conference table, staring at him, waiting. When he looked in his briefcase for the roster, the one document he actually needed, he couldn't find it.

Probably it was in there. He had to pee. The room lacked a clock. His chair was no good, and somehow he was sitting at the seam between two crooked tables, which called for awkward pedaling with his legs, and that didn't bode well. Already he'd sweated through his T-shirt into the button-down he thought he should wear. Everyone waited. They weren't dressed up. His glasses were smudged. The students wore bright shirts made of parachute material. Cruise clothes. Was this even the right class?

Fuck it. This would get worked out. He said hello and welcome, making the obligatory referential comment about how ridiculously *weird* it was to be studying writing on a cruise ship, of all places, which no one laughed or smiled at or even acknowledged facially. Perhaps they didn't know they were at sea. Was there a certain percentage of people at sea who lacked the knowledge that they were at sea?

Really, anyway, Fleming insisted to them, location shouldn't matter, because this was serious work they were doing, and this was a serious class, to be done anywhere. If possible, they should, you know, forget about the outside world when they were in here and focus on literature.

Their faces were grave and their eyes, already, seemed to be closing.

So, great. His first lesson to them was to ignore the outside world, which he'd just said had nothing to do with real literature. Splendid advice for writers. And it would be fairly easy to follow inside this airless kill box. This was going very well.

They went around the room and said their names, along with some other data he'd requested—favorite books and writers, past classes taken—which they surrendered with quiet hostility, as if they were corpses who had been fed some rejuvenating pulp that would allow them to release a few more sentences before dying again. You brought me back to life for *this*? their bodies seemed to say.

The first story they considered was by Timothy, who had an amazing beard. This didn't disguise the fact that he was no older than twenty-two. Even if it had been a white beard, even had he walked with a cane and maybe pushed along an IV bag on a gurney—like a child playing an old person in the theater— this boy would look young. Yet somehow he had raised a beard of Bunyan density, and the sight of it reproached anything facial Fleming, maybe thirty years the boy's senior, had ever attempted.

In Timothy's story an old man sat on a bed and thought back on his life, which featured some activities he regretted, which he would now tell us about in great length. The end.

A woman named Shay started the critique. She shrugged, said she had trouble believing it, and then paused, failing to elaborate.

That did rather sum things up, Fleming thought. Sort of a brave piece of thinking. Maybe true of almost everything created ever: paintings, books, houses, bridges, certain people. None of them are finally believable, when you really think about it. But, well, there they are. Whole schools of philosophy had fought with that one. Looking at Shay, and the confidence she projected, it was clear that belief was her holy grail and she probably rarely found it. She didn't believe *this,* she didn't believe *that,* it was all so unbelievable. Many years from now Shay would be dying somewhere nonspecific—Fleming's imagination couldn't piece together a good deathbed location—and she would declare that she couldn't believe it.

Did Shay want to suggest anything Timothy could do to make his story more believable? Fleming asked.

"No. I don't believe in meddling with other people's art. No way. And I don't want anyone to meddle with mine."

Well put, and good on you, he thought, but then *what the fuck are you doing here?*

He almost said, Okay, so what do other people think of that? The classic workshop whirlpool everyone might happily drown in for a while. Let's all go down together! But he stopped himself, because that would be like asking, Who else thinks that we have no purpose here? And even if he verged toward the affirmative himself, he'd better pull this ship back to dock pretty fast.

How come a ship metaphor, when actually on board a ship, seemed embarrassing, even when kept to himself, whereas on land it was perfectly acceptable?

Relying on experience, Fleming waited. It was about the only trick he had when he was in the gladiator pit. Ride out the silence. Stare the fuckers down. Someone else in the room was likely to find the pause unbearable before he did. And, sure enough, up stepped Timothy's defender, Rory. Cheerful, permissive, simple, friendly, handsome, healthy, well adjusted, insane: someone who should never have become a writer.

Rory thought the story was great. So great! That man, on that bed. Wow. Rory could just see and feel him there. The whole thing was *so real* and he wouldn't change a thing. This was perfect stuff. It almost could have been a movie! Rory smiled, and it was clear that no one had ever disagreed with him, ever. Or, more likely, people *had* disagreed with Rory but he wasn't aware of it. The bliss it must be to be Rory.

So the poles had been set, approval and dismissal of Timothy's story, and now it was Fleming's duty to string critical latticework between them, ricocheting between praise and criticism until everyone had gotten their money's worth. Later, Timothy could pick from this web of provocative suggestion as he got going with his revision.

Slowly the workshop roles emerged. There were the miniaturists, who wanted to look at a certain line on page 5 and wonder if maybe it shouldn't be airlifted earlier, which might seismically alter the story and bring the whole thing scarily to life. Mightn't it? There was the person who said that the story really began halfway down page 2. Apparently these people were everywhere, even on boats. The *your story starts here* people. What about saying that the story begins right after it ends, right here, on a page you haven't written yet, and then throw a balled-up piece of paper at the writer? There was a young woman named Britt who felt the story should be switched from first person to third. First person, to her, at least in *this* story, allowed confessional overtones that seemed to let too much self-pity creep into the story, which defeated a reader's ability to care for this man. If he feels sorry for himself, she explained, it makes it harder for us to. Not bad, Britt, Fleming thought, keeping his face neutral. A strange dose of reason on the high seas. But her comment was ignored and then there was the person who confessed that this story really wasn't his thing so it wasn't even fair for him to try to evaluate it. He'd better pass. He wanted to pose this response as an apology, like saying he was sorry, he didn't read French, so what could he do? I'm sorry, man, your shit isn't my thing.

Ah, one of those guys. The one from last semester had been

named Sean. This one, the cruise version, was Carl. Exempted from value exchanges because of his immensely idiosyncratic place in this world. Not really *his* world, just a world he is grumpily visiting. That's what Carl should have said: I'm sorry, I have to pass, I'm not actually a human being. Whatever Carl's real *thing* was would be a closely guarded secret until he turned in his own story, and everyone—or so it usually went—once they saw it, would strain to detect the slightest difference between Carl's writing and the work of the peers he'd spent so much effort distancing himself from.

Fleming jumped into the discussion and said that Timothy was brave to write about something so distant from his life, and for this he should be commended. Brave or silly, though, he wondered? Often it was hard to know the difference. To the students he said this was powerful material. A man who will die soon, wondering what went wrong in his life. And he's alone. His mistakes have left him alone. He's done this to himself, it's his fault, there's no one else to blame, and yet we somehow, *potentially,* feel for him. It's really tragic. Cheers, really, to Timothy, because this stuff is big. But could the story maybe, who knows, use a scene? Sometimes an actual scene carries feeling really well, at least if that's the goal here? Possibly not. Possibly not. Expository narrative can be really, important pause, interesting. Can anyone think of examples of this?

Of course they couldn't, and he panicked, because suddenly he couldn't, either, even though he'd once taught a whole class on the subject, "Tell Don't Show," one of those kill-the-father courses that resulted in a literary body count of zero. But no one seemed to care. They didn't want examples. The era of illustrating a point was long gone, which made teaching easier, if lonelier. Years ago Fleming would tackle a discussion to a halt, to recommend books, even while his students would look suddenly unplugged, drained of life, because Fleming hadn't just changed the subject, he'd made them forget their names and why they were there. He would describe the plots of these books, their styles, their techniques, why they were important, and no one ever made a note, even to write down an author's name. They would blink at him, waiting for his seizure to flare out. In his evaluations, Fleming would learn that students viewed these endorsements not as the kind of resource sharing that universities were meant to enable, but as digressions, beside the point. *Stalling,* one student called it. And so instead he talked and talked and talked about Timothy's story itself, devoting more language to it than it contained, a body of criticism outweighing a work that would never be published, trying to praise Timothy without alienating his classmates, most of whom sensed that the story was muted and unreal, an exercise. But Timothy couldn't be shut down here, Fleming knew. He needed to be encouraged. Get the young man on his back, lift up his shirt, and rub that fucking belly. And yet at the same time Timothy's classmates could not think their teacher was an idiot pushover who simply praised whatever he read, particularly writing like this, because then what was his praise worth if it ever actually came their way?

Fleming danced the tightrope, throwing coins to each side of the line. If Timothy did not actually purr out loud, at least he seemed content. Fleming's neutrality in the end must have only made him seem spineless. A politician of the classroom, pleasing precisely fucking no one.

There was time at the end for Timothy to ask questions, and he just thanked everyone. He really appreciated it, nodding through that wondrous beard, rubbing his hands together.

"No questions? That's it?" Fleming asked.

"I mean, yeah," said Timothy, sitting back, pleased. "I wrote that story in like two hours so I'm surprised anyone liked it at all."

.  .  .

Lunch was a buffet. Fleming loaded his plate with pasta, rolls, salad. What he wished was that he could take the food to his room. The walk would be long, the elevator ride conspicuous. He'd have to carry his plate through telescoping dining rooms, up carpeted stairs, then out across the sun-blasted pool deck and along the railing, where you had to practically tiptoe single file or else go overboard. By then his shame would be complete, his food cold. The package he was on didn't include room service, which meant eating above decks, and that risked eating with students. Or being seen eating alone by students. He wasn't sure which was worse.

They found him at the kiddie pool, on dessert. There was pretty good-looking pie here, so he'd gone with a piece of chocolate cream. The kiddie pool had a shaded canopy so he could eat without getting reamed by the sun, which was on a tear today. Large men his own age with very different lives stood shin-deep in the pool holding barrel-sized drinks, their shoulders boiling and blistering like the surface of a distant planet.

"Hey, Professor Fleming." There were maybe five of them, hovering awkwardly. Writers in the sun. Just asking to get shot.

"Hey, guys, sit." He welcomed them as if this were his own little porch.

They pulled up chairs and sat and looked at him, waiting again. He couldn't really eat chocolate pie under that kind of scrutiny. Jesus, he thought, did he have to keep entertaining these monsters, even though class was over? This was break time, which meant he needed to replenish his stores of fraudulence for the next round. How else could he summon his artillery of deceit without some pretty serious alone time? He needed a different body to wear around when he wasn't in the workshop. Or, at the very least, a T-shirt that read: I'M OFF THE CLOCK, BITCHES!

"So what do you think of class?" one of them asked. This

would be Franklin, the quiet one with translucent skin. Franklin was a thin, pink person who was either a genius or, well, not one. Chances weren't.

"I should ask you guys that, right?" Fleming tried to smile through a mouthful of chocolate.

He knew he shouldn't do this, but he couldn't help it. It was like asking Erin if she loved him, the conversational sugar he sought out like an addict. What was she going to say? It looked so desperate, so helpless. Maybe because it was. Class had hardly started and here he was groveling for student approval.

"Seriously," he said. "Does class seem okay?"

They burst out laughing and looked at one another. A merry laughter, he supposed, but still. Already with the knowing looks! They'd hardly even met and here they were being conspiratorial at the fucking kiddie pool.

"We never know when you're joking," explained Helen, as if they had discussed this issue at some length. Maybe Helen was the spokesperson.

He smiled. As in *when* did they not know? What was the phrase that was either funny or serious? Let's get out the transcript and take a goddamn look. He had yet to joke with them a single time that he could remember.

Here's a clue, he should have said: I haven't been genuinely funny in a very long time.

They were back at it in the afternoon. The story was a pastoral, with a nameless man walking through the landscape—the powerful, moody landscape—thinking. The writer, George, was older than the others. He had a large, sad face and he was bald. These men were everywhere. The cattle in our lives we hardly even see. Slowly they are herded into the dark shed to be killed. Fleming hoped he didn't look like George, but he suspected he looked far worse. Older, sadder, balder, one of the cattle who'd gotten out alive, survived the air gun to the head. A little bit soft of brain, but holding his own. To look like George would be lucky, probably. If he went home looking like George maybe Erin would be intrigued. She'd smile and throw her arms around him, yelling, "Sylvie, your handsome father is home!" The force field around Erin would lift. Love would surge through the house, and people in the surrounding neighborhood would fall to the floor in sympathetic orgasm. Just because Fleming was slightly less fat.

On the first page of his story George had written a note for the workshop:

"Hey everyone! I can't wait to meet you. Thanks so much in advance for reading my story. Your time means a lot to me. I'd love to hear what you think. Best, George."

"I don't know," said Franklin, cautiously. "It doesn't seem like anything happens."

"Can that be okay?" Fleming asked, eyeing the room for a taker. "Do things need to happen?"

Franklin blinked little crumbs from his eyes. He seemed to decide the question was not for him but for the group at large. He retreated in his chair, started to doodle. He must have been exhausted from that amazing opening comment.

Timothy jumped in. "It's landscape porn."

Everybody laughed, except George, who seemed bewildered. Was this a compliment?

"What's landscape porn, Timothy?" Fleming asked.

"It's just masturbatory images of mountains and lanes and creeks and desert and there's no drama to any of it. It's not a story," said the young bearded man who himself had not written a story.

"Like, what if I described a teacup for five pages? Would anyone care?"

More laughs. George was scribbling notes, as if this was the most helpful critique he'd ever had. But what could he possibly be writing? Fleming wondered. *Story is no better than description of a teacup?*

"Okay," said Fleming, looking at George across the table, determined *not* to mention the French New Novel, which by now had grown quite forgotten and old, and perhaps should be renamed the French Old Novel, or the French novel that recently died but that once mattered to a few people he knew, themselves also old. "But maybe instead of diagnosing what it is and isn't, let's try to talk about the experience of reading it, and maybe see if that discussion might be of use to George."

This the class didn't much want to do, and Fleming carried the weight of the thing. Frankly it was George's fault. He had written some passable description, at least sort of, and he'd made the whole thing pretty moody, but, it was true, *nothing happened.* Could this, Fleming ventured, be the descriptive intermission in a story that hasn't been written yet? Perhaps we are only looking at the thigh of the beast. We can say *nice thigh,* but beyond that we are in the dark. His metaphor was out of hand, running amok. Maybe they hadn't noticed.

Britt alone picked up on Fleming's desperation, while George transcribed the discussion ever more furiously, and she tried to help, reminding everyone of the inherent drama of landscapes and how charged they could be, how story resides in the land—had she really just said that?—and our best stories come from our relationship to nature.

"That's your opinion," snapped Shay, suddenly bothered.

Britt didn't flinch. "Right," she agreed, cheerfully. "Am I meant to be representing someone else's opinion?"

"Do what you want," said Shay, apparently not sure if Britt's response was an insult.

Carl made a cat sound, clawing the air, hissing.

"Oh, shit," said Rory, and he suddenly seemed at a loss with no friends around to high-five.

George raised his hand, usually taboo for the writer, but Fleming seized on it. Saved by the sad sack.

"This is really incredible," said George. "Thank you, everyone. I really appreciate it."

So this was George's shtick, thought Fleming. He was a professional thanker.

"I guess," said George, "I have one question for you all, given the remarks."

"Okay, shoot."

"If this was set in a city, instead of out west," asked George, hopefully, "do people think that would make it better?"


Britt followed Fleming out after class. He wanted to stand in the sunshine, look at the sea, maybe let the salty air purge his face from the worrisome things he'd said, and lash him for the helpful things he hadn't.

They were at the railing and the boat was really hauling ass. But when he didn't look at the water they suddenly seemed not to be moving. Behind them a terrific whooping arose from the pool, where kids had lined up at the slide, zooming down the bright chute into the water. How amazing if he could get an hour alone with that pool, guarded from spectators, streaking down the slide, exploding against the water, only to pull himself back up the ladder to do it again.

"Why'd you start with two men today?" Britt asked.

"What do you mean?" Dear God, what did she mean?

"The class is half women and you could have discussed one of each today, a man and a woman. Wouldn't that have been more fair?"

He had no answer. He'd given no thought to this.

"It'll balance out," he said, trying not to look at her.

Britt struck a puzzled look. "It seems to indicate clear bias on your part, to let two men go first, and I don't see how that won't disrupt the balance of the class going forward, if the women collectively feel that you do not think highly of their work. So much so that you've delayed its discussion in favor of the work of two men who hardly seem—*in my opinion*—talented enough to have gone first. I just wanted to pick your brain about that."

Very crafty, little Britt. Let's solve the problem of your bias together, you old, sexless fossil. I care about you and want to help. Now drink this poison and lie back while I chop at your expired genitalia. That's good. Even though you're going to jail, I still care for you.

Britt had pale hair, wore no makeup, and seemed so at ease with him it was disturbing, like one of those precocious children who is only friends with adults. Even Erin adopted a more formal tone than this, seemed a stranger to him sometimes when they spoke. He liked Britt. Clearly the feeling wasn't mutual.

"Look," he tried to explain, though he had no explanation. "Going first, as you call it, is no big deal. Certainly it's not a privilege. I'd say it sucks to go first, actually, because no one knows each other, we have no rapport, and we're not at our best, critically, yet. We haven't vibed as a group. People who go first are at a disadvantage, actually."

This sort of sounded half-believable to him as he said it.

Britt took this in, winching her eyebrows as she formulated her rebuttal. He braced himself.

"So today, if I'm hearing you correctly, you were *punishing* Timothy and George by making them go first? You deliberately put them at a disadvantage? Perhaps I misread your bias. Maybe it's men you have a problem with. I will say reverse discrimination is no less worrisome. It is, arguably, more hidden, more sinister."

"Sinister?" He sighed, starting to protest, but Britt bent over, laughing.

"Oh my *God,* I totally had you!" she shrieked. "You totally believed me! I wish you could see your face!"

Fleming had seen his own face enough times, in this life and the next one.

Britt threw herself into him, spasming with laughter, claiming she really had him going.

"What?" he said, quietly, trying to push her away, even though the contact felt good. "Which part was a joke?"

Britt grabbed his arm, tugging down on him while she recovered from her fit of laughter. "You are hilarious," she shouted. "Oh my God, you are so funny!"

She kept crashing into him as if she couldn't stand on her own. Was he meant to hold her up? People would be watching. This no longer felt good.

"You thought I was one of those insane feminists," she gasped. "You actually thought that!"

"Why wouldn't I?" he snapped. "Not insane. Maybe it was a reasonable point. Am I not supposed to believe what you say?"

Just then Helen found them, walking up with a sly smile on her face.

"Hey, you two," she said. "What are you guys up to?"

You two? *You two?* And here was Britt pulling on him and laughing as if they were together. He extricated himself, again, but Britt threw an arm around him and told Helen it was nothing, a silly joke, and they were just hanging out watching the ocean go by. Wasn't the ocean amazing?

Helen looked out at the water, frowned, and carefully agreed that it was. It seemed she was on the fence about it. This ocean, she told them, reminded her of a story, in fact, a very long story, slowly told, that got hung up in a complicated preamble about the first time she had told the story and who was there and why it had been a sort of hard story to tell. Apparently it still was. The old story about a story trick. An act of sheer violence to its audience. Fleming wanted to turn to dust.

He begged off, saying that he needed to go work, which wasn't true. He had no intention of doing any writing on this boat, but maybe there was something good on cable. Or something bad on cable. Or maybe the wall in his room was doing some interesting shit that he could stare at while he held his balls. Anyway it was clear that if he wanted to escape his students—yes, yes, he wanted to—about the only place he could do that was in his room. But as he left the pool area he heard Britt shouting his name. She caught up, breathless. It was just that she was curious what room he was in, on what level, because such-and-such was her room number, on the such-and-such level, you know, just in case, and was he going to be around at the bar later?

Fleming told Erin about it over the phone. This was the best way to defuse all prospects. Confess before it happens, then it won't happen.

"It was so awkward. And on the first day! Right on the ship railing where everyone could see us."

"What am I supposed to say?" asked Erin, sounding tired. "That it's cool a student is attracted to you? Good for you?"

"No, of course not. I think it's funny. I mean, me. She can't really be attracted to *me*."

Erin let that one go. Apparently she agreed.

"Okay," she said, in the classic way she ended her phone calls. As in, Okay, I've had enough, this is over.

"Well, I miss you," challenged Fleming. The phone was sweaty against his head. He wanted out of this conversation, too. But it seemed dimly important for them to exchange intimacy.

Nothing.

He broke. "You can't say one nice thing?"

"I can say many nice things."

Just not to *you,* being the implication.

"All right, well, I don't know what I did, but I'm sorry."

"How can you apologize if you don't know what you did?"

Here we go.

"I'm not sure how, Erin. But I apologize, I really do."

"We'll talk when you get back."

"Let's talk now."

"I really, really, really, really can't."

*Really?* he wanted to say. But he couldn't honestly blame her, because he didn't want to talk, either.

"I'll call you tomorrow," Fleming said. "I hope you feel better."

Fleming was asleep when someone knocked on his door. He tried to ignore it. What time was it, anyway? The knocking persisted. It was a quiet knock, which he found sort of queer, because there was nothing polite about being woken up in your *cabin.* Ever since he'd boarded this ship he'd been systematically chased into a corner as he searched for privacy. Now they'd found his corner, too, and he was left with—and here he modulated his interior voice into something menacing—*nowhere to hide.* He laughed out loud. Clichés like this were perfectly acceptable when you thought them to yourself, particularly in theatrical voices.

The knocking continued. The knock of someone who knew he was in here. The knock of someone who wasn't going away. The knock, no doubt, of a crazy if highly attractive person named Britt. A powerful, yet subtle knock. Tomorrow in class they should critique knocking styles. He hadn't told Britt his room number, but it wouldn't have been hard for her to figure out. Maybe when she saw him in his big-and-tall sleep shirt, a ring of hair puffing up from where his sleep mask was, maybe then her resolve to seduce a corpse would, as they say, *wane.*

It wasn't Britt. At the door stood one of the ship people, a young man in a strange white suit holding a clipboard. The purser, perhaps.

"Mr. Fleming?" he asked.

"Yes."

"Okay, good," and he checked off something on his pad. "Is there anyone else in there with you?"

Peering in, snooping, the little perv.

"No," said Fleming, hesitating. Why did he feel nervous if it was true? Oh, because maybe it *wasn't*? Because maybe Fleming had been up to some evening blood sport without knowing it, partitioning his overdeveloped psyche in order to, uh, tolerate the unbearable moral strain of his secret passions: abduction, captivity, taking his pleasures from people wearing hoods. How amazing if it were true. How dull that it wasn't. Fleming was fully, finally alone. If he had a secret life it was a complete secret.

"Do you want to come in and search?" Fleming offered. Come on in my cabin, smell my sleep.

The man looked at Fleming with alarm. "No, no, that's fine, thank you."

Fleming had behaved like a suspect when there obviously hadn't been a crime. Maybe he *wanted* to get arrested. Maybe that was the only way off this boat.

As the purser left, Fleming asked what this was about. You don't knock on someone's door in the middle of the night without explaining yourself.

"Just a head count," the man said.

"A head count."

"Don't worry. We've counted you. You're here. We've got you."

. . .

At breakfast the students were buzzing. Someone had gone overboard, they speculated. The ship's crew had been to their cabins.
They were trying to figure out who was missing. Perhaps, Fleming thought, this was the only good thing about the Midwest. You
couldn't go overboard. Except for the lakes. There were the lakes.
The virtues of the Midwest shrank back to zero again.

Franklin was chiding Carl, who sat there grinning, looking
otherwise like sheer hell, as if he hadn't slept. Come to think of it,
Carl had on the same outfit as yesterday.

"I saw you at the bar all covered in sex," teased Franklin. "How
many heads did they count in your cabin, you little faggot?"

Carl nodded proudly, gave a lazy thumbs-up.

Fleming must have looked pale, because Franklin grabbed
his arm.

"I can call him that because he's not one, and I am."

Sort of like if I called you a writer, Fleming thought. *Oh,
except that wasn't fair.* Be nice to these people, he reminded himself. And he knew that his assessment of others had never borne
out over the years, with the least likely of his students always,
always, enjoying the most success. In fact, he had better be nicer to
Franklin. Franklin would probably be hiring him someday.

Class went okay. Britt's story was disappointingly good. Talented
writers can also be sexy little nut jobs who play mind games on
boats. Her story described seven or eight different houses, which
the narrator had lived in from birth until her death as an old woman.
The writing was cold and beautiful, executed with severe control,
and Britt leaped through the years of her narrator's life, changing continents, changing marriages, until the narrator was alone
again, inside a house not so different from where she was born,

thousands of miles away. It was effortless, formally original, and Fleming was a little bit jealous.

Rory didn't get it. "I guess," he said, uncomfortable, as if he had never said an unkind thing to anyone in the world, "it might have been more interesting if it was the same character who lived in these houses, rather than so many different people of different ages in these different places. I couldn't keep track of them, and I wasn't sure what held them together."

Shay cracked up laughing.

"What?" said Rory, blushing.

"Nothing." Shay smiled, drunk on schadenfreude. "That's awesome."

"It's the same narrator," sneered Carl, who still looked debauched and exhausted from whatever he'd done last night. Not too tired to trounce the dumb blond man across the table, apparently.

Fleming felt that this called for a vote. "Did anyone else think there were many different narrators throughout the story?"

No one else raised a hand.

"Anyone?"


At lunch, arranging his papers, Fleming found the class roster. There were indeed supposed to be ten students in his class rather than the nine who had been showing up. The missing student's name was C. L. Levy. He e-mailed the university office from the ship's public computer terminal, which was embedded in a wall of foam-colored naval ornaments, as if long ago pirates stood here and checked their Facebook pages, yelling to the next pirate in line to wait his fucking turn.

A reply popped into his inbox a few minutes later, saying that all ten students were paid in full. No one had canceled at the last minute. No one had written in for a refund.

That was a lot of money to be paid in full, only to not board the ship, or to board the ship and not attend class. In the afternoon workshop session he asked his students if anyone knew of this C. L. Levy, but none of them did. "Man or woman?" asked Helen, thoughtfully, as if that might determine her answer. He didn't know. "Alive or dead?" she asked. And that he didn't know, either. They seemed to think that C. L. Levy was just another writer he was recommending to them. Professor Fleming was stalling again.

After dinner Fleming went to the front desk to see if C. L. Levy was on board. Of course they couldn't give out that information.

"Isn't there a passenger manifest?"

Yes, there was a passenger manifest, but it wasn't for passengers.

Back in his cabin, Fleming told Erin about it on the phone. The missing student, the possibility that someone had gone overboard last night, and the ensuing head count that woke him up.

"Huh," she said.

"Weird, right?"

"I guess. I mean it's not really that weird. It's normal for them to do a head count. Is that what you said was weird? Or was something else weird?"

Dear Jesus, what was going on between them?

He took on the overly patient tone she hated. Explained it slowly. Offered a short course on the uncanny for his wife. Theories and origins of strangeness. And then, when he was done, Erin had been proved right, again without speaking. None of it seemed particularly weird. When you put it that way.

"I feel concerned, that's all."

This surprised Erin. Had he never expressed concern before? "I don't know why you're telling *me*. If you were really worried, wouldn't you have done something about it instead of calling me?"

"Okay, I won't talk about this to you anymore, I promise."

"Oh, you're going to pout now?"

"Gosh, Erin, I still haven't stopped pouting from last time. But

I have more pouting saved up after this pouting is finished. Don't worry, I'll let you know when the new pouting starts."

She hung up.


On the way out of his room, Britt was waiting for him in the hallway, waving a black glove.

The little stalker had found his room.

"How come you're not writing?" he asked, as if he'd run into her in public somewhere. Some cheerful patter, instead of screaming his head off in fright.

"How come *you're* not, Professor?"

Did Fleming have this to look forward to every time he came and went? Could he get a new room? He'd sleep in the fucking lifeboat if he had to. He'd play it off cheerfully, using the deep reserves of cheer he stored in his infinitely sized happy place. He had cheer to goddamn spare. Maybe he'd get another room just to stash his extra cheer. How other people, Erin most of all, shook off moods, or, more impressively, pretended not to have them in the first place, was entirely beyond him. Except what wasn't beyond him? Was there anything?

"What's going on with the glove?" he said, like a person to whom this was really happening. "It's warm out."

"Well, I'm glad you asked."

Britt gave him a weird smile. There was food in her teeth. He didn't know her well enough to mention it. Thank God.

"This, sir, is a brand-new glove. I just took it from its package." Britt flopped the glove against her face—a gesture of, what, self-harm?—then added, blushing, almost too quiet to hear: "No one has been pleasured with it yet."

Fleming studied the glove, leaned in, and pretended to sniff it. "That you know of," he said, in his scientific voice.

Britt laughed. "You *are* funny. We've been debating this. I've had to *defend* you. They think you're *so* serious. But you're not! You, my friend, are catching on."

She swished the glove at his face and he leaned away from it.

"I *am* catching on, Britt. You might try that glove on someone else. Go throughout the longship, trying it on every young oarsman."

"But I don't want to go throughout the longship. I have traveled far, good sir. I am home now. I have *found* the owner of the glove."

She baby-pouted up at him.

"No thank you, Britt."

"You don't know what you're missing!"

"True," he said, walking off.

And neither did she. What Fleming was missing was a home and family and self that had never quite come to be, which was maybe why he was on a boat now with strangers, pitying himself. How could you miss something that hadn't happened? There was a certain feeling at home with Erin and Sylvie that sometimes, rarely, despite the prickly ways they fought, swept through them, for reasons he could not understand, little gusts of unexamined happiness when he and Erin smiled at each other for no reason and when they stretched out on the rug and played blocks with Sylvie and when Sylvie would roll over and suddenly yell "Pants!" kicking her naked legs in the air. A serious call for pants from his young daughter that made them laugh so hard. That's what he missed, but it stood alone. Had it really even happened that way? And if something like it happened again, who knows, Fleming or Erin or both of them would react differently, would look away from each other, embarrassed that they'd suddenly been caught living while poor Sylvie shrieked with joy under the cold gaze of her functionally dead parents.

.   .   .

From the house phone outside the restaurant Fleming dialed the ship's operator and asked to be connected to the room of C. L. Levy.

"I have no such passenger," said the operator.

"As of when?" asked Fleming.

"I'm sorry?"

"Did you ever have a passenger by that name?"

"You mean ever on the ship? That's not really something I can look up."

Oh, but you fucking can, you master of the database. "I mean up until yesterday. Was there a C. L. Levy yesterday and now there is not one today?"

"But we haven't put into port yet. No one has left the ship."

Fleming paused. "It does stretch the imagination," he admitted. He pictured C. L. Levy, just a shadow, standing on the ship's railing, tilting out of sight. They say you can't hear the splash. He bet to hell you could hear the splash. Something that awful could never be silent.

"Sir, I apologize, I'm not sure I can help you."

"Thank you," said Fleming. "I understand."

But he didn't, and he wouldn't, and he couldn't. The encounter joined too many others in the bottomless gunnysack he lugged around for situations that didn't, maybe never would, make sense. He'd become a bit of a collector, but was the material worth anything? Everything unbelievable in his whole life that had nevertheless still happened. It would need to be probed for secrets.

Out on deck it wasn't dark enough to hide. His students would be roaming the ship, drinking, waiting behind fake bushes so they could jump out at him when he walked by. The stars were close tonight. Not just exquisite pricks of light leaking through a tear in the fabric of some other world, to quote a writer he loved. These stars seemed to have fallen too low. They looked shapeless and dirty. Cast outs, perhaps, from the world of finer stars that knew enough to keep their distance. Or maybe the ship was climbing, lurching straight up out of the water like a slow rocket. He could close his eyes, feel the air rushing down on him, and believe that. Why was that so easy to believe, and it wasn't true, yet what was true was so finally impossible and unconvincing? The stars—close and dirty and shapeless and false, the sort a child might draw, and what did children even know?—were not credible. The sky, the whole night, his conversations. These things did not fucking ring *true* anymore, they needed *work*. What happened to him needed to be revised until he could find it believable. Or, *he* needed to be revised. Fleming. He needed to change himself so what was real did not seem so alien and wrong. Do you do that with tools, with your hands, with a bag over your head? Do you do that by standing on the ship's railing at night? Fleming would tuck himself over behind the pool, behind the games floor, where the sun umbrellas were rolled up, stacked, and chained. It was a kind of bed. It wasn't so bad. The dark night was a kind of room, and it would do better than where he'd been. This was the perfect place to miss out on the next head count, should it come. No one would find him here, at least until morning. They could never check off his name. Maybe that was what was called for, for the next head count to go around, for the ship and its rooms to be searched for its living, viable people—its human beings!—and to be finally, once and for all, counted out.

# The Dark Arts

On a dark winter morning at the Müllerhaus men's hostel, Julian Bledstein reached for his dopp kit. At home he could medicate himself blindfolded, but here, across the ocean, it wasn't so easy. The room stank, and more than one young man was snoring. The beds in the old gymnasium were singles, which hadn't kept certain of the guests from coupling when the lights went out. Sometimes Julian could hear them going at it, fornicating as if with silencers on. He studied the sounds when he couldn't sleep, picturing the worst: animals strapped to breathing machines, children smothered under blankets. In the morning he could never tell just who had been making love. The men dressed and left for the day, avoiding eye contact, mesmerized by the glow of their cell phones. The evidence of sex failed to show on their faces.

Julian held his breath and squeezed the syringe, draining untold dollars' worth of questionable medicine into the flesh of his thigh. He clipped a bag holding the last of his money to the metal underside of his bed. His father's hard-earned money. Not enough euros left. Not nearly enough. He'd have to make a call, poor mouth into the phone, until his father's wallet spit out more bills. Under his mattress he stashed his passport.

He left the hostel and took the stone path down to nothing good. This morning he was on his way, yet again, to meet Hayley's train. Sweet, sweet Hayley. She would fail to appear today, no doubt, as she had failed to appear every day for the past two weeks.

More and more it seemed that his lovely, explosively angry girl-friend, who only rarely seemed to loathe him, wouldn't be joining him in Germany. Even though they'd planned the trip for months, googling deep into Julian's unemployed afternoons back home, Hayley pinging him sexy links from work when she could. A food truck map, day treks along the Königsallee. First they'd destroy England and France, lay waste to the Old World, then drop into freaking Düsseldorf for the last, broken leg of the journey.

It was going to be a romantic medical tourist getaway, a young invalid and his lady friend sampling the experimental medicine of the Rhine. Hayley promised to break bitter pieces of Ger-man chocolate over his tongue as he stared at the ceiling and wished his life away. But they'd fought in France, and he'd come to Düsseldorf ahead of her. Now he waited not so hopefully, not so patiently—dragging himself between the hostel, the train station, and the Internet café, checking vainly for messages from Hayley—while seeking treatment up at the clinic on the hill.

*Treatment,* well, that might not have been the word. His was one of the doomed conditions. An allergy to his own blood, he not so scientifically thought of it. An allergy to himself, was more like it. His immune system was mistaken, fighting against the home team. Or his immune system knew *exactly* what it was doing. These days autoimmune diseases were the most sophisti-cated way to undermine yourself, to be your own worst enemy. In the States, with such pain and such striking blood work, they merely soaked you in opiates and watched the clock. They dug your hole and wrote your name in stone. Not so in Germany, a shining outpost on the medical frontier, where out of wisdom, or denial, or economic opportunity, they tried what was forbidden or unconscionable elsewhere. And for a fee they'd try it on you. *Massive doses of it.* You could bathe in its miracle waters. You could practically get stem-cell Jell-O shooters at the bar on Thursday nights. So long as, you know, you waived—yes, waived—it good-bye. Your rights, your family, your life.

It was not such a terrible trade. The clinic brandished a very fine needle on Julian's first day. It gleamed in the cold fluorescent light of the guinea pig room, and they sank it into his back. From his wheezing torso they drew blood and marrow, his deep, private syrup—boiled it, then spoon-fed it back to him until he sizzled, until he just about *glowed*. Of course the whole thing was more complicated than that, particularly the dark arts they conjured on his marrow once they'd smuggled it out of him. They spun it, cleaned it, damn near weaponized it, then sold it back to him for cash. Zero sum medicine, since he'd grown it himself, in what Hayley, digging into his ribs, had called "The Julian Farm." Except the sum was a good deal larger than zero. He might as well have eaten his own arm or sucked elixir through a straw punched into his heart.

Back home he'd tried it all and felt no different. The steroids, the nerve blocks, the premium plasma. He ate only green food until it ran down his legs. Then for a long time he tried nothing. He tried school, then tried dropping out. Now he was trying, in his midtwenties, his old room in his father's house, which Hayley always said *impressed* her. The courage it must have taken for him to decide to *really* live there with his father. Maybe. Through it all, though, he was mostly trying Hayley, as in really, really trying her, and he could see how very tired she'd been getting. Imagine that you're the girlfriend of a long, gray, twentysomething man who is ill in a way that no one understands. Or is he? It was Hayley who'd pushed for this trip, so Julian could finally have a shot at the new medical approach they'd read so much about, a possible breakthrough with rare autoimmune disorders.

In Germany they treated you with yourself. You were guilty of hiding your own cure inside of you, you selfish fuck. They salvaged and upgraded it, then returned it to you with a vicious needle while you trembled in your chair. After a few weeks you'd be better. Hmm. In his wellness fantasies, Julian always pictured himself scrubbed clean, nicely dressed, suddenly funny and charming. All better, in every goddamned way. Maybe even a name change. Of course throughout these treatments, as he'd discovered, your frowning doctors hedged and balked and shat caveats, until the promise of recovery was off the table, out of the room, nowhere near the building. But at least on the way toward oblivion you got to, you know, feed on yourself, suck your best parts free of promise. You got to try the finest of what medicine did not legally have to offer.

This morning he ducked the stares of shopkeepers, who guarded their doors against him, the pale American who spent no money. They must have come to recognize his sickly figure by now. What was left of it. God knows they'd gawked. To Julian it seemed they could see right through his clothes, and they were not amused. You'd need more than clothing to hide a body like his. You'd need a shovel, a tarp. Tarps were *designed* to cover men like him. *This is what you call a person? This is not a person.* Tombstone inscriptions like this just came to him. He had a certain gift for the form.

The shopkeepers—little men protected by bibs, youngsters with ghostly mustaches—stood and stared as Julian snuck down the street. Was this friendliness? Was it love? Julian could only walk faster, wincing until they released him from eye contact. Had anyone, he wondered, ever studied the biology of being seen? The ravaging, the way it literally burned when you fetched up in someone's sight line and they took aim at you with their minds? He wanted to summon a look of kindness and curiosity in return, a look that might forgive his miserly ways, his trespass on their ancient, superior city. But his face, as no one had ever needed to tell him, lacked the power to *convey*. He'd stopped trying to use it for silent communication, the semaphore you performed overseas, absent a shared language, to suggest you were not a murderer. Such facial language was for apes, or some mime troupe in Vermont. Mummenschanz people who emoted for a living. He ate with his face and spoke with it. Sometimes he hid it in his hands. That should have been enough.

It took him just one sucking sprint on a cigarette to reach the train station, a domed building in rust-colored stone. After a few mornings inside, braving the crush of travelers who reeked of chowder, he figured he didn't need to enter the dank space just to wait for Hayley. A granite ledge opposite the station offered a perfect view of the decamping passengers. Every morning locals poured from the building wrapped in hemp and straw. The fancier ones wore the waxed canvas coats of hunters. Occasionally an American or two spoiled the tasteful palette with vacation colors, releasing high-strung moods as if by megaphone: *I have arrived in your historic city and I am the happiest person you will ever know! Let me rub my joy on you!* They shot into the town square like clowns fired from a cannon, mugging their snack-smeared faces at some imagined camera, dreaming of paparazzi.

No one disliked American tourists more than their own kind. Or probably they did. Probably there was widespread competition in this arena, hostility toward the first world animal spreading its lucre abroad. Julian could picture the American tourist problem resolving in a civil war, a snake not eating its own tail, but maybe doing something nastier. Giving it head, its snake jaws popped out of joint to apple bob the shaft.

It was only upon leaving New Jersey, flying east toward higher civilization, that the demise of his decadent homeland seemed so overdue. But some higher power, or some covert, stateless, ideological power, kept forgetting to stick the pig. America kept charging the horizon, its lancet drawn, a milky substance leaking from the tip, refusing to perish. Now he had to look at these muffin-tops from home ready to speed-learn German culture, their sneakers swollen like parade floats as they bounced around outside the Hauptbanhof, trying to keep warm in the bitter German air.

Two weeks went by like this. Trains rolled in from Paris, Salzburg, Dresden, Berlin, failing each time to spit from their insides the girl Julian had fought with in Strasbourg. A disappointment of trains. He and Hayley, in fact, had fought in several cities in the Western Hemisphere on this trip, a road show of freeze-outs and recriminations. For the most part they warred silently, with so much stealth that sometimes Julian wasn't sure whether or not they were even quarreling. Even in bed, as she hobbyhorsed on top of him in pursuit of her sexual quota, with the focus of a child doing homework, grimacing when her time came, he wondered if she was mad at him. Their mating activity was hardly much sexier than a needle in the back. But at least he got to see her naked. Hayley could look so serious beneath her pixie haircut. She was too stubbornly self-contained, too confident, too okay with it all, which was decidedly not okay with Julian. A self needed to spill out sometimes, a body should show evidence of what the hell went on inside it. But Hayley had built a fire wall around her feelings and moods. There was no knowing her, and fuck you if you tried to pierce her privacy. You were a creep and an invader and you'd be rebuffed, then shamed. Hayley would fall quiet if Julian suddenly touched her hand, when all he wanted was to be touched back. That was the consolation prize available to the bottoms in a relationship, right? The mules, the dinguses, the shitbags? Touchbacks were supposed to be free. And she'd be clearly annoyed at the transparency of Julian's desire when out of nowhere he pounced. Poking her to be cute, which was not, he knew, *cute*. Was there a subcategory of shit-eating grin, depending on whose shit you ate? He'd gone to a different school of etiquette, the school of no shame, the school of I need *more* from you. He'd been fucking homeschooled in emotional helplessness, scoring off the charts. By touching Hayley and waiting for her response, Julian could pursue the kind of emotional research you didn't get to conduct in graduate school: dissertation-level inquiry into the limits of revulsion regarding people who ostensibly love each other. Which would always turn out to be a really stupid move. Hayley would snap and he'd feel his face burn, getting ready to be rubbed in something. She'd smell his need and it stank, it really, truly stank. Why did he always have to *confirm* a good thing, asking about it and asking about it, Hayley wanted to know? She told him to put his hellish thermometer away, to stop prodding her with his goddamned thermometer, obsessively trying to gauge how she felt so much that he kept *ruining the mood*.

Which proved that he loved Hayley. Somewhat. A lot. Awfully. God help him. First of all, she didn't leave him, even though his salient feature as a man was his leavability. He created occasions for departure in others. Tombstone. And until now Hayley had hung in there. Her loyalty alone was an aphrodisiac, even though his medication sometimes gave him the useless crotch of a mannequin. Hayley also believed in Julian's illness, found it true and real and even pretty damn interesting, a faith that had turned out to be rare. Julian's father and Hayley and the occasional stranger on the Internet, where the ill go in search of each other, humping each other's empathy slots. These were the believers. Even if, sometimes, maybe just a little bit, Julian did not really believe in the illness himself.

Hayley wasn't coming. It was pretty obvious. Julian sat shivering in the chill, listening for the 9:13, the 9:41, the 10:02. He was tired. In winter he sometimes caught a fever. His arms and back burned hot, as if a flame were being held to his skin. This was the dying of the nerves, an Internet confidante had explained. Of course his immune system wanted him dead. *It knew*. It was making the call on behalf of the wider society. It was taking him out. In the larger project of the universe, of which he must necessarily be kept in the dark, his own existence appeared to be an obstacle. So the species makes an adjustment. Tombstone. It redacts.

No one else waited outside today. No one else was stupid enough to sit and freeze on a granite ledge in middle Germany, watching the trains come in. People here knew where their loved ones were. A loved one's coordinates were simply available. Such was the nature, the very definition, of a loved one. People didn't need to risk exposure and illness waiting outside and wondering, letting their minds work up end-time scenarios. The vanished, dead loved one. The disloyal loved one, licking a stranger in another city. They did not need to dream up future sorrows for themselves, a life lived without the loved one. Slap an ankle bracelet on your loved one if you must, *must* know where they are at all times, but solve the problem, he told himself. Get it done. Track your fucking people or cut them loose.

After the first trains of the morning failed to produce her, Julian stood at a café for a scorched espresso, then returned to his lookout to wait. Later, when Hayley still hadn't come, he took shelter at the crepe stand, where they'd already cloaked the day's crepes in black jam. A death bread, for two euros. The thousand-year-old remains of an old man, now just a wedge of tar. This is you in the future, you poor, rotting thing.

He wasn't hungry. He was never hungry. But some dim sense of duty haunted him, his father's voice, gentle and girlish, suggesting that food might help. Food, food, food. Please, Julian, eat something, his father was always saying, as if noxious, soon to be spoiled material from the earth was going to do anything but poison him further. For Julian's whole life his father—small, kind, and so selfless Julian wondered if he had any needs of his own—stood at the stove and made pancakes for him, grilled cheese, oatmeal, eggs, burgers. Later, when the alternative care community had thrust nutritional strategies their way, when the Prednisone and Lyrica, the off-label intravenous immunoglobulin, and the chemotherapy worms had fattened and ruined and bleached and burned and defeated him, his father steamed bushels of kale. But Julian only ever picked at what polluted his plate, as if dissecting roadkill for shards of glass. His father, especially after his mother traveled underground to spend the rest of eternity inside a luxury coffin where no one could disturb her again, removed Julian's untouched food and scraped it into the trash. Only to try again a few hours later, smiling and kind.

So now he thought that eating something might be smart, but the tourist's gesture for plain crepe eluded him. Or the vendor enjoyed watching Julian pretend to scrape something foul from his hand. Scraping it and scraping it, souring his face to indicate his distaste for the jam, while the vendor grinned at him and winked, as if Julian were demonstrating something the two of them might do together later, in private. Why were these gestures always considered sexual, one hand doing something untoward to the other hand? Why wasn't it seen as semaphore of the beginning of the world, God the creator digging life from the soil and brushing it off, sending it without a headlamp into the darkness? He might finally consent to play charades, *maybe,* if instead of celebrities the pantomime could be restricted to events surrounding the big bang. Religious scenarios. The cold narrative of physics. Reenactments from the very, very beginning of time. Very fucking very. And on the eighth day, God made his creatures so lonely they wept. Picture that charade, he thought. The people of this world weeping into their hands.

Julian was early for his transfusion. This was probably good, because he had to navigate a ritual confusion at the clinic front desk. It concerned the very existence of Hayley.

"You do not come alone?" the receptionist quizzed him, as per fucking usual. She rose from her chair, which gassed, and peered behind him. He stepped aside so she could see the emptiness.

"I do."

As in, *regardez* how goddamn alone I am. See it once and for all.

There seemed to be no way to permanently establish the fact of his solitude. He shrugged at her and showed, via sneer, what he considered to be justified disgust. It made his face ache.

The receptionist failed to notice.

"You are not supposed to be coming alone," she insisted, waving the form.

It was true. He'd agreed to be accompanied—they didn't give a shit by whom—because the treatments left you weak, woozy. The treatments left you worse than that. Supine, prone, drooling, horny. Tombstone. Never mind how problematic that was, how much that suggested that *treatment* was the wrong word. The very, very wrong word. What should you call it when afterward you needed to be led from the premises? When, due to the obliterating immunosuppressants, which preceded the perfectly refreshing speedballs of marrow, the body lacks the power to remove itself? Probably they didn't care, at this first-class medical establishment, if the body was dumped in the Rhine. Just get it out of the clinic. Did they call it *the body*? Did they ask each other, peeking from behind their German curtain: has *the body* gone? It is all clear, *Ja*?

He wasn't racist, he was just tired. Anyway, he'd done fine most days without Hayley, weaving through the granite lobby after his treatment, baby stepping down the broad, white stairway overlooking town. On some days, well, at least once, he'd even felt strong and alert, with a fresh dose of doctored stem cells running through his blood.

Julian leaned in, showed his teeth. These were the gray teeth, he knew, of someone not threatening to bite you, but to crumble his mouth on your face, leaving bits of horrid ash.

"Would you like me to leave?" he hissed at her. "Because I will. Is that what you want?"

Ooh, boy. What a tremendous threat, to not follow through on his *own* treatment, which his father had already paid for! He really had her now. He'd backed her into a corner!

The toddler threatens the parent:

*If you don't give me what I want, I'll refuse to eat this candy!*

The receptionist sighed. She was a human being after all.

"This person exists for you?"

"Not just for me."

"And you say she is coming?" The receptionist struck a hopeful tone.

Oh, God, he thought, let's not be hopeful anymore. Where has it gotten us, really?

"No," Julian said. "I'd say she is not."


In the waiting room, once he'd been buzzed in, he shut his eyes against the wheezing shrieks of the ill. Or was that a computer, booting up like a Tasered horse? It was possible that no one within earshot was screaming, but shouldn't someone be screaming right now? Anyone? In places like this Julian imagined death throes around every corner, a gowned man twitching on the floor while a crowd of doctors leg-blocked your view.

When he'd first arrived, the clinic wasn't what he expected. The place lacked a porch with rocking chairs, where dignitaries convalesced deep in thought, staring out over a thundering gorge. Nurses did not come by with blankets to cover your lap. You did not take the clean, healing air, or hike up mossy trails into the mountains. Hadn't the Germans pretty much popularized convalescence, established it as the solution to life among functional people? What a huge disappointment this place was, and if it weren't for the illicit product, unavailable stateside, tombstone, he might as well have been home in New Jersey.

The Bensdorp Clinic seemed free of any kind of Bavarian mountain heritage. Convalescence here was presented as an essentially professional activity, like day-trading. The reception lounge was smartened up like a bank, the treatment rooms hidden in vaults. Photographs of athletic prowess, framed in metal, lined the hallways. Bodies performing impossible maneuvers, glistening, mostly nude. These images were hung, no doubt, to flatter the rumored celebrity clients, who must have had their own entrance, their own goddamn *wing,* because Julian never saw them. Rich and arthritic American athletes, willing to take injections of liquid horse penis or whatever into their stiff joints, able to afford exceedingly rare and hazardous attacks on their bodies. Sea sponge in the neck, cartilage-fortifying worms, administered via cream.

In the waiting room patients gazed at their phones or read or looked anywhere but at one another. A certain shame, along with the exhausted indifference of the dying, lingered over people going out of pocket on experimental health care, paying too much to keep feeling worse far from home. How humiliating to be seen like this, failing to rage, rage against the dying of the light. Failing even to fucking *complain*.

When his name was called, the technician led him to the semi-private room where patients reclined in blue vinyl chairs, watching television they could not understand. Here they pretended, or didn't, that their procedures were going to work. Even the hopeful tilted over their own graves, a boot at their back.

In transfusion chair number 3, Julian submitted to the usual pretreatment shenanigans. He confirmed his name and birth date, signing, yet again, a German-language consent form. A nurse-practitioner arrived to stick him for blood, filling a vial from his leg until it shined like a long, black bullet. She waved it at him and it foamed.

"You are okay," she said.

"I am?"

"Yes," she smirked. "I know this." She tapped her head. A universal sign of certainty. He needed to remember to tap his head when he spoke, no matter what. He should always tap his head.

Yesterday he'd had a scan and some other tests, so today he was relatively in the clear, time wise. Today's transfusion would only take an hour, the nurse told him, and then he was free. He'd have some daylight when he got out and maybe he'd wait at the train station. He didn't have to pay for his seat on the ledge, licking his wounds, pretending to watch for Hayley. And if he returned to the hostel too early, he'd have to hide under his sheets until the blinding overhead lights were shut off for the night.

"Ready?" asked the nurse, and he nodded to her. He wasn't.

She wheeled up the apparatus and switched it on. Inside its wire frame rested the clear bag sloshing with his new life, frothy and pink, and it produced a not-unpleasant hum.

He let his arm fall into the syringe basket and closed his eyes, waiting for the dreams that sometimes came on when the long needle, loaded with marrow, was raised over his body.


After his treatment, Julian's father assured him from the lobby pay phone that money was not a problem. He'd wire it over on his lunch break, which meant Julian could get it later tonight. But how was he feeling, his father wanted to know, and how were his side effects, and was he able to sleep? Because you don't get better if you don't sleep well—tombstone—that's just common sense, and of course the city must be tempting, the museums and the old opera house and the Latin food festival that opened last night, according to what his father had read online—what an exciting thing for Germany to be doing! his father said—but he shouldn't go crazy, even though the delights of Düsseldorf must be so tempting. The delights! Is his hotel clean? He should take care of himself, and money seriously was not a problem.

This, Julian knew, was his father's way of not saying that money *was* a problem, a very big problem, and that his father worried about it night and day, but never spoke of it. Never. Julian was simply allowed to lick money from his father's body whenever he wanted to and his father had pledged to never cry out in pain.

They would find a way, his father said. He'd send more than Julian asked for, because worrying about money was the last thing Julian needed right now. He needed to heal. Was he healing?

Julian glanced at his needle-kissed arm. He pictured the German blood product sluicing through his body, trouncing free radicals, convincing his white blood cells not to eat through bone.

He guessed that he was healing. Quite.

"How's Hayley?" his father asked. "She keeping you fed?"

Julian pictured Hayley prying his mouth open with her fist, pouring sauce down his throat.

"She's fine," Julian answered. No doubt this was true. Hayley was probably having a glass of wine, smoking, sitting at an outdoor café somewhere north of here. France, still? Berlin?

They'd spoken of Berlin in a vaguely flirty way, as if they might like each other more there.

"Is she with you now? Can you put her on?"

His father and Hayley and their whisper time. They were his armchair doctors, his medical curators, who earned their authority because they cared more about his health than he did. Julian was supposed to walk away after handing over the phone, to give them privacy, usually at Hayley's place when he hadn't come home for a while and his father was starting to worry. His caregivers needed to huddle and the patient was a nuisance.

"Oh, she went ahead to scout a good place for dinner. I'm starving."

"That's what I like to hear," his father said.

How about that, having something you like to hear. For Julian it would be, what, exactly? Maybe something Hayley-related. Hayley saying something un-Hayley-like:

*Hey, Jules, it's me. I miss you and I'm on my way.*

Would it be possible to hear that, or something like it, soon?

"Okay, Dad, well, thank you."

His father breathed into the phone. He could tell, all the way from Germany, that at home in New Jersey his father was okay, maybe even smiling. He could feel it. This was something nice, too. It was very nice. It would do.

Shouldn't he never, until the very second he died, stop thinking and thinking and thinking that he had a father who would do anything for him? What a crime to forget this. He was a criminal if he ever stopped thinking this for even a minute.

Julian thanked him again and tried very hard to sound sincere.

"I love you, honey," his father said, and they hung up.


Julian took a shortcut to Old Town, up along Adersstrasse, dipping around the Graf-Adolf-Platz. Germany was deadly cold this time of year, the trees slick with ice, the grass so scarce it seemed the whole country had been poured in cement. The weathered stone, the weathered people, even the language was weathered. All around him flowed the gravest-sounding speech. It was genius, Julian thought, to create a language from strangled cries, deathbed wheezing. There was perhaps no truer way to communicate. If he spoke German he could sound solemn and serious. His inanities would escalate into parable. Everything out of his mouth would be a eulogy. German was *the* end-time language, the only tongue worth speaking on the last days. If the sun shrank and went cold, the world falling dark, everyone should squirm in the soil intoning German phrases. To honor the final minutes of the world.

Instead, Julian was stuck with whiny, nasal English, in which every word was a spoiled complaint, a bit of pouting, like children's music sped up on the record player. In English, no matter what you said, you sounded like a coddled human mascot with a giant head asking to have his wiener petted. Because you were lonely. Because you were scared. And your wiener would feel so much better if someone petted it. How freakishly impolite, how shameful, to let these things be revealed by one's language. English, a whiner's tongue, a language for people who had to beg for sexual favors. At least overseas he didn't speak much English. He didn't speak much anything.

Julian ate no dinner. He found a wine bar and drank cautiously from a communal bottle of something red and sparkly, a kind of alcoholic soda. He sat in a sea of couches and every now and then some grinning celebrant poured a swallow into his glass and raised it vaguely at the others. A kind of listless cheers, offered to the room. Each time, Julian raised his own glass in response, nodding his head. Cheers indeed. When the bottle was empty, and he'd paid far more than he owed, he walked back down to the station and took his position on the ledge.

There was something fine about not looking out for Hayley tonight, a desire he'd pledged to destroy. He would take an evening off from feeling incomplete without her. Paid vacation. Nobody had to know that he wasn't pining for her full-time. He'd done this shit on his own so far, and if Hayley had been here he would have tried to scrape her, day and night, for pity and understanding. She would have been empty by now, empty and seething, but he would have kept scraping, using a spoon, digging deep into her sweetest parts until they were long gone, and still he'd scrape at her, maybe until he could see through to the other side. He'd been doing fine without Hayley and he would do fine and he fucking *was* fine. He sat and he froze and he shivered, and it was perfectly terrific. Somehow he'd ended up with nothing to be ashamed of. He didn't even know the train schedule tonight. A wonderful thing to be ignorant of. The trains could do what they liked. He had no good reason to be down at the station—what day was it anyway, and what time was it, and what was his name again?—and yet so far, since he'd arrived, this was his best night in Germany. He even felt sort of *healthy,* although it made him nervous to think so, and damned if he even knew what healthy meant anymore. He'd long ago lost track of how he was supposed to feel, and on days like this, nights like this, treatment or not, it was hard not to be worried, a little bit, that some of the reactionary, conservative doctors whom Hayley had railed against at home, the ones who'd diagnosed Julian in the merely normal range, might actually have been right. He was fine this whole time. He wasn't legitimately sick, at least when it came to conventional measurements.

This was just what it felt like, perhaps, to be alive.

Or so these doctors seemed to be saying.

Did other people, he wondered, feel this same way—listless, strange, anxious, dull, scared, you could pretty much go shopping from a list of adjectives—and did everyone else just clench their jaws and endure it? Suit up for the day and fight it out on the streets? Were people barely okay and yet not running, as he did, to the doctor, again and again, and was no one discussing, out of some deep personal bravery, what they were so quietly and politely enduring?

For hours, it seemed, no trains came into the station. The tracks were quiet and the whole city was perfectly still, as if perhaps there'd been some agreement, deep in the brain of the city, that the machines would shut down at this hour, the vehicles grounded. Cars and trains and buses. A scheduled hiatus of activity on this clear, cold evening in Düsseldorf.

Down at the station, commuters still occasionally pushed out through the tall glass doors, locals mostly, pulling dark suitcases across the ice. How they'd come to town without a train was a mystery, until he realized that striding across the square, faceless in the darkening evening, were simply people who had arrived from elsewhere hours ago and waited inside, where it was warm, for someone to come and get them. These were the arrivals. Arrivals wait. Not all of them get met. They'd been staring out at the square all night as the tiny, fuel-efficient cars ripped here and there without them. Finally they must have realized that their rides weren't coming, so they bundled up, took matters into their own hands, and walked out alone into the cold.

That night at the hostel, a visitor came to Julian's bed. Some uninvited man crept under his covers, *while he slept,* and Julian woke up—suddenly, rudely, confused. This man was *taking liberties.* Before much could happen—before disgrace and shame and, who knows, the implication that he was even remotely okay with this—he'd fled to the bathroom.

His heart was blasting, his sleep shirt wet and twisted. From the bathroom, looking back out into the gymnasium, the air thick with sleep, there was no sign of anything. No man, no sounds, just beds and bodies and darkness. As if the stranger had vanished. Hands had been on him while he slept, but when he thought about it he kept seeing himself lying there *reciprocating.* He couldn't piece it together. What in the goddamn hell had happened? He checked his body everywhere, testing. For evidence? Damages?

He'd been touched, *that* he was sure of. He'd been touched, it had happened, and now there was nothing to be done. He caught his breath, paced around the bathroom, splashed water on his face. He could shower, but he had no towel and it was too fucking cold, anyway. Someone had really been touching him. Now it was over.

He crouched in a bathroom stall, trying to think. Some scene in whatever he'd been dreaming—he'd been having some kind of *intense* dream, oh God—had allowed for this to happen, made him stay longer than he should have in bed. A bit too long, as if he'd enjoyed it. At first whatever was happening seemed perfectly okay, just unreal enough. He was holding on to someone. It wasn't really a sexual dream, per se. It was more like cuddling. He'd been dreaming of cuddling, and not with Hayley, but big deal. That's how it worked. You could date the whole world in your dreams and it was okay. You could, actually, date-*rape* the whole world in a dream, too. You could kill and clean up after yourself. Or not, you could leave evidence all over the world and get caught and go to jail forever and wake up crying. So fucking what? The point is, he was cuddling someone in his dream, and he was doing it in that squirming way, he had to admit, that he hoped might lead to more, and then he woke against a body and what were you supposed to do? There was *no way* not to respond. Anyone would. He was aroused, technically, but he certainly did have to pee. Usually after a pee that issue resolved. Usually. But he was aroused *before* the man had crawled into bed with him, so this was bullshit.

But was he? Oh, God. He wanted to cry foul.

In the morning he tried to explain the situation to the front desk. He spat his useless English and he gestured and he slammed his hand on the counter. They were only puzzled, behind the glass partition, by what he told them, as if to say: Someone tried to hold you and you fled? But why, sir?

He imagined someone calmly explaining: Don't you know, sir, that this is why people *stay* at Müllerhaus?

Instead he asked about other accommodations, and they offered him a private room, for twice the money. Then, no, they withdrew that offer, because it seemed those were taken. The only available beds were in the Turnhalle, where he was staying, and if he would like to change beds, he could do that, for a fee. Maybe a bed in another part of the room? Maybe that would be better for Sir?

He lurked outside the hostel, watching the men light their cigarettes and head into town. They filed out silently, squinting against the day. Which one of them had done this? He scanned their faces and wanted to challenge them to have a dream like that, so sweet and comforting, very nearly a wet dream of cuddling, and then to wake up against a body—the heat, the moisture, the smell—this kind of thing is ancient and overpowering and we're helpless before it—and not feel some slight rush of arousal. Really slight! You couldn't do it. It could have been a *dog* and he would have nuzzled into it, feeling something. He might have given in and not cared. So what? Because it wasn't really about the sexual parts of what lived and breathed right next to you. Man or woman or whatever. You were sort of aroused, if you got aroused, by something else. Not the person's *parts*.

Oh, it was pointless. He realized, standing out on Schützenstrasse, once the men were gone from Müllerhaus and the locals had zoomed into the homes and shops that would keep them during working hours, that he was exaggerating his indignation. The whole thing was a wash. He was worked up for nothing. No one was watching and he was putting on the fucking Ritz, for God's sake, as if there was something so terribly wrong with someone kissing him at night.

Was he really supposed to care at this late date who kissed

him? Wasn't it enough to be kissed by someone? What was the saying: beggars can't be complete and total losers?

At a restaurant called Altstadt he ate a full breakfast of cold cuts and long potatoes. It was early but he ordered a beer, and it tasted so good he ordered another. He smoked and had a coffee and sat looking out the window at a small, distant piece of the Rhine. Then, on his way out, he realized he was still hungry and sat down again for a piece of chocolate cake. He pointed at it through the display case and they brought over, instead, a cake that turned out to be citrus and ginger, which he devoured. He had another coffee and could have sat there all day but he had plans to make and if he didn't get moving, he was going to be late.

After his treatment that afternoon, Julian woke to a surprise.

"Your friend is here," said the nurse.

Friend, thought Julian. Not possible. The word made him picture animals. Pets he'd never had.

"Your friend waits there now," said the nurse, pointing up.

If he followed that direction, he'd leave the building and float through the sky before crashing to the ground. Head in this direction, sir, even if it takes you over a cliff. Waiting for you, maybe, will be someone who cares. Trust us.

Julian cleaned up in the patients' bathroom. On the way out a nurse flagged him over to the doctor's office, where his very own doctor, who he hadn't seen for days, was hanging film in a light box.

The doctor greeted Julian and waved him over to a stool.

Julian, instead, stepped up to the light box. The scan was mostly black, a portrait of darkness.

"Is this me?" Julian asked. "My head?"

The doctor nodded.

"We are looking at your scan while you are here this day."

Julian studied the doctor. He was trim and his skin glowed. Like most doctors, the fanciest ones, he seemed offensively healthy, as if he kept the real secret of vitality to himself. He would live forever and people would crumble and die around him. You were supposed to feel like death after seeing him, in terms of your complexion, your posture, your whole body. If necessary, this doctor would eat you to survive.

· "Well, we see something sometimes," the doctor was saying, "in this kind of white blood person. The scan is really. This is why we scan. And," the doctor continued, "we have this discovery to show you."

The doctor pointed his pen at a scuff in the film.

"A little discovery. You can discover it here."

The doctor traced the outline of nothing that was, perhaps, a shade lighter than the nothing around it.

Maybe Julian could see it. A very small shape, like a cloud. *In his brain.* Weather passing through. If you could draw a headache, this is what you would draw.

"This is a concern," said the doctor, looking at Julian hopefully.

"Okay," said Julian. "Where is it?"

That mattered, right? His entire personality could be explained by this cloud. A cluster of rogue cells pushes on a nerve, blocks a vessel supplying blood to the deep limbic system, and suddenly you're funny, witty, and charming. That's what a personality was, the blood thirst of rogue cells, a growth in the mind.

The doctor pointed again at the cloud.

"It is here," he said, more slowly.

"No, I mean in *me*. Where is this thing?"

Julian tapped his head. Maybe it wasn't in the brain itself.

"This is not our work."

"You didn't make this tumor?" Julian grinned.

"Well, tumor," the doctor said, as if there might be some doubt. "We see a shape, yes? We do not make that name for it. We do not work on this kind of area? We do not fix this."

"Does anyone?"

"Someone who must know what this is. Who treats the brain where you live."

Yes, someone must.

"We will be sending this scan to your American doctor. And we think that the stem cell transfusions is not, for now, a good idea. Until this."

The doctor pointed at the cloud and tried, again, to look stumped.

"This first. To understand this. Then, maybe."

Julian was impressed. The doctor had devised a pretty good tombstone.

*This first. To understand this. Then, maybe.*

Julian laughed.

"What is it?" asked the doctor. As in, thank God this moron is going into denial now. He's going to be one of those people who cracks jokes after getting news of a tumor. I will not need to wash his tears from my doctor's coat.

"It's just that, if you tell me it's all in my head now," said Julian, "you won't be lying."

"Aha. I see what you say. This is truly funny. But we will not be lying to you ever, Mr. Bledstein."

Oh, feel free, Julian didn't say. Lie to me all you want.


The nurse brought in the papers to terminate his treatment, seal off liability, severing connections between Julian and the clinic. He signed and signed and signed. His writing surprised him, his ability to do it. It wasn't a language-blocking cloud, but, then, what was it blocking? What was it allowing? And how long had it been there?

The doctor, frowning thoughtfully, trying to make conversation, stood by.

"I am sorry we do not have a way to give you your money back," the doctor was saying.

"I could help you," Julian said, "if you want."

"Excuse me?"

"I could show you a way to give me my money back," explained Julian. "You know, how to transfer it back to my credit card. It's not so hard."

"Oh, you must misunderstand." The doctor blushed.

"Yes, I must," said Julian.

Outside the clinic, standing on the plaza steps in her long corduroy thrift store coat, nearly hidden by a plaid scarf, was Hayley. She gave him a shy little wave, sheepishly smiling, forgiving, forgetting, denying, all in one cute fucking face. How on earth?

"Jules! Oh my God, you took *forever*!"

"I took forever?" He tried to sound arch. Here his Hayley actually *was*. Jesus Christ.

"It's freezing here." She laughed.

She had a gift for killing off oddity, making shit like this—sudden encounters in foreign countries—seem routine.

Julian agreed that it was cold. Germany in February and all that. But he stood his ground. Specimen Hayley, trying to make good. How interesting. He'd see where this led. He probably had cancer.

"Are you okay?" she asked. "You *look* good."

How nice if that were true. He'd never looked good, even as a baby. Even before he was a baby, when he was just somebody's fear. Once he was only dread in the pit of his mother's stomach. He was born sick, conceived by his parents as their sick little boy. Was there a sexual position favored by his parents' generation that guaranteed they'd birth a forceless runt, someone who would desperately need their help his whole life? Hayley should be ashamed of herself. *He looked good*. Still, he had to applaud her strategy. Cheer, denial, exuberance. If only he could. Tombstone.

"Come here already!" Hayley shouted. "Come hug me, you stupid bastard. How are you? Oh my God, I can't believe I'm *seeing* you."

He succumbed to Hayley's hug, giving little back. Whatever he had done, or not done, to himself, not just over the last two weeks, but over the years, too, had rendered him immune right now to the pleasures of her small body wrapped up in his, to her breath, to the way her hair got on his face. Even the warm kiss she gave. Immune, indifferent, cold. Once it had been his choice to resist these overtures. He used to watch himself taking the low road, hogging the lane, during Hayley's flirtations with forgiveness. But no longer. It was like being hugged by a machine. He held his breath and waited for it to end.

"Oh, you," she kept saying. "I missed you, you know."

He didn't answer.

"*You know*?" She nudged him.

Julian said they should probably start walking before they died. He didn't want to die in Germany.

They walked through the icy streets of Düsseldorf, hugging the Rhine, stopping to sit and shiver on a cold metal bench at the Rheinturm.

Julian took Hayley through Old Town, along Carlsplatz,

pointing out cultural zones with the indifference of a local. And he lied, effortlessly, about places he'd not even seen, like the Kunstakademie—looking at art was the last thing he'd wanted to do—even inventing a day trip to Cologne. Which he took last Wednesday? Or maybe Thursday? Hayley beamed up at him, her brave and adventurous American boyfriend, snuggling into his coat as they walked.

Hayley kept saying that she couldn't believe she was here. I mean, could *he,* she asked Julian? Could he believe it? And he disappointed her by saying, that, well, yeah, he could, because she was supposed to come, wasn't she?

"I know, but it's crazy, right?" she said.

Julian steered Hayley clear of Müllerhaus, but he kept it in his sights, a secret back door he could fall through. He didn't interrogate her on her whereabouts these past two weeks, on the matter of who or what had detained her through the brighter, more exciting ports of Europe, and she didn't mention it. She hardly spoke. Maybe they *hadn't* fought and maybe they weren't still, in some quiet, effortlessly Zen way, fighting right now. One day, people would swab each other with animosity sticks, and there'd be no way to hide it. Just as you could be tested for cancer, you could be tested for fury. Your anger would show, or your resentment, your detachment, your ambivalence, your reduced sexual attraction, no matter what you said or did. Your mood would be a chemical fact and if you lied about it then, poor, poor you. You'd be found out! Looking at Hayley, seeing her radiate, feeling her cozy up against him, it was ridiculously hard—in fact it was impossible—not to feel that this affection that she was suddenly smothering him with was meant for someone else.

Maybe that person shared his name, and looked like him—the poor fuck—but so what. Hayley wanted a stranger—*you are dead to me,* he wanted to say to himself—and Julian couldn't help her.

Instead of breaking up with your girlfriend, could you break up with *yourself*?

"So I talked to your dad," Hayley said.

"Why?"

"Well . . ." She looked at him funny.

"Because I wanted to know where you were." She punched him softly in the arm.

Maybe she wanted to say: play along with this, Julian, please, please, because this is how it works. I am trying so hard right now.

"You knew exactly where I was," he said. "I've been right here the whole time. I've been at the clinic every day for two weeks. Where else would I be?"

"I wanted to know that you were doing okay, and, you know, where you were staying."

"So you asked him?"

"I knew you'd have been in touch with him."

"Yeah."

"I can care about you, Julian."

"I know you can, Hale."

She could care about him in theory, and maybe in real life, too. But he must have migrated to some third place, because both of those territories seemed very far off to him now.


They crossed the Oberkassel Bridge, where the wind destroyed them, and finally Hayley admitted to being impossibly, horribly cold. And hungry. The poor thing's nose was running and her face was red and she looked ready to freeze. Could they maybe head back now, she wanted to know? Would he mind so much if they left now?

"Where?" he said.

"To the room."

"Room? There is no room." Tombstone.

"At the Am Volksgarten. You know, where we . . . They had rooms. I didn't know where you were and you weren't checked in there."

"Oh, are you Madame Düsseldorf now? What have you been here for, like eleven minutes? Plus, I have a place to stay. And there isn't room there for you."

"What do you mean?"

It took all of Julian's strength to look away.

"I am perfectly lodged, thank you." Tombstone.

"Would you please stop it?"

"I doubt it."

"Jules, please. I want to stay with you tonight."

He crossed the avenue where they'd stopped and she spoke his name, but not so urgently. This is what a favor looks like, he thought. Probably there was a favor being done right now. Except as he turned uphill and left Hayley behind, he had to wonder who, exactly, was actually doing this favor, and who was the fucking favor even for?

It was getting dark. Soon the hostel lights would go off. The men would tuck in and some of them would be snoring in seconds. The whole room would hum with desire, forty or fifty men trying not to be seen for a little while, even if they crept out at large, into the world. They required darkness for their work. This was where Julian belonged. He wanted to be in bed and ready. Maybe if he was lucky, his visitor would return. His visitor might give him another chance. This time he'd stay in his bed, no matter what. He would not bolt. He'd listen all night for footsteps. If none came, then perhaps he would be the stranger. He would find someone sleeping in the Turnhalle, someone who needed badly to be visited, and he would oblige.

Julian would reach out his hand and he wouldn't say it out loud, but he could certainly think it. He'd been thinking it for so long now. *Wouldn't you like to join me?* And wouldn't that most perfect phrase serve as the prettiest inscription on the tombstone they would finally place, when the time came, over his grave?

# Rollingwood

t's still dark when the weeping erupts, so Mather knows it's early. How early he isn't sure, but he won't be able to fall back asleep, so it doesn't matter. He pulls the extra pillow over his head, tries to smother the sound, but it's still there, the distant siren of the boy crying in the other room.

The boy is wedged under the machine when Mather goes in. The machine has run dry again, streaks of pink fluid smeared inside the hose, the tank in the crib issuing an exhausted wheeze. It's a terrible design. Under the clouded tank is a cavity just large enough to conceal the boy if he crawls in, which is what he does when he wakes up too early and no one comes for him. So Mather has to wedge his fingers beneath the thing, which barely fits in the crib, anyway, and lift it just enough to grab the boy and pull him out.

Of course the boy has been crying. *Crying* isn't really the right word for it. He has been explosively weeping, maybe for a long time, and when Mather picks him up and holds him close, the weeping escalates, the boy breaking down in Mather's arms.

Mather tries to set the boy down in the dark kitchen so that he can make coffee, but as soon as the boy is released he bursts into sobs again. As usual, Mather talks to him, tries to calmly reassure him, but the boy's crying is so loud that Mather cannot even hear his own voice. He sits on the dirty kitchen floor and gathers the boy in to try to soothe him, but the boy squirms from his grasp and goes on wailing, so Mather leaves the kitchen and shuts himself in the bathroom, triggering even higher-pitched cries from the boy.

When the doorbell rings to signal that Mather's ride to work is here, he isn't ready to go. The boy's diaper was dry when he got up, which meant that he hadn't had enough water, but Mather could not get him to drink anything. The boy twisted his head away when offered a bottle, so Mather tried to interest him in different cups, even his own coffee mug, which the boy usually tried to pry away from his hands. Finally, the boy took a few greedy gulps from the mug, with most of the water running down his chest. He wouldn't eat the egg that Mather had prepared for him, but he did steal Mather's toast, which he squeezed into a gummy mass in his fist while wandering around the living room, still half crying.

Now Mather has to quickly force the boy into his clothing as he struggles to get away. From the hallway, he grabs the same day bag he used yesterday, and the day before, packed with the same spare clothes for the boy and the same dry snacks that he never seems to want.

No one says hello when Mather opens the door of the carpool vehicle. They have had to wait for him in the unlit garage, and he can tell that they've lost patience. There's no car seat installed today, no space reserved for the boy, and he won't hold still in Mather's lap. The woman next to Mather is not amused when the boy throws himself across her legs, trying to crawl toward the window. She sits back, hands up, indicating that Mather must remove the boy himself. Mather apologizes and pulls the boy back, holding him tightly so that he can't escape. This makes the boy shriek and squirm with surprising strength. But Mather does not relent. He has no real choice.

They pass the old bald hill and the spire, then get waved through at the Faraday gate, where they join the line of cars that form a single file to climb to the top. The little trees out the window are bare and the grass is colorless this time of year, but it's a bright, clear day. Mather wishes a window was open, but he doesn't feel that he can ask. No doubt someone decided, before they picked him up, that they'd ride to work with the windows closed, breathing one another's stale air.

In the parking lot, overlooking the valley, the boy wants to walk under his own power, but there are cars pulling in and it's too dangerous. Mather finds a little patch of grass for the boy to run around in. It isn't much, and it quickly drops off into a steep decline, so he stations himself to keep the boy from running down the cliff. For a while the boy staggers around, grabbing little sticks, which he holds up to his father with pride.

When the work bell sounds, Mather lines up at the service entrance and waits his turn for the security check. The boy tenses in Mather's arms as they approach the nursery, but when Mather hands him off to the caregiver, the boy does not let himself cry. Even at this age, he is trying to be brave. Mather watches through the high window as the boy is quickly placed on the floor of the playroom, in front of a bucket of blocks. The caregiver disappears into an office, but the boy does not seem to notice. He picks something out of the bucket and puts it in his mouth. Mather gives him a last look, then heads up the ramp to the elevator.

The boy is one and a half years old and his name is Alan Mather, and already he has dense black hair on his head. To Mather, Alan is a name not for a baby but for a grown man. When they were naming him, he had let the boy's mother choose, thinking that he should pick his battles. She had been so sure about it, and Mather had found that he could not think of a single name that didn't make him feel uneasy when he said it out loud. Mather has tried to call the boy "honey" instead, and maybe if he keeps doing so it will come to feel more natural. The boy has a quiet, wet cough and pink-rimmed eyes, and he's already capable of sustained, piercing eye contact that his father can never quite match.

At his lunch hour, Mather takes his thermos and sandwich down to the nursery. The boy is in a crib, but he is not asleep. He has the same little foam object in his hand, and it's been chewed to shreds. When the boy sees Mather, he starts to cry, but softly, as if he had already cried himself hoarse. The respirator in the nursery hasn't been turned on, and when Mather checks the log to see if the boy has received his medication, there are no entries for today. The boy has the kind of asthma that keeps his lungs from properly lubricating, so he has to inhale moisture through a mask every four hours or his lungs will start to dry out. It's not serious, the doctor told Mather, but he should try not to miss a treatment. The director of the nursery seemed to be concealing a smirk when Mather first introduced him to the equipment, as if Mather had simply brought in one of Alan's favorite toys.

After Mather holds the mask to the boy's face and the boy obediently inhales the wet air, his little brow wrinkled in concentration, they return to the patch of grass outside. Mather tries to eat while the boy sits in his lap, facing downhill. The boy wants to hold Mather's sandwich, but when Mather lets him he won't eat any of it, and when Mather tries to rescue the sandwich the boy squishes it into a ball. Mather isn't hungry for the sandwich, anyway. When he hasn't slept well, he wants only a sugared muffin with a Coke. His sandwich is cucumbers with olive spread, between slices of thin, black toast, and it smells like potting soil.

It's a bright, clear day, and Mather can see all the way down to Rollingwood, the neighborhood where he grew up. He can't see his old house, but he can see the street where it would be, behind a hooked cul-de-sac of narrow homes. His old elementary school's clock tower rises out of the trees. The clock stopped at 3:15 a long time ago, and unless you stand beneath the tower you'd think the little hand had fallen off, because it's perfectly hidden beneath the big hand.

Mather's son won't go to school there, because they live far away from Rollingwood now. Mather doesn't even know where the public schools are in his new neighborhood. It's not so much a neighborhood as an exit off the freeway, but it's pretty, in its way, with circular grass parks and housing staggered down the middle. In the spring, it's one of his favorite parts of town. Something about the absence of trees makes the light seem perfect. It's hard to imagine that he'll still be in the same apartment, at the same job, in the same city, when the boy starts kindergarten in a few years. But of course the boy will attend kindergarten wherever his mother is living at the time, so Mather isn't even sure why he's thinking about the schools in his neighborhood.

Mather points out landmarks to the boy—the old Rotterman Dam and the shipping depot built of natural black bricks—but the boy doesn't look. He hangs on Mather's outstretched arm and tries to swing from it. Mather stands up and swings him around and the boy laughs, but the laugh turns into a whimper, and Mather isn't sure if the boy is frightened or happy.


After work, they take the bus to the boy's mother's apartment, but she isn't home. She has repeatedly asked Mather to return his key, given to him during friendlier days, but it's times like this that persuade him to hang on to it. Otherwise he'd be waiting forever on the narrow balcony of her building and the boy would be imperiling himself by trying to squeeze through the bars.

Mather lets himself inside and medicates the boy with the old ventilator in the living room, then looks for something to give him for dinner. There is only a chicken salad, so Mather spreads it on a cutting board and begins chipping it fine. The boy refuses the first spoonful, but Mather leaves the bowl on the coffee table, and after the boy has finished running around the apartment he discovers the mashed chicken and starts to awkwardly feed himself while Mather watches from his chair.

It's late and dark when the boy's mother comes home. She's with her boyfriend, who excuses himself to the bedroom without even taking off his coat. Mather has done his best to accept the boyfriend, has always been cordial and said hello, but the boy-friend won't look Mather in the eye and never stops to talk.

At these drop-offs, Mather and the boy's mother, Maureen, do not say much. They confirm the next exchange and discuss Alan's medication, what he's eaten, how he's sleeping. They stick to factual matters and flatten their tone of voice as much as possible, disguising their feelings. But today Maureen says that she needs to talk to him and asks him to sit down.

Mather hides his excitement. Maureen never wants to talk to him. Usually she seems disgusted by his presence, critical of how he fathers the boy, indifferent to anything Mather says that is unrelated to the boy's care. It is as if she had stored up disappointment that she is determined to show him during the ten minutes they see each other twice a week. So for a moment Mather imagines that Maureen has grown suddenly tender toward him, even with the boyfriend lurking in the bedroom. She misses Mather, maybe, and would like to talk to someone who really knows her. Someone who understands, because they once went through a lot together.

Except that's not it. Maureen needs a favor. She tells him that she can't take the boy right now. She's going away tomorrow.

"Okay," Mather says carefully, wanting to sound cooperative. He'd love to do her a favor, because she thinks he is selfish. If he shows resistance, she'll be upset and they'll have another fight.

"Thanks for understanding," Maureen says. "I appreciate it." She gets up as if the discussion is over.

But Mather doesn't understand. What is she telling him?

"I guess we need to wake up Alan," Maureen says, and she heads for the curtained-off hallway where Mather put him to sleep in the portable crib.

"Where are you going, can I ask?" Mather says. He's not sure why he sounds apologetic.

"To Robert's hometown."

Robert is the boyfriend. Mather thinks that Robert is lucky to be alone in a dark room right now. Maybe Robert is standing at the door, still wearing his winter coat, listening to them.

"Why can't you take Alan? It's your turn. He can't go with you?"

"No. Alan can't come."

"Well, when are you coming back?"

"Really soon. I'll call you. I'll make up the days."

"So you're just going off in the middle of the workweek?"

Maureen looks at him sharply, and it's clear that she doesn't think she needs to explain herself. She picks up the boy and starts whispering to him, her voice losing its scolding tone, dissolving into singsong. She bounces and hushes him, even though he's not crying.

The boy clings to his mother. When she bends over the couch to change him, he clutches her as if he were a baby animal, and she has to peel him away. She tells the boy that he will be staying with his daddy for a little while longer, and that she will miss him so much. She will see him soon, and they will do fun things and she will give him lots of kisses because he's her little boy, isn't he, and she wants to kiss him all the time. Should they go on a boat ride when she comes home? Does he remember the boat ride they once took? Would he like to do that again? That's what they'll do. She'll come home and they'll go down to the river and take a nice boat ride.

Mather stands there in the dark living room. There won't be

a boat ride. He knows that. She's showering so much love on the boy that he will become dazed by it, then Mather will have to take over and the boy will be bitterly disappointed again. To Mather, these intense displays of love are what he must help the boy recover from. Fatherhood has somehow become about helping the boy not love his mother too painfully.

Maureen hands the boy off to Mather, and the boy registers the change for one perfectly quiet second, then screams. He's never liked parting from his mother, and now they've woken him up late at night only to make him suffer the sudden separation. Mather closes his eyes and takes a deep breath. There's nothing he can do. He'd like Maureen to seem more obviously guilty, but she shows no sign of having done anything wrong. It is, apparently, Mather's fault that the boy does not love him with the same terrible desperation.

There's no one else at the bus stop, and from what Mather can tell, after reading the posted schedule, the next bus will come in one minute, which is lucky for him, because the boy is not pleased, outside in the winter at night. Except when one minute passes, then two, then five, it becomes clear that the bus must have come already and now the next one isn't due for half an hour.

Alone, which is what he was supposed to be tonight, Mather wouldn't care. He'd sit on the bench and read, enjoying the cold night. But he has the boy with him, and the boy is fully awake after all his screaming and will be cold soon. This isn't the sort of area where empty taxicabs drive around looking for fares. Mather calls information and gets the number for a car service, then speaks to a dispatcher. They can send a driver in forty-five minutes. Mather tells the man that it's late and his baby is tired and hungry, and the man repeats that he can send a car in forty-five minutes. More like an hour, actually, to be honest—as if he were doing Mather a favor by lengthening the estimate.

Mather starts to walk home, carrying the boy, along the bus route, even though it's less direct. He figures that the bus, when it comes, won't cruelly pass him by if he stands in the road and waves. The roads are so empty that Mather wonders for a moment if something terrible has happened, and everyone is at home watching the news, knowing better than to go outside. He stops walking and listens. It's the quietest he's ever heard his city. The boy, too, seems transfixed, staring into the darkness. But then a bus rolls into sight and Mather stands right over the white line, waving. He doesn't want to take any chances.

Maureen doesn't call the next day, or the day after that, and then it's the weekend. On Sunday, Mather's parents visit, but they're so tired they don't leave their chairs. Mather's parents have been to Lisbon, and they tell him of eating fish seared on the rocks at the harbor. The flat rocks are heated by torches overnight, and when the morning's catch comes in a man cleans whole fish to order and lays them out, butterflied, on the hot stone, which is black and oily from the cooking. When you salt this fish, it's the best thing you've ever eaten. You eat it with your fingers. Even the locals eat it, which, of course, is the best endorsement.

Mather's father studies him for signs of enthusiasm.

Mather nods his approval and says that he'd love to try it sometime.

The boy goes to the front hallway and grabs his little white shoes, then brings them over to Mather. Then he carries first one, then the other, of Mather's old maroon work shoes, dumping them loudly at Mather's feet.

"He wants to go out," Mather mumbles.

Mather's parents smile with abstract pleasure but do not move. When he doesn't hear from Maureen by Monday afternoon,

Mather calls and gets her voice mail. He would like to know her plans. The boy is doing fine, he tells her. He's actually eating, and he gets up twice at night, but Mather downgrades this to once in his message, because somehow the extra night wakings might seem like his failure. He asks Maureen to get back to him so that he knows when to drop Alan off.

He gets no call the next day. The day after that, at work, the nursery is closed. The lights are off and the door is locked when Mather carries the boy over in the morning. Mather waits outside while his colleagues head upstairs. He calls the nursery number and gets no answer. He bangs on the dark glass. Finally, when he is going to be late for work, he takes the boy up the ramp to the elevators and brings him into the suite of offices.

Mather asks someone named Drew what's going on with the nursery today. Drew has pictures of kids on his desk. He must have used the nursery at some point. But Drew shrugs and looks at Alan in Mather's arms as if Mather has smuggled contraband into work.

"I'll go see Ferguson, I guess," Mather says.

Ferguson is the supervisor and maybe he'll understand.

"He's not coming in this morning," Drew says, his face arranged in an unconvincing look of concern.

Mather heads to Ferguson's office, anyway, and asks his assistant if he can see him.

"And you are?" the assistant asks.

"It's just for a moment," Mather says. "It's an emergency." He holds up the boy as proof. See my emergency.

The assistant doesn't look. "Your name?" he asks.

"Mather," Mather says. "I work over there." He gestures at the cubicle with his head. There's a young woman working at his desk. Sometimes temps from the night shift set up at empty desks for their red-eye projects and have to move when the full-timers come in. He's going to have to ask her to leave and she's going to be annoyed, even though it's his desk.

"How's Friday at eleven?" the assistant asks.

"The day after tomorrow?"

The assistant is irritated. "That would be Friday, yes."

"Could you please let him know I've had an emergency and need a personal day?"

The assistant eyes him carefully. "You'd better write that out yourself to be sure the message is how you want it."

But Mather says that he trusts the assistant to get it right. It's not very complicated.


At home, he phones Maureen's office and the call is routed to a receptionist. Maureen is not available. But he'd like to know if she's there, if she's actually at work today. The receptionist repeats that she's not available to come to the phone and would Mather like to leave a message?

He says that it's about her son and would she please call him.

The boy won't nap, but he doesn't cry. He sits in his crib quietly, and Mather notices that his breath is coming heavily, with a faint whistling sound. Under the boy's dark hair, Mather thinks, the scalp looks unusually red, and when he touches it the boy flinches. He gives him the humidifier mask and the boy takes hungry gulps of the wet air. When Mather tries to remove him from the crib, the boy protests, points back to his mattress, so Mather leaves him there, and the boy crawls under the tank of the humidifier.

Mather checks on him later and he is still awake, but he cries when Mather tries to pick him up. The tank is empty, so Mather rinses it out and fills it with more distilled water. The boy returns the mask to his face and Mather can hear a whinny in his breath now. Is he getting worse? The redness on the boy's scalp has spread beyond his hairline, down his face.

Mather's mother, before she retired, was a nurse, so he calls her.

"You worry too much," she says. "Leave him alone. Children are remarkably strong. They're much stronger than us. You never got sick, never once. You never caused us any problems."


The next morning the car-pool vehicle does not come. Mather has been up for hours and is packed and ready to go. He's lost track of whose turn it is to drive today, so he can't even make a phone call. He's been so grateful to be part of the car pool, since he has no car of his own, that he's paid more than his share of the gas, to be sure that nothing goes wrong. He tries not to make trouble, particularly on days when he has the boy. But there's no car today, and if he doesn't leave right away he will be late for work.

On the bus there are no empty seats, so Mather stakes out a position for himself against a pole. The boy is pale inside his snow-suit. His face is dry and peeling. His skin seems nearly translucent. His cough is small and weak, and it could be that he's dehydrated.

The bus lets him off downhill from the Faraday gate. With the boy in his arms, Mather hikes up the side of the road as a stream of cars pass them on the way to work. He sees some people he knows, but no one stops. He's never hiked this road, and it's much steeper than he would have thought. He's drenched inside his winter coat, and the boy's face is flushed, even though he's not exerting himself. At the gate, Mather has to show his credentials and they ask to pat down the boy, who goes with one of the guards without complaint. He doesn't even seem to notice that someone else is carrying him.

The nursery is closed again this morning. Someone has taped a notice to the door, but it's since been ripped down, leaving the tape fastened over a shred of blank paper. Mather brings the boy up to his office and there are two temps sharing his desk. He stands there holding the boy, needing to put him down so that he can figure out what to do.

"All right," he says to the temps, trying to sound cheerful. "I guess I have to get in here."

He has no idea what he's going to do with Alan today, but at least if he gets his desk back he can settle in and maybe make a play area for him on the floor.

The temps look up at him and blink. "We're here until noon," the young man says. Probably he's in his early twenties, but he looks like a boy.

"Well," Mather says, "you need to move to the conference room or somewhere else, because this is my desk."

He shouldn't have to say this.

"Mr. Ferguson told us to work here," the other temp says impatiently, a young woman who is so striking he's afraid to look at her.

The boy wriggles out of Mather's grasp and sets off away from him, not even looking back, so Mather excuses himself to follow him, until they bump into Ferguson, who is speaking with some executives outside the conference room.

"Well, who do we have here?" Ferguson says, addressing the boy.

Mather leans over the boy, as if he needs to formally present him to his supervisor. "This is Alan," he says.

"Alan. Is that right? Are you helping your father get his stuff, Alan?"

"My stuff?" Mather asks. "What do you mean?"

"I had a note that you were leaving."

The executives standing with Ferguson smile at Mather. Ferguson smiles, too.

"No, no, no," Mather protests. "I had to take a personal day yesterday. His mother is supposed to have him and the nursery was closed. I'm sorry for the misunderstanding. I'm not leaving."

"Well, that *is* a misunderstanding," Ferguson says. "That contradicts the note I received."

His face has clouded over. When someone like Ferguson exceeds the allotted time for encounters with employees in the hallway, he does not try to hide it.

"No," Mather says. "I'm here, I'm here. I'm not going anywhere."

"Okay," Ferguson says, and he looks down at the boy, who's still in his snowsuit, pressed against the glass of the conference room. "But what about today?" Ferguson wants to know. "What's your plan?"

What he's going to do is check the nursery again, Mather tells Ferguson, because maybe they've opened it by now, and then he'll be right back. But of course the nursery is still closed when he gets there, locked and dark, with no note on the window. He asks the security guards if they know anything, but they don't. From the guard booth, they look over at the unlit nursery room as if they've never seen it before. So Mather has no choice but to go home with the boy in his arms, who is so light it feels to Mather that he is carrying an empty snowsuit.

At home he calls Maureen again, but her voice mail is full and she's not picking up. Mather would try Robert, to reach Maureen, but if he was ever told Robert's last name he can't remember it now. Mather knows nothing about him, let alone where his hometown is.

There are a few of Maureen's friends to try, but Alma is the obvious one, the loyalist, whose negative forecasts about Mather were always, according to Maureen, 100 percent accurate.

"If Alma is so smart," Mather once asked, "then why is she fat and alone?" He wanted to think that this was an innocent question, prompted by irreconcilable pieces of information.

"Of course you'd ask that," Maureen said, smiling. "Of course." She always seemed genuinely happy when Mather was at his worst.

And of course you'd have no answer, Mather thought, back at her, in the unspoken way he often fought with her, but then Maureen did have an answer, at least about Alma's weight. A gland or a duct or perhaps an entire organ had begun to work overtime, could not stop laboring inside Alma, as if there were always unfinished work to do. Or was it the reverse? The result was that incredibly pale skin Alma had and, yes, it was true, some extra weight. A depressed metabolism, because Alma actually ate less than the rest of us. But Mather didn't even deserve to know that, Maureen assured him. He wasn't even worthy of knowing that about Alma.

She picks up on the first ring, stating her full name, Alma Ryan, which everyone does at her office, a publishing house specializing in children's books. Mather quickly says that it is him, and that she shouldn't hang up, because this is about Alan, and does Alma know where Maureen is?

"What happened to Alan?" Alma asks in a careful voice.

Mather explains that nothing has, but Maureen is still not back and this isn't like her and it's causing problems for him. He's home with the boy now when he needs to be at work. He might even lose his job because of this.

"I'm sorry to hear that your child is an inconvenience to you," Alma says.

Mather curses at her, freely and at length, and Alma hangs up. Then he calls her right back.

"Alma Ryan."

Mather explains that he is sorry and he needs her help. Alan is no inconvenience to him. Alan is his son and he loves him. Alma has to believe that, no matter what she thinks of him. But the boy needs his mother, too. Mather explains that Alan is too little to be away from his mother for this long, with Mather not even knowing where she is or when she's coming back. Maybe Alma does not know the details, but Alan is not well. His asthma. This is not fair to Alan.

He explains this to Alma, but when he waits for her to respond she isn't there. The line is dead. It is possible that Alma hung up as soon as she heard Mather's voice. She doesn't pick up again.

In the late afternoon, the boy won't breathe through his mask. He covers his mouth with his hands and turns away. Mather tries to listen to his breath, but the boy won't stay put. Still, Mather hears a whistle in the boy's lungs, and he pictures them shriveling inside the boy's small chest, as dry as paper curling up in the heat. He knows that if the boy would inhale the vapors from the mask his lungs would lubricate and he would feel better, but the boy is stubborn and the more Mather tries to press the mask over his face, the more he twists out of reach.

Mather reminds himself that it isn't serious. The treatments are supposedly optional, meant to increase the boy's comfort. It is only asthma. But the boy is pale and certainly too little for his age, and he sits listlessly on the rug after his nap, uninterested in the toy cars that Mather has arranged around him.

Mather schedules a sitter, and the next morning he shows her around the apartment while the boy clings to him. Mather demonstrates the ventilator to the sitter, but it is clear that she has already decided that it is too complicated for her to operate.

Mather was going to leave early for the bus stop, to be sure that he wasn't late for work, but then his doorbell rings, and he runs downstairs to the car-pool vehicle, the boy crying behind him in the sitter's arms. A proper good-bye would only have made it worse, and the boy will recover faster this way. In any case, Mather needs to go to work. This is how it has to be.

In the dark car, no one so much as looks his way. Mather wonders what happens day after day in this car before he is picked up that makes for such grim silence. They stare ahead while he settles in and buckles his seat belt, and for a moment Mather feels the enormous relief of traveling alone, even if there are mute coworkers pressed against him. He has no one to take care of and he can relax.

Mather lowers his window when they pull out of the garage, and the woman beside him huffs. He'll consider himself scolded. They turn onto the Hills Parkway and the car picks up speed. Outside, it's a flat, gray morning, but the air is warm, and Mather lets the wind cover his face. There are sweet, smoky streaks in the sky, the kind of clouds that scatter if a bird so much as flies through them. Mather almost feels that he could sleep, and he wishes the ride were longer. He'd love to stay in the car like this all day, driving around town, sleeping a little, looking out the window, doing nothing, while someone else keeps the boy busy at home.

The temps are at his desk when he gets to work.

"Okay, guys, break it up," he says, wanting to sound jovial.

They're engrossed in their work and don't look up. It's the same two temps from yesterday, and a third one leans over them, staring at the computer screen. They have coffees and food wrappers cluttering the desk, and Mather's own inbox is nowhere to be seen. There's hardly room for him to put down his briefcase.

"I'm back," Mather says, this time more softly.

"We're pretty hunkered down," the young man from yesterday says. Mather isn't sure, but the young man's hand motion may be waving him away.

Mather says, "I can see that." It's important to stay friendly, extend an olive branch. He was a temp once. There's no reason to lord his rank over them. "Would you guys like to take a minute to find another place to work?"

The young man seems to consider this but mentions their deadline and how settled in they are at Mather's desk. He says that they're good where they are, but thanks for the offer.

Of course it's a misunderstanding, and a small one, but Mather feels that he hasn't been at his desk in ages and he'd like things to return to normal. How long has it been since he's had a normal workday? He looks around for some sort of backup, commiseration from the other full-timers, but his colleagues are hopelessly entranced by their computers. Unfortunately, he has to go higher up on this one. He'd have liked to avoid that, but the temps have given him no choice. Ferguson's assistant tells Mather that his appointment isn't until eleven.

Mather says, "I didn't make that appointment. Remember? I need to see him now. The temps are at my desk and I have to get to work. It's already after nine."

"So are you canceling the eleven o'clock?" the assistant asks, crossing something out in his book.

"No," Mather says quietly, "because I never made it."

"Never made what?" a voice booms behind him.

It's Ferguson walking in, acting as though he'd missed the beginning of a joke. Mather wonders if Ferguson ever gets tired, smiling like that. The assistant disengages, returns to his work.

"I never made an appointment with you," Mather explains, realizing that this will only confuse Ferguson, but Ferguson has the ability not to show confusion, perhaps not to even experience it. A man like Ferguson can remain impervious to all messages beyond his own internal script, which drives him with purpose from room to room.

Ferguson pats Mather on the back.

"So you got rid of him, huh?" he asks.

"Who?" Mather says.

"Who!" Ferguson laughs. "The kid! You finally fobbed him off! Good work!"

"Oh," Mather says. "I did. Yeah."

"Just a quick thing," he says to Ferguson, using a serious, professional tone.

He would like Ferguson, if possible, to resolve this situation with the temps, he says, because he needs to get back to work, and why does he always have to vacate people from his desk every morning? It's stressful, if Ferguson wants to know the truth, and Ferguson nods with sympathy. The temps should have marching orders and time frames before they even sit down at someone else's desk. Mather explains that it creates tension and it's maybe not a great idea for office morale.

"The temps left at eight today," Ferguson says, "as usual. But let me introduce you to our new team. We've made some pretty killer hires. Morale couldn't be better."

At Mather's desk, Ferguson presents the three new hotshot employees, but Mather doesn't listen to their names. Ferguson is boasting about the marketing initiative they took as temps and how they're the first temps in a year to move up the ladder like this. Straight up the ladder. Fire at their heels.

The three of them, still caught up in the seriousness flowing from Mather's computer, are flushed with Ferguson's praise, as if they believe that soon they'll be running the company. And somehow Mather is supposed to feel happy for them, which he tells Ferguson he is, but of course, this is his desk, where his unfinished projects remain and can't the new team work somewhere else?

Ferguson says that he and Mather should go talk at the elevator. His voice is soft, and he tries to shepherd Mather away, placing an arm around him.

Mather imagines Ferguson obeying his internal voice: *Walk employee to a quiet place. Present bad news in positive terms.*

About the only way that Mather can have an edge on Ferguson is to hold his ground and force this conversation to happen right here. He can feel his coworkers pretending not to look at him.

Ferguson says, "I think the next step is a good strategy talk down in H.R. They'll have a really tactical perspective on what might be next for you. It's never a bad time to talk strategy. You think you've considered all your options, but you never have. There's always something you haven't thought of."

Mather's cell phone rings and he doesn't recognize the number, but he feels he must pick up, even though the timing is bad. It could be Maureen calling from someone else's phone. Maybe she lost her phone, which is why she hasn't picked up for so long. Maybe she's calling to say she's sorry, and how is baby Alan, and can she see him soon?

Except it's not Maureen, it's someone with poor English, on a poor connection, who asks several times for Mr. Mather.

"This is he," Mather says, as Ferguson and the new employees look at him with polite curiosity.

The caller asks again for Mather, and again he says, "This is he," until it occurs to him that she doesn't understand the expression.

"This is Mr. Mather. Who's calling, please?" Without people watching him, he might have hung up already.

Mather figures out that it's the sitter, and what she's saying to him, over and over, is the name of his boy. She's saying "Alan," except with her accent it sounds like "Allah." She has little ability to elaborate. Something is wrong with the boy. She needs him to come home right away.

Mather stays calm.

"I have to go. It's my son."

"I guess you can't get rid of him that easy!" Ferguson laughs.

Mather rushes to the elevator, and behind him Ferguson calls out that business about H.R. again and scheduling an appointment.

"Strategy!" Ferguson shouts, as the elevator doors close.

It's not until Mather gets on the bus that he realizes precisely what has happened. This is how it's done. No doubt Ferguson took a workshop to learn the exact language. Perhaps he was excited to practice it on Mather. Firing is an opportunity, the start of something wonderful and new.

While Mather is on the bus, the sitter calls again, but there's nothing he can do. He's on his way, she has to hold tight, and he will be there as soon as he can.

His phone rings once more as he approaches the back of his building. This time it's Maureen.

"Finally," he says. It's as if the whole crisis were over, simply because she has called. He's not even mad, just relieved.

"Where are you?" Maureen demands.

"Where am I? Where am I?" Mather can't believe it. "Are you kidding me? Where the fuck are you?"

Then he sees, across the parking lot, at the entrance to his building, Maureen talking on her phone. Robert is with her, and he's got the boy. Next to them is the sitter, and even from here Mather can see that she's crying hysterically.

"You left him with a stranger," Maureen hisses into the phone. "I can't go away for one minute. I can't leave him with you for a single second. A stranger who knows nothing about children."

Mather sees the full hatred in her body, how she'd like to crawl into her phone and kill him as she stalks around the parking lot.

"I'm right here," Mather says. "Look up," and he watches her uncoil.

Maureen sees Mather and takes the boy from Robert. They've got him wrapped up in his snowsuit, and he's wearing one of those white stocking caps they give to babies at the hospital. Somehow it still fits him.

"We're leaving," she announces, and Robert falls into step behind her.

Mather approaches and the sitter rushes at him, frantic.

"I don't give them Allah. They take Allah. It's okay they take Allah?"

Mather tells Maureen to wait, to hold on, there's a lot to talk about. She can't just barge over and take Alan like that. She has a lot to account for.

"Really?" Maureen says, and she looks almost excited, as if she can't wait to tear into Mather over this.

Mather wants to see the boy, and, when he approaches, Alan looks at him with his pink-rimmed eyes, crusty and dry in the corners, and his skin not so much pale as yellow. Mather goes to touch the boy gently—this is his little son, he would like to give him a kiss—and the boy cringes, nestling further into his mother.

Mather backs away.

"It's okay, Mr. Mather?" the sitter says. "It's okay they take him?" She's acting like Mather's only friend.

"You're asking the wrong person, you bitch," Maureen says. But Mather calms the sitter down and says, "Yes, it's okay, don't worry."

"Leave my friends alone," Maureen spits. "Don't call my work. Don't call us."

Robert looks at Mather, and there's not even malice in his eyes. Just boredom.


Mather watches them drive away and he goes upstairs, alone, to his apartment. It's not even noon. He'll start by doing laundry, all the boy's clothes. He takes everything down to the machines in the basement, then upstairs he vacuums, opens the windows for air.

From the boy's crib he removes the humidifier. What Mather will do is take off the tubes and soak them in a good, hot solution. The plastic water tank has to be soaked, too. The mask pulls easily from the hose and it still smells a little bit of the boy, his sleeping breath. When Mather puts it back together it will be as clean as new.

Later, Mather will go shopping and he'll buy the boy's favorite foods. He'll stock up on distilled water for the tank. He'll even lay in some candy, for those times when nothing else works. If it's not too late after that and he has the energy, Mather will take the bus down to Rollingwood to the toy store he loved when he was young, if it's even still there, and he will pick up something fun for the boy. There has to be something that Alan will love to play with, maybe a train table, which he's too young for at the moment, though not really for long. He's growing up. It's not a bad idea to start thinking about getting the right train table built up in the living room.

At home tonight, Mather will lay the pieces out on the floor, and he'll start building, because it could take a few days to get it done, and this way he'll have a head start. He wants to be ready for next time. He wants to bring the boy in and present it to him and see the look in the boy's eyes when he lowers him into place and pushes that very first train into view.

2

# On Not Growing Up

*—How long have you been a child?*
—Seventy-one years.

*—Who did you work with?*
—Meyerowits for the first phase: colic, teething, walking, talking. He taught me how to produce false prodigy markers and developmental reversals, to test the power in the room without speaking. I was encouraged to look beyond the tantrum and drastic mood migrations that depended on the environment, and if you know my work you have an idea what resulted. The rest is a hodge-podge, but I don't advocate linear apprenticeships. A stint in the Bonn Residency. Fellowships at the Cleveland Place, then later a *stage* at Quebec Center. I entered that Appalachian Trail retreat in 1974, before Krenov revised it, but had to get helicoptered out. Probably my first infant crisis, before I knew to deliberately court interference. The debt to Meyerowits is huge, obviously, if just for the innocence training. Probably I should have laid off after that, because now it's all about unlearning.

*—Unlearning as Kugler practices it? That radical?*
—I skip the hostility to animals. I skip the forced submersion and the chelation flush. That's proven to be a dead end. But Kugler is a walking contradiction in that respect, isn't he? He keeps a horse barn. He does twilight childishness, and now he's suddenly oppos-

ing the Phoenix baby-talk crowd, who I think are not as threatening as he makes out.

—*They're not registered.*
—True, but they're pro-family, and I still believe, when I'm out in the field, in a pro-parent regimen, in supporting those with maturity fixations.

—*Which is contradictory, isn't it, given how many adult families you've worked with, and how many of them have ultimately disbanded?*
—The term *adult* is problematic, I think, and it's too easy to say that my childwork is directly divisive to Matures, particularly Rigid or Bolted Matures. I may help accelerate a latent behavior, I may enable conflict vectors along the lines of the Michiganders, who fasted as a form of warfare, and I feign indifference to familial tension, but I think that success itself has been fetishized, and a certain nostalgia for growth has spoiled our thinking. I can be pro-family without coddling actual families. I can support familial fear-based clustering even if it involves admitting that we are most likely members of the wrong family. There is that famous German phrase, which I can't remember exactly, that describes a certain way to hold a gun to someone's head. The literal meaning of the phrase is that you love that person deeply, just not at the moment. I argue for a love that functions perfectly in theory.

—*But you have destroyed an unprecedented number of families.*
—I don't destroy anything. I do question the term limits of parents, and I'm not the first to promote child-driven power reversals. We have to remember how much thought Benner-Louis put into this subject, and how resonant her geological metaphors were. If prodding an object for flaws causes a momentarily resolved family to unravel, then what you're saying is that we should stay silent

and paralyzed, the classic demand placed upon children. It is not my problem that families are hurt when we notice how they have hardened into stone, how they stoke each other's failure instinct, and if Matures are not powerful enough to admit a stagnation, they are welcome to blame me, but that's merely evasive. I give choices to children, and I supply functional tunnels to those who have yet to become children. This is mapping as Parsons envisioned it: you don't map a route that has been spoiled by the progress of others. Adulthood looks like an exhaustion farm. Who would knowingly purchase a ticket to that? In my work, I re-child certain people who have presumed a premature adulthood, and, most importantly, I question adulthood as a retreat from the power of infancy. I'm a supplier.

—*Which brings us to Maryland.*
—My tantrum work is still being fine-tuned, but you could reference an entire series of Chesapeake catastrophes that might seem now like open wounds, even as our daily perspective, as time passes and fewer of us can recall the perished, will refresh itself to show how essential, for instance, something like the Lake Maneuver was. Assertive Submersion may not be pleasant, in the lived sense, but if the values of a social group are being collectively ignored, forcing Matures, through panic, to relocate their child-state, it is an adequate way to broadcast a set of perspectives and beliefs that have been conveniently forgotten. Behaviors are advertised and promoted all the time. Why should we be penalized for making our case so powerfully that people nearly die from the overwhelming logic of it?

—*But can you sketch for me a picture of your ethics?*
—I think that fixed moral boundaries are harmful, even if they provide momentary comfort and save lives. I think our ethical

duty is to eliminate the behavioral corsets that are cinched over children just as their explosive energy is at its most threatening. Is a tantrum disruptive, or does it point to an emotional tunnel we're afraid of entering? The doctrines of the tantras involve meditation, mantras, ritual, and explosive behavior. We're talking about ancient ideas that are elementary and obvious to high schoolers. My ethics? I'd like to shed the strictures of adulthood and make maturity an optional result of a freely lived human life, not the necessary path to power and success, lorded over by depressed, overweight, unimaginative corpses. The twenty most central mantras have their roots in baby talk. No one disputes this anymore. A syntax comprised of these mantras, which should not be confused with NASA's failed language, can marshal the force of an entire infant society, but—and this is key—this syntax is not capable of instructional phrasings, so nothing can be taught, which keeps maturity and its death mask perfectly at bay.

*—Has it been necessary to denounce such important figures in child development as Dr. Spock? Where has that adversarial approach benefited your child program?*
—Dr. Spock reviewed existing children, but he didn't promote new ones. His art was to survey the past and ensure a predictable persona outcome. He devised solutions for the escape of childhood, very good ones, I might add. I think that some of his approaches are worth modifying, if only in service of a kind of dark science. We can bottle that kind of curatorial approach to behavior, but it won't save anyone. These were tonics for escape, and they should have been marketed that way from the start. I've simply asked for honesty. Spock's entire approach presents infancy as a problem to be managed, to be grown out of, and I'm not alone in finding this condescending. Physical growth is (mostly) a necessity (although we'll soon see about that), but emotional growth is something

Matures crave strictly for others. Rarely is it satisfying to the person who accomplishes it. There's a missionary zeal around this dirty word, *development,* and it's exerted on otherwise defenseless people. A spell has been cast on us, and it leads to a spectacularly depressing failure we have come to call "adulthood." The artwork of children is so often discarded because Matures cannot accept, let alone decipher, the chaos and disorder children depict after only briefly gazing at the crushed and gargantuan figures that supposedly parent them. Children's art perfectly captures the sloppy, disordered, ugly world that awaits them if they choose the path of maturity.

—*Many people would disagree with that.*
—And I bet they're old and "adult" and reasonable, accumulating comprehension as if it were food. It's a laughable mistake, this certainty compulsion. Your entire line of questioning revolves around the notion that if not everyone agrees with me, there must be something wrong with my ideas. This is a classic rhetorical tactic—I think it's called the Consensus Chalice—for a Mature. *The Fear of the Infant* wasn't merely a successful film; it depicted a real aversion to the kinds of discoveries that might be possible if Matures didn't operate with such staggering fear. Baby talk has tremendous potential, despite its obvious dangers and its near-total incomprehensibility. The only reason you don't embrace it is your abject terror.

—*What's next for you?*
—Meyerowits, for all of his accomplishments, died as an adult, and it has shamed his entire family. His legacy, in the end, means nothing, because he left this world knowing and thinking too much, headed down the wrong road, with a body that weighed as much as six children. He attacked his own theories, in fear of the com-

plexities and richness of innocence, and now he's dead. I want to die as I am, looking out at a world that I can admit is too complex to know and far too terrible to join. I want to die as a child: barely able to walk, careening through the fog of objects and people I can never know, wearing nothing but the tattered onesie my first mother bought me. This is my goal.

# My Views on the Darkness

*—People are pursuing different strategies during the hardship, and yours would seem among the most severe. How long have you advocated the cave?*

—*Advocate* is the wrong word. If I occupy a life raft out on the ocean, and people are drowning, I don't "advocate" the raft to them. I enjoy the raft and my relative security. If the people in the water choose to survive, they will swim to me and petition the raft, and of course I'll give fair consideration to their request, weighing the relevant factors. In such a case, advocacy of the raft is hardly necessary, and the same is true for what you call the cave.

*—So you don't need to promote what people cannot live without?*

—Right. But even if I hold a deep conviction about survival, particularly during the hardship, our species is too complex for me to assume that everyone wants or needs to survive. There will be people, to follow this life raft example, who must stay in the water and perish, for reasons peculiar to them, and it's not my business to probe their motives. Oceans require people to drown in them. That's not only a line from a popular song. To me it's beautiful that our survival strategies are wonderfully diverse and not all of us can succeed.

*—In other words, you feel that people who do not agree with you about the cave have a death wish?*

—My feeling about other people and their wishes is not important. What I think doesn't interest me, just as survival is not a theoretical project, at least as I practice it. When you outlast everyone addicted to unprotected space—Americans, as we call them—you don't much care to hear the ravings of the newly dead. Every species is defined by death and every creature has a role to play, even if some of those roles appear negating or doomed, or beguilingly marginal. If I was assigned a death role, if I was meant to die tonight, for example, which I'd be prepared to do if such an event could lift the shadow, you might still hear me disputing the reigning survival narratives, perhaps even arguing that death is the most radical form of survival. It is a necessary imperfection of the species that we each believe we are in the right.

—*So the cave is a survival narrative?*
—It's not a cave any more than a house is a cave.

—*It's underground.*
—A relative distinction, and a sloppy one. Caves have entrances, in any case, so your terminology is moot. Let's try to think outside of our disease. It's enormously difficult to penetrate a true underground space, and I'm hardly an absolutist when it comes to subterranean levels.

—*Explain.*
—Most of what you call the underground was once cold, blue space that is now simply clotted with matter. It's the old adage we learned in grade school: solids attract, space is a punishment. Are there ideal clottages of matter that feature high survival ratios? Perhaps, but it's not so simple. I look for below-grade cavities that are aperture free, but I'm not interested in fixating on pure coordinates because I don't believe in compassing. These foolish

tools are just treasure maps to one hell or another. Areas of high solidity, which often occur at extremely low altitudes, are simply safer. The sea-levelers have lost access to light and power and laid themselves bare to every sort of attack, yet still we have to listen to their sentimental justifications and old-fashioned cries for the good pastures and prairies which are graveyards now. I don't believe in some absolute mineral intelligence, but you'd have to be a moron not to notice what is surviving and to wonder very seriously how to model it.

—*To the outsider, this looks like you're burying yourself alive.*
—I would agree with the word *alive* here. I put a premium on life, even while others wring their hands and object to the "idea" of the low home, or other safe zones, all the while groping in cold darkness with no food, at an altitude—where our buildings used to be—with a remarkably grim survival rate. Drs. Moskin and Ruefle have repeatedly refuted the idea of an absolute sea level. Why are we even having this conversation? We key your dangerous coordinates into a GPS and find ourselves headlong over a cliff. What good will it do me to grab on to you if we're both falling to our deaths?

—*But we're not falling.*
—Said the remarkably uninformed man. The whole idea of a boundary between the earth and the air is problematic. It is one of those intellectual wrong turns that has marked us with a terrible shadow. The scar around our necks is where sea level used to be.

—*What scar?*
—It's an expression. Altitude itself has been fanatically idealized since early mythology. We've been banning the wrong books. The beauty of flight, the freedom of space, the supposed poetry of

birds: glories or cautions? To me it's strikingly obvious that we should seek to be supported by matter on all sides, a suit of earth, as Frehlan put it, whether in person-sized cavities or elsewhere. Altitude, even as a concept, has failed. Evolution teaches in the negative, but we are terrible students of the future.

—*Is it the Anchorites you side with?*
—Who said that if you want to watch someone die, befriend an Anchorite? There's a narcissism to people who flee to the mountains, and I'm not just singling out my father. The flight of the Anchorites is self-centered and historically minded—in the worst way—and to me they are like characters auditioning for a novel. Pick me, pick me! They are begging to be noticed and they cry when wounded. The preening quality of their isolation has no appeal to me. They have a fondness for exposure, and we might as well watch them decay before our eyes. But my opinion on this is merely personal. I care about results. In terms of efficacy, which is what matters, Anchorites die. Six of them will die during this conversation.

—*Is that your final measurement for people, whether or not they die?*
—That measurement predates me, and it will outlast me, too. I'd be curious to learn of a more revealing criterion.

—*You've given up many things in pursuit of the cave: your family, your home, your job.*
—I'll have those things again. They might not take the same shape or form, it might not be the same family, home, or job, but those things will return to me even stronger because of my survival work.

—*But do you miss your actual family?*
—I feel relief. Relief and gratitude. Gratitude because I can expe-

rience strong feelings for those people. How many of us really have that intense flood of emotion, like being drugged? Feelings are a gift, and I am lucky. In some sense, my feelings toward my wife and children are more intense when the moment is not complicated by their presence, and there is no accounting for the magnification that happens when we are swaddled by earth, fully enclosed, necessarily free of people.

—*As a father and husband, are you responsible for the survival strategies, flawed as they may be in your view, of your wife and children? Is there an obligation here?*
—I am not here to talk about particular people I may have known. There's no need to cripple our thinking with specificity. But I presented an airtight survival case to those individuals, and my views on this are well documented. Families necessitate energetic concealments of the obvious, to be plain about it. To be in a family is to work strenuously to suppress the truth, for reasons I cannot determine, and the shadow, when it came, caused competing strategies in the family I occupied. My wife tuned her intelligence to a dilemma altogether different from the dilemma at hand, and I was confirmed in my belief that survival cannot be outwardly imposed, even within a niche group like a family. Responsibility, during a hardship, is a luxury, and it is a luxury I strove to enjoy, even as it compromised the project. It was decadent of me to show so much responsibility for my family, as it was then defined. I admit to this indulgence of youth. We have our weaknesses. One of mine was loyalty. But hardships necessitate that we forgo luxury, and in this case I needed to move from my own comforts toward the necessarily desolate work I'm doing now.

—*Survival, then, but at what cost?*
—That question doesn't become you. I choose to be alive in order to measure the depth of my sacrifice, if any. Are we supposed to

gloat from the afterlife that we avoided difficult choices and took the easy way out? If other people, including my affiliates, do not choose to navigate hardship by seeking out full earth swaddling, then I cannot help them.

—*In a time of intermittent sun and fee-rationed power, I am curious if you are worried about the people above, as you have called them.*
—My views on the darkness are well known. I have found that after the first bracing moments, stepping into an ossified berm of shale, or what have you, when your hand appears ink-soaked and then invisible, and when sounds are suddenly so heightened that you can hear your blood rushing through your body, a release occurs, a lightness, and it is in this space that a great feeling arises. I can only wish that such a feeling has become available not just to those people you name, but to everyone. The shadow has made new experiences possible. In the end, it should not matter how deserving we are, and the people above should not be punished for their mistake. I would hate to think that only a lucky few of us could feel the safety of stone, protecting us from all sides, where we can let ourselves believe that beyond our private walls, another good person might be resting and waiting. If our sight was such that we saw only bodies, and not the stone and earth that encloses so many of our survivors, a floating web of people would appear before us, and such a diagram of the species, hovering there and breathing just fine, would be beautiful.

3

# Watching Mysteries
# with My Mother

don't think my mother will die today. It's late at night already. She'd have to die in the next forty-five minutes, which doesn't seem likely. I just saw her for dinner. We ordered in and watched a mystery on PBS. She kissed me good night and I took a taxi home. For my mother to die today, things would need to take a rapid turn.

My mother has her share of health troubles. She lives alone, which increases the likelihood of death. I could wake to a phone call and learn that she died shortly after I left her tonight. I'd like to say that the odds are against my mother dying today, since so much of the day has already passed. She needs only to survive at home, in her bed, for less than an hour, and then she will have lived through the day, proving me correct. But I don't know enough about odds. It would seem to me that the underlying premise of death—the death of an old woman alone in her apartment—is that it does not participate in man-made conceits like odds. People are often said to beat the odds. But then, perhaps, whoever keeps the odds—if he or she is intelligent—must account in advance for the odds being beaten and adjust the odds accordingly. Odds keepers cannot be ignorant of the claim that the odds are often beaten. This must disturb them. And then would they not adjust the odds, in order to make the odds more accurate? I don't know. Odds should be odds, and they should never be beaten. If they are, then the odds are incorrect and should be changed.

If my mother knew that she only needed to survive for under

an hour—in order not to die today—would her chances of living increase? If I phoned her now and told her to hang on, so that she didn't die today, would her odds change? In other words, does it increase our chance of survival if we consciously try to live? It wouldn't seem likely, not that she'd even pick up the phone now. It is late at night. She is tired. She was even tired at dinner. When we watched our mystery, she fell asleep. The phrase for people of a certain age, in certain circumstances, is *nodded off*. My mother nodded off. I paid her the courtesy of not seeming to notice, even though I watched her sleep under her blanket on the reclining chair she loves. I noticed how her hair no longer moves, not even a strand of it, no matter what position she is in. She woke up throughout the broadcast, and she actually grasped more of the plot than I did. It is possible she'd seen this mystery before.

The people who work in kitchens, in castles in England, at least in the mysteries my mother and I watch, are far more intelligent than their employers. The kitchens are vast stone rooms with gorgeous pots hanging from hooks. Sometimes the difference in intelligence between employer and servant is striking, a fact my mother relies on for her solutions to the mystery.

I understand, of course, that these mystery stories are invented, but I also understand that the people who invent them are hopelessly bound to what they've seen and heard. As much as these people might dream of a kind of pure fabrication, imagining out of whole cloth an utterly new Victorian British society in which petty domestic crimes take place, they cannot do it. They hew, like it or not, to what has already happened, to what people have already done, and what people have already thought. In this case, working-class characters are functional geniuses compared to the slow-thinking, wealthy, overfed people who rule them. The popularity of their shows depends upon it. I depend upon it. My mother depends upon it. Even if, at times, while the shows play in her living room, she sleeps.

People are reluctant to admit that they have slept, particularly, perhaps exclusively, when they've done so in front of witnesses. Just when it would seem impossible to deny, people deny that they nodded off. A point of pride is perhaps involved. So I never confronted my mother with the fact that she had slept through the second act, even though I watched her sleeping, arguably more than I watched the mystery. Why would I harass her with the truth? I do my best not to watch my mother when she is sleeping. I think it is impolite. Yet sometimes I fail. When she is awake I do not get to watch my mother so carefully, for such extended periods of time. If it is impolite to stare at someone while they sleep, it is more so when they are awake, aware of your scrutiny. It is not only more impolite, it is essentially impossible to closely look at another person for a long time while they are awake. A code prevents it. I would never think of following her around, staring. I am generally aware of the things I should not do.

And yet the crime is the same: staring at another person. Awake or asleep should not matter, but clearly the fact of being seen while staring at a waking person aggravates the transgression. If a third person could be in the room while my mother nodded off and I stared at her, and this third person—not my father, obviously, oh, God, no—witnessed me staring at my sleeping mother, has my offense thus escalated? I do not know.

When I think of her sometimes forgetting her medicine, forgetting to eat much more than a rice cake, neglecting to drink water, I must wonder if my mother could live longer if only she tried.

Servants in the kitchen, especially the daftest ones who appear idiotic in the first act, end up being the most devious. Look out for the stupid ones, my mother will shout, whenever we watch a mystery. She wags a finger at me and smiles.

I try to get her to drink water and she says the water tastes awful. She feels she's drinking water that someone soaked his teeth in, even if I have only just drawn the water from the tap. It tastes like a stranger's mouth, she'll yell. As if the water would be acceptable if only it tasted like the mouth of someone she knew. A person's determination cannot—can it?—have too much to do with when they die, unless they are choosing to die, which is another topic. If determination played a role, allowing people to deliberately live longer, death would undergo a fundamental change, and people would exert their will in disruptive ways, living so long it would antagonize their families. I do not like to imagine the kinds of things that would happen in such a world where people could delay their own deaths.

On the other hand, there is a long history of people who, without moving a muscle, have fought for their lives. A person inert in a hospital bed, rigged to bags and lines, is referred to as a fighter. Upon observation, no visible fight can be detected. But a will to live is cited in these situations. The family, gathered at the bed, can detect it. Even when their loved one dies, they say she fought so hard. She was such a fighter. She put up an unbelievable fight.

Such circumstances have always concerned me, and not just tonight, as I wonder about my mother's resolve to live at least until tomorrow, whether or not her resolve, as discussed, even comes into play.

If I am the patient in the hospital bed, and I am urged, even by a stranger, to fight for my life, will I know how to do it? It simply is not clear, has never been clear, how exactly one fights for one's life, with no tools, no weapons, no training, no information whatsoever.

Even the doctors, standing there personally watching me die, will not tell me a thing about what I can do on my own, right now, to extend my life and not succumb to what is killing me. Why is this information kept secret? A stranger might cheer me on, exhort me to dig deep and fight—and I say stranger because I did not marry and my brother and sister have passed. A stranger would, by necessity, attend my bed. Or no one. No one is more likely. Why would a stranger stop in my room, stand at my bed, and exhort me to live? What kind of stranger does things like that? And if the answer is a good kind of stranger, I must wonder if it is then my duty, not tonight, because I am busy, but sometime soon, to enter a hospital at night and find a patient alone in his or her room, preferably a patient on the brink of death, and urge them to fight, and fight hard? I should strive to be a good stranger, is that not correct?

My mother, if she were able, would attend my bed, and possibly even urge me to fight for my life, although I cannot picture her issuing such a command without laughing. It is her stated idea that many things we know and say and feel are ridiculous. I would think that by the time I am in my hospital bed being urged to fight for my life, my mother will be dead. She will have already fought for her life and lost. But now, on the brink of death herself, though not today, I don't think, I fear my mother is similarly in the dark. If I asked her to fight for her life, assuming a calamity brought her to the hospital, she might politely agree, if she could even speak, but to herself she would be forced to admit that she could not carry out such an action. The technique is beyond her. It has been beyond everyone in our family. None of us possess the skill to fight for our lives. One by one we pass away. If the known people of the world were ranked according to their ability to fight for their lives, my family would not score well.

I will hold my mother's hand and ask her to please hang on. She will want to please me because she has always wanted to please me, and so she will agree to fight for her life, to please me, but when it comes to actually fighting for her life she will be baffled. She will have spent her entire life having no control whatsoever of what happens inside her body, with her blood and cells and bones, not to mention the organs and nerves, and now, eighty-six years into this seasoned indifference, allowing the insides of her body to conduct their own affairs, she will be urged to suddenly pay attention and control her body to such a degree that it does not die. How could anyone ask this of a frail old woman?

In the nature films the behavior is clear. When their lives are threatened, animals shoot through the grass, faster than they've ever run before, sometimes shitting out of fright, or they turn and crouch, meet the attack. When they fight for their lives there is compelling evidence, whereas people are meant to fight for their lives without moving, without showing the slightest effort. A strictly internal struggle, not even detectable by medical machinery.

The scullery maid often has a confidant. The confidant might be a beautiful homosexual man, who has his own tricks to play. Someone on the staff has access to the secrets of the wealthy family they work for but at the same time feels too much allegiance to betray them.

I must wonder if I am terribly wrong to think my mother will not die today.

Someone who could easily address the question of odds is my father. He was a statistician by profession. A probablist is the official term. The question regarding the odds of my mother dying today would be an elementary one for my father and his colleagues, most of whom came from India. A fertile country for mathematicians, my father reportedly said. Or, perhaps, only for probablists. My father passed away, so he cannot address the question, and I cannot refer to my father's publications, some of which I have here with me, because they do not treat matters as elementary as these.

My mother's odds of dying increase every moment of her life. Right now, sleeping in her bed, she has never in her entire life been in greater danger of dying. So it would seem to me that I shouldn't be so secure in thinking she will not die today, not that I am particularly secure anymore, if only because it is more likely than ever that she will die right now. This statement, whenever I make it, will be true for the rest of her life. It will be true even if I do not make it. Even if I do not think this thought—that the danger my mother faces has never been greater—it will be true, which suggests to me that there are then likely many more thoughts I have not had, some of which are true. Many more. A tally of the thoughts I have not had would be impossible. Surely some of these thoughts I have failed to think bear down directly on the matter of my mother's life and death. Of the many things I have failed to think, and within that category those thoughts that are also true, which of them, if only I could think them now, would reveal to me more about my mother and her prospects for survival today?

And, if I should not be secure in thinking that my mother won't die today, it occurs to me that I would do well to return to her now, so that I might enjoy her company for her last moments alive.

You see, I aim to do what is right with regards to my mother and her last living days.

I need to consider this more carefully, though. By this reasoning, I would never be able to part from my mother again, since whenever I left her I would be doing so at the direst moment in her life when she was more likely than ever to pass away. This will be true, assuming my mother lives through the night, whenever I see her again. I would say good night, wish her well, and depart knowing that her risk of death was increasing while I walked away, while I left her apartment building, nodding to the doorman, and then walked the quiet side street to the busier avenue where the taxis gather. It would be difficult not to wonder at such times what kind of son walks away when his mother is in ever-greater danger of dying. Who does that? Kisses an old woman at her door, his own mother, knowing the whole time that she has never been in more danger?

It would appear that I do that. Every time I have left her, I have done that. If she lives through the night, I will do it again, take my leave knowing that even though yesterday her risk of dying was terribly high, today it has grown worse. It worsens as we speak, and still I must say good-bye to her as if I don't care that she is in increasing danger of dying.

I did it to her as a child, too. I said good-bye and went to school. I said good-bye and went to camp. I said good-bye on a Saturday morning and who knows when I came home. When I did this, I left my mother dying. In doorways, in kitchens, in living rooms, on lawns. Sometimes even when she was sick with a cold in bed, I said good-bye from the bottom of the stairs, just as her chances of dying had peaked. I said good-bye and went to college, when she was even more likely to die. And when I came home to visit, it wasn't long before I departed again, leaving her to die. Just as tonight, after watching a mystery on PBS, I said good night to my mother and left her at home to die.

We speak of having one foot in the grave, but we do not speak of having both feet and both legs and then one's entire torso, arms, and head in the grave, inside a coffin, which is covered in dirt, upon which is planted a pretty little stone.

The castle is always the same castle. Despite the mystery, despite the show, despite the cast, despite hundreds of years spanning different periods of time, it is always the same castle. A castle acquired for this purpose, perhaps, rented out to anyone needing to make a British mystery. Once there were real people living real lives in this castle, just as we, living in our own homes, consider ourselves real, with real lives. And if we consider that one day our own homes, as with the castle, will be used exclusively for the filming of television shows about people much like ourselves, it gives us a certain feeling about the destiny of our homes, where people hired to portray us will scamper about reciting sentences to each other, while off-camera the contemporary men and women, with up-to-date perspectives on life, devour unimaginable snacks and laugh at what simple, blind fools we must have been.

It is not untoward to believe that at some other location, so many years from now, an old woman and her only son will sit and watch this television show, or whatever it is called then, enjoying their dinner, not saying much, one of them sleeping, the other one looking on, waiting for her to wake up and declare something wonderful.

I am tempted to say that it would serve me right if my mother died today. Because I have chronically abandoned her, each time at the height of an ever-increasing danger, from the moment I could first walk, in some sense it would serve me right if she died. I would get what was coming to me. Her death, today, would be fitting. A comeuppance. However, when I think this through, and realize that I would deserve it if my mother dies today, it occurs to me that her death then becomes contingent on behavior I have or have not produced. Her death is a payment in response to behavior of mine. She cannot die unless I am fully deserving, although since I have been deserving for some time now, from a period beginning right after I was born, my mother has enjoyed a lengthy period in which she could die and I would be found deserving.

I am helpless then to wonder if there is someone in the world who would deserve it if I died. If, for instance, a person's death occurs as a punitive measure to some other person, as my mother's death, should it occur today, would certainly seem to me, then whose comeuppance is it when I die? Is there, for each of us, a culprit who will have had it coming when we go?

Well, of course, not every death needs to serve as a punishment of others, even while an attractive ecology is suggested by such a theory. So many things would suddenly be explained. Yet some deaths—my own, for instance—might be independent events, not designed as rebukes or scolds for anyone on earth. Deaths not really meant to trigger guilt in anyone. Deaths perhaps not meant to cause any feelings. Self-contained events without impact. Certainly the ecology of death would need to sustain variety in this regard. Or not certainly. I have no authority on this matter. There is the slight possibility, additionally, that the person for whom my death, when it does occur, is a comeuppance, will never learn of my death, never know that it served him right or that he had it coming. He might be in another part of the world, distant from the news sources that could alert him to my demise, if any news sources report the event. He might live out his days never knowing that I died, thus avoiding, forever, his comeuppance.

The butler, these days, is kindly, having endured long decades being stereotyped as cruel. Always now the butler is bottomlessly kind to everyone concerned.

It is perhaps the phrase, "The butler did it," that guarantees now, on the PBS mysteries my mother and I watch, that the butler will never have done it. The butler is now too nice to have done it. On the other hand, the current blamelessness of butlers, in mysteries such as these, suggests that the perfect villain must now again, or soon, be the butler. My mother explained once to me that the key to solving these mysteries, at their outset, is to identify the least likely culprit. Often this person ends up being the villain. She said that of the many revelations she'd had in her life, this was among the saddest, since it cruelly ruined any mystery she ever watched. Figuring things out, she said, is such a sadness. You didn't really know your father, she said, but he wasn't very hard to know. And that was the problem. What do you do once you know someone?

My father and his colleagues from India, as probablists, must have been considered master odds keepers, the most gifted of the people in the world who keep odds. Had they not passed away, I could turn to one or the other of them now with my questions of odds, but since they have passed away, they no longer keep the odds. Well, have the Indian probablists passed away, along with my father? Even if they have, there are, no doubt, successors. Each field of inquiry creates successors who desecrate and then improve upon the work of their mentors, and the mentors soon pass. No matter how masterful the mentor is, there is a successor waiting in the anteroom. There must be new Indian probablists, probably several new Indian probablists every year, a stream of successors flying in from India. Even my father must have had a successor, after he passed. Someone succeeded my father, the master odds keeper, whose gift I never got to witness. My father must have bequeathed his odds to this successor, who now keeps them. Even if my mother and I do not know this person's name or his where-abouts, we can safely believe that right now there is, at large in the world, a successor to my father, keeping what my father once kept. When my mother dies, though not today, and then, eventu-ally, when I die, will the successor to my father be considered our survivor, even if we did not know him? The thought offers some comfort.

Physicians who sign autopsy reports, listing a person's cause of death as unknown, attribute their momentary ignorance to the blind spots of science, which will one day come into view. Eventu-ally every cause of death will be known, in most cases well before the death. It is only that we now live in a curious time when some things cannot be known until after they happen. One imagines that years from now this will be viewed as a touching limitation to our way of life: having to wait for something to happen, like a mother's death, in order to know about it. People won't be able to imagine being so docile and patient as we are today, obsessing over the distinction between old-fashioned notions of before and after. They will love us tenderly for waiting around for our mothers to die, for being victims of time, but they will also feel superior to us, and some of them will make a cogent argument that in many ways we were not so different from animals in our ignorance, worthy of tremendous respect, but animals just the same.

If my mother did die today, she would not—I am nearly certain—be discovered until tomorrow. Tomorrow, at the earliest. To be discovered today, someone other than her son would have to think, out of nowhere, late at night, right now, to ring my mother's doorbell, and then, receiving no response, would need to summon the building superintendent and gain entrance to her apartment. Aside from the unlikelihood, which is considerable, this would take time. Tomorrow would have come before this person had even reached the super. The super's phone might be off. Perhaps there would be an option to page the super, but it is doubtful the super would respond fast enough, with a key, in order for my mother to be discovered today.

It is bewildering to consider that while these mysteries are being filmed, there are young men and women standing off-camera, wearing contemporary clothing, holding contemporary views of sexuality and ethics, grinning behind their hands at the sad animals strutting in front of the camera.

Even if the super picked up right away. In addition, there would be other explanations for an unanswered doorbell, and the super would have to be mindful.

There is often a young girl in the wealthy family, unbearably beautiful, in league with the servants.

It is late at night and most people are asleep. Old people go to bed early. If my mother has gone to bed, which I hope she has, and fallen asleep, which I hope she has, it is likely she will not hear the doorbell.

The girl is the sole object of sympathy from the wealthy classes, suggesting that not all rich people from the old days were evil.

The super would make this same argument, would be reluctant to use his key to gain entrance to my mother's apartment. He would want some proof that something had happened. The worry of a neighbor could not count as proof. Blood under the door would be proof. But even if she had died, it is not likely there would be blood under the door. Proof would be very hard to come by.

A constable always comes, but a constable never solves the crime. No body, no crime, my mother sometimes shouts from her chair.

The super would be justified in wondering why a neighbor, in the middle of the night, had decided to ring the doorbell of an old woman, demanding entrance to her apartment. This is not a neighborly action.

There is a pecking order regarding who can answer the door, such tasks being left usually to the footman.

The super would make a case for waiting until morning, thereby guaranteeing that even if my mother died today, she would not be discovered until tomorrow.

If, on the other hand, my mother were to die loudly, creating some commotion, and neighbors were to hear, it is possible they would reach her in time, not to save her life, necessarily, but at least to discover that she died today. To find her today, leaving very little surprise for tomorrow. There would be my own surprise upon receiving the terrible phone call alerting me to the unfortunate event inside my mother's home. Many people would know of my mother's death before me, a thought that does not please me. I feel that such an event would be mine to know about first, which I realize is the explanation often given by murderers—they wanted to be the first to learn of an important event, and the only way to be in that position was to cause the event itself, so they killed people, thus learning of the event before anyone else. But my motive in this respect is altogether different. To some of these people my mother's death would be old hat by the time I found out. Other people in the area may have died in the intervening hours, displacing my mother in their thoughts. On the world stage many thousands of people would have died after my mother, yet before I was alerted. If she fell on the stairs and cried out. If she collapsed from some mishap to her circulation. Perhaps instead of crying out, my mother would have the strength to dial her phone. She might lack the energy to cry out loudly enough to be heard. Screaming requires a terrific summoning of muscle. It scares me to think that one day I will be too weak to scream when I most need to scream. I will produce only small sounds, barely audible even to myself. If, crawling on her hands and knees, severely disabled from a circulatory event, my mother reached the phone and dialed it, she could conduct a quiet conversation, alerting the party on the line to the circumstances. Help would be called, and help would come.

The question of discovery becomes complicated here. If, for instance, my mother is able, by telephone, to alert the party on the line to her medical situation, dying shortly thereafter, does this information constitute adequate discovery for the later determination that my mother died today? I think not. I think the remote party on the line can learn that the medical crisis began today, precipitating my mother's telephone call, but unless she died while talking on the phone, before midnight, it would not, from this evidence, be possible to definitively declare time of death. Even if she, because of death, dropped the phone, the remote party, unable to see her, would lack definitive proof that she suddenly died in the middle of the conversation. The remote party might only conclude that my mother could no longer speak or make sounds, or, also, move, because the remote party would hear nothing if indeed my mother, against the odds, died today. There would be silence. But silence is not enough.

If I want my mother to survive, as I continue to say that I do, so she is not discovered dead in her apartment, should I not hire a companion for her? If people who do not live alone ultimately, per the studies, live longer than people who do, and if I have not rescued my mother from living alone, is it not the case that I am enabling her to die sooner rather than later? This would be a factor I could control. This would be *me* fighting for *her* life, since my mother cannot, as established, fight for her own life, just as none of the people in our family, of which we are the two surviving members, can. And if one living partner increases the life of both parties, would not two living partners add that much more time to my mother's life? Unless there are diminishing returns. But, even so, returns are returns, however diminished, and one must guess that the more people who reside with my mother, the longer she will live. The reasoning hereafter becomes troubling. At what point does it end? Can I continue to acquire companions for my mother, thus sustaining her life perhaps well past her natural point of demise, adding companions to her entourage each day so she never dies? The logistics collapse around such a project.

A crowd employed to accompany my mother would need to be paid and fed, they would need to be lodged, and then, at certain times, such as when I visit for dinner and television, the crowd, at my command, would need to disperse, so I could be alone with my mother and enjoy her company. Together we'd sift through the takeout menus, making a show of choosing, of looking at the entrees for the Afghan place, and the delicious side plates offered from the Turkish place, but settling, as we always do, on Italian, which is what we both love, getting our pastas, requesting extra bread, and sometimes, but not always, sharing a salad. If we are feeling wicked, I will draw up stools by our chairs so we can, as we say, eat and watch, and more and more we are feeling wicked. And yet, when I dispatch the crowd and give my mother only the lone companion, me, am I endangering her, creating a sudden withdrawal from the people who were saving her life? Is this not another way of killing her, making me a murderer? She has thrived with a large population of life-extending companions, and now, her selfish son sends them away so she can die sooner, in exchange for a private moment—even though they hardly speak—of which the selfish son has had far more than his share? He is her son and he has kept his mother to himself his whole life, even when his brother and sister briefly lived, and his father the odds keeper briefly lived, vying for the attention that was always aimed first at him, as if through a bright, golden cone, but all he ever did was say good-bye to her, nearly every day of his life. All of those paid companions, waiting outside—blocking traffic, because there are thousands of them by now, he has spent his last penny on them—the companions crowded together looking in the window at mother and son, eating dinner in front of the television set, wondering how he could do this to her, leave her alone like that. What kind of son is he?

Someone always has a past, and someone's past is always returning, ruinously. The past, in the mind of the person who had it, is terrible and shameful, but to the television viewer the terrible past this person had is only ever endearing. The illegitimate child is one of the more common shameful pasts dramatized on PBS. This plot troubles my mother. She does not care for it. Once she said that all children are illegitimate, and I laughed, but she shot me a look. Illegitimate children grow up into illegitimate adults, only to die and become illegitimate corpses, buried illegitimately. Soon she fell asleep and I learned that the illegitimate child, who was an heiress, had taken a scullery position in the very mansion where her unwitting family lived. My mother woke and angrily declared, seemingly out of nowhere, that this girl would be the first suspect in the episode, and she would be shamed and abused and shamed again, but in the end they would discover that she did not do it. There is always a first suspect, quickly forgiven. Nowadays there are several suspects who wind up innocent. That's what you want to be, my mother advised, pointing her finger at me. The first suspect. Be the first suspect. The first suspect never did it.

If my mother did die today, she would die while I was writing. Years from now someone might ask me what I was doing when my mother died and I would have to answer that I was home, writing. This scenario implies that I will one day meet someone who will take the familiar with me, because there is no one presently in my life who would think, I think, to ask me such a question. Does a stranger, even a well-intentioned one, ask such a question? I would have to meet someone who would, quickly or slowly—I'm fine with either—gain enough familiarity with me to pose this personal question. Perhaps this man or woman would be someone with whom I would grow close, even though I would be an older person by then with little to offer in terms of romantic maneuvers. We'd pose each other questions on couches, chairs, park benches, beds, in cars and on buses and sometimes walking through fields, or so I imagine, seeking to overcome each other's defenses, hoping that personal questions, asked and answered, would come, over time, to pass for intimacy, but wondering, sometimes, if that's even how it's done, and if that doesn't somehow seem too strenuous a method of getting someone finally to love you.

This question of what I was doing when someone died, however, does not seem to be asked about the death of unremarkable citizens. We only seem to ask after someone's whereabouts when it comes to the death of celebrities. So I can perhaps count on the odds that—even if I do gain a companion in my life going forward, an event that I would welcome—I won't be asked what I was doing when my mother died. No one will have to know, unless I volunteer it. Odds are. Unless, in my eulogy, which I would have to write very quickly, I declare my whereabouts when she died.

It's often the young, wild-haired simpleton, whose accent is more cockney than the others, indicating the deepest possible underdog. She assists the cook and the cook treats her poorly. Everyone treats her poorly. Her very employment is a matter of charity. They underestimate her. Not my mother. Early on, even during the opening credits, my mother wags her finger and says, Look out for that one!

What I will be able to say, without lying, is that when my mother died I was at home thinking about her, since in order to write about my mother I must first think about her, and in that sense she is very much in my thoughts. In order to increase the chances of this being true, it would seem that I should not stop writing, or at the very least thinking, about my mother, at the risk of thinking of something else and then having her suddenly die.

If, for instance, I get up from my chair and become distracted at the refrigerator, deciding that I'd like a taste of cold yogurt, and then for those moments cease thinking about my mother, I run the risk that she will die, alone, in no one's thoughts, while her only son ate from an open container and stared into nowhere, thinking, for a moment, of nothing.

I cannot let this happen.

Episode after episode, watching mysteries with my mother, I look out for the wild-haired simpleton. I watch the wild-haired simpleton, waiting for her to strike, and yet her endgame is slow, her long play is invisible, so much so that by the time the credits roll the wild-haired simpleton has yet to pounce. She is frequently back where she started, working in a kitchen, having come to nothing. She has nowhere to go, and nobody loves her, and the wild-haired simpleton herself, with her soft, gray teeth, seems incapable of loving anyone else. My mother nods and says, Don't write that one off.

The credits have rolled, the show is over. The contemporary people standing off camera with their up-to-date views on the world have wandered away to go home. The actress portraying the wild-haired simpleton resumes her normal, highly educated accent, yanks the tangled fright wig from her head, returns to her trailer to shower and put on her smart clothing. My mother, though, watching the credits and smiling, looks at me with sharp eyes.

Next time, she promises. That one isn't done. She's got more fight in her. She's a fighter, that one. She'll get them next time.

# The Loyalty Protocol

The phone call said to come alone, but he couldn't just leave them. Perhaps they'd been called, too, and didn't remember the procedure, which would only figure. His father was not good with instructions. Worse, his father was fatally indifferent to what people said. Other people spoke and the man's face went blank, as if any voice but his own was in a foreign language. Perhaps his father had not heard the phone. Or maybe he mistook the message for a prank and hung up.

Later, his helpless parents in tow, Edward could explain the mistake, if necessary. By then it'd be too conspicuous to leave them stranded in the road while everyone else left town.

Owing to the roadblock that would be set up on Morris Avenue, Edward parked at Grove and Williams and trekked through muddy backyards to the apartment complex. He cursed himself, because he'd have to lead his parents back the same way, down a wet slope where his car would be waiting. In the many configurations they'd rehearsed at the workshop, somehow he had not accounted for this major obstacle: herding his parents in the dark down a steep, wet slope.

His father was awake and packed already, wandering through the apartment. When Edward walked in, his father started to put on his coat.

"Where's Mom?"

"Not coming, I guess," his father said.

"Dad."

"You try. I tried already. You try if you want to. I'm disgusted.

I'm ready to go. Do you know how many times I've had to do this?"

"Did they call you?" Edward asked.

"Did who call me?" His father was on the defensive. Had he even slept? Had he been up all night, waiting?

"Did your phone ring tonight?" Edward asked, trying not to sound impatient. There were cautions against this very thing, the petty quarrels associated with departure, which only escalate during an emergency.

"I don't know, Eddie. Our phone doesn't work. I'm ready to go. I'm always ready. We're down there almost every night. Why not tonight?"

Edward picked up the phone and heard an odd pitch. More like an emergency signal than a dial tone.

"You don't believe me?" his father said. "I tell you the phone doesn't work and you don't trust me?"

"I trust you. Let's get Mom and go."

His mother was in bed, sheets pulled over her face. It felt wrong to sit on his parents' bed, to touch his mother while she was lying down. Standing up, he could hug and kiss his mother with only the usual awkwardness, but once she was prone it seemed inappropriate, like touching a dead person. He shook her gently.

"C'mon, Mom, let's go. Get dressed."

She answered from under the sheets, in a voice that was fully awake. Awake and bothered.

"I'm too tired. I'm not going."

They'd been told that, at times like this, old people dig in their heels. More than any other population, the elderly refuse to go. They hide in their homes, wait in the dark of their yards while their houses are searched. Often they request to die. Some of them do not request it. They take matters into their own hands.

But there were a few little things you could do to persuade them, and Edward had learned some of them in the workshop.

"Mom, you don't know what you're saying. You really don't want to be here, I promise you."

"See what I told you?" said his father from the doorway.

"Tell him to shut up," said his mother.

"You shut up," his father barked. "Don't ever tell me to shut up."

"Shut up," she whispered.

They waited in his parents' room, where he'd come and snuggled as a child, a thousand years ago, and he couldn't help siding with his mother. It would be so wonderful to fall back asleep right now. If only.

"Mom, if you don't come with us, who knows where you'll sleep tonight. Or you won't sleep. I can guarantee that you won't like what will happen. It will be horrible. Do you want me to tell you what will happen?"

He could hear his mother breathing under the sheets. She seemed to be listening. He paused a bit longer for suspense.

"I could spell it out for you. Would you like me to do that? I have to say I'd rather not."

Something wordless, passing for surrender, sounded. Edward left the room to give her time and it wasn't long before she joined them in the front hall, scowling. She'd thrown a coat over her nightgown and carried a small bag.

"Okay?" said Edward.

They didn't answer, just followed him outside, where the streets were empty.

"Where's your car?" his mother grumbled.

He explained what they'd have to do and they looked at him as if he were crazy.

"Do you see any other cars here?" he whispered. "Do you know why?"

"Don't act like you know what's going on," his father whispered as they trekked out. "You're as much in the dark as we are.

You have no idea what's really happening. None. Fucking hotshot. Tell me one fact. I dare you."

When they reached the hill and had to navigate the decline, his mother kept falling. She'd fall and cry out, landing on her rear end in the grass. He'd never heard her cry in pain before. His father was beside her holding her arm, but she was the larger of his parents and when she stumbled his father strained and couldn't hold her up. He lost his temper and kept yelling at her, and finally, softly, she said she was doing her best. She really was.

"Well, I can't carry you!" he yelled.

"Then don't," she replied, and she stood up and tried to walk on her own, but she went down again, with an awful cry, sliding through the mud.

In the car she wept and Edward felt ashamed. This was supposedly the easy part.


The gymnasium was crowded. A motor roared, which must have been the generator, because they would have lost power at this point. They signed in, then looked for their settlements, divided by neighborhood. This was the drill. Edward would have a different settlement from his parents, which he'd tried to explain to them, but his father had trouble with the terminology.

"It's not a settlement," he'd said.

"Okay, I agree, but that's what they're calling it."

"It's ridiculous. We'll be staying there for what, a few hours, not even, and they call it a settlement? A settlement is a place where people stop and stay. You know, people *live* in a settlement."

"Dad, I don't think it really matters. I think what matters is you find the area where you're supposed to be and then go there."

"But it won't be the area where *you* will be, am I right?"

"That's right. But I'll be nearby. I'll be able to check on you and Mom."

"You don't know that, though, Eddie. How could you know that?"

When Edward brought his parents to their settlement, he could not get them admitted. A young woman he knew as Hannah had the clipboard. After scanning her pages, she shook her head.

"They're not on my list."

"They live in this neighborhood." He gave her their address, their apartment number. For no real reason he gave her their zip code, the solitary zip code for all of them.

In the crowd that had already registered were several of his parents' neighbors, huddled against a wall. There were retirees from his parents' building. Neighbors who knew his parents. This was the right place. He waved, but no one saw him.

Hannah stared from behind her clipboard. He could sense the protocol overwhelming her mind. A street address, recited anecdotally, was no kind of evidence. Anyone could deliver that information. Edward was only a man talking.

"Do you want to see their driver's licenses?" he asked, a bit too curtly. Not that he'd brought them.

"No. I want to see their names on this list, and since I don't, I can't admit them. I have the most straightforward job in the world. If you have a problem you should discuss it with Frederick, but something tells me I know what he'll say."

From under her shawl Edward's mother said, "Eddie, it's okay, we'll go with you to yours." She sounded relieved. That would solve everything and they could be together.

Edward looked at Hannah, who simply raised her eyebrows. She and Edward had once been on a team together at the beginning. She had seemed nice. Very smart, too, which explained her promotion. Unfortunately, Hannah was impossibly striking. He had been so desperately compelled by her face that he had instantly resolved never to look at her or show her any kind of attention. Everything would be much easier that way. It was troubling now to discover that Hannah ran his parents' settlement. Was this how things were now? Had everything shifted again? It meant he'd have to see more of her and regularly be reminded that she would never be his. She would never kiss him or get undressed for him or relieve his needs before work or stop trying to look pretty for him, which was the part he liked best, at least when he played out futures with women he'd never speak to. When someone like Hannah, not that there'd ever been someone like Hannah, let herself go and showed up on the couch after dinner in sweatpants and a long, chewed-up sweater. It was unbearable.

Edward knew that he shouldn't do this, but Hannah would have to understand. He broke character and pleaded with her.

"There's nowhere else to go. Can you please take them? Please? Is someone really going to come by later and match each person to a name on your list?"

She hardened her face. She wasn't going to drop the act, and she seemed disgusted with Edward for having done so himself.

"Did they get a phone call?" she asked. Even this question seemed beneath her.

He started to answer, figuring he could lie, when his father blurted out that their phone was broken. How could you get a phone call with a broken phone?

"I assumed they did," he confided to Hannah. "That's the truth. Why wouldn't they get a call? Look, their neighbors are here. People from the same building. Why would my parents have been left out?"

At this last question she looked at him flatly. Why indeed.

"They're not supposed to be here," Hannah said. "You shouldn't have brought them. You might consider . . ." She seemed reluctant to say what she was thinking. "At this point you've made a serious mistake and you need to decide how to fix it with minimal impact on the community."

She glanced pitilessly at his parents, then muttered, "I know what I would do."

Edward figured that he knew what she would do, too.

He leaned in so he could speak into her ear. "Are you carrying?" he whispered. "Because if you are, and I could borrow it, I could kill them right here, and it would be a lesson for everyone."

She was stone-faced. That wasn't funny. "There are people behind you. I have a protocol to run."

Don't we all, Edward thought. But his protocol, to keep his parents safe, could not be achieved here.

"Okay, well, thanks for your help," he said, sneering. "Good teamwork. Way to go."

She kept her cool. "So you want me to make a mistake, arguably a bigger one, because you did? Let's say your mistake was an accident, which possibly it was, although I can't say. I'm guessing you're not an imbecile, although this is only a guess. You want me to consciously break the rules. You want your error, a stupid error, if you ask me, to beget other errors so we're both somehow to blame, even though I do not know you and have no responsibility for you? How does that do you a favor? How does that help you? At this point you need to fall on your sword. I don't understand what's so hard about that."

Why was it so much worse to be shamed by an attractive person? Somehow he felt he could handle this critique from anyone else in the world.

Just then the lights switched on in the gymnasium and a hush fell. Frederick, leader of the readiness workshop, walked in with his wireless microphone. Everyone watched him. He stood at center court, tucked the microphone under his arm, and started to clap methodically, as if he were killing something between his hands. Soon everyone was applauding, moving in close to hear what Frederick would say. The drill, apparently, was over.

He thumped his mic, said *Hello, Hello,* and everyone fell silent. He was such a cock, Edward thought. An impossible cock.

"So," he said, in his quick, high voice. "Fair work tonight. Not terrible. We made okay time. Maybe we're a half hour slow, and I don't need to tell you what that means."

"Boom!" someone yelled from the crowd, to an eruption of laughter.

"Boom is right," replied Frederick. "But it's not funny."

The laughter stopped.

"We would have lost people. A certainty. I would have faced a decision, a certainty, even as some of you drove up in your cars. Some of you wouldn't have made it. You'd have watched us leave and, believe me, you would not have been permitted to follow. I won't spell that out. You'd be alone now and it would be getting colder. You'd wonder how much gas remained. You'd wonder about the power grid, the water supply, the food supply. You'd determine, correctly, that you know nothing about these things. Nothing. You'd need a leader. Or would you? Maybe you could decide things as a group. You'd start to quarrel. You'd divide. It would get colder. This is supposed to be the easy leg. We didn't even do the highway drill tonight. Do you know how much time we'll lose on the highway?"

"Too much!" the crowd yelled.

"That's right. The highway is an ugly variable. There's a reason we have not shared the details with you. The highway. We cannot find a way to speak of it that is not disturbing. Whereas this"— Frederick gestured into the gymnasium—"this you can control, down to the second. Which means I'd like to see us shave off that half hour. Maybe forty-five minutes. We need breathing room. We need to join our settlements without panic, with time to kill. Next time we do this I want time to kill. Tonight we had no time to kill. And you know what?"

Someone from far in the back of the gym shouted, "What?"

"I'm disappointed," Frederick said. He shut his eyes. The gymnasium seemed to groan.

"But do you know what else?" Frederick asked, staring from his expressionless face.

No one responded.

"I'm proud as hell of you. Every single one of you."

Except me, thought Edward. He was pretty sure that Frederick wouldn't be proud of him.


They broke out in groups for the critique and Edward sat in a circle with his settlement. His parents, because they weren't meant to be part of tonight's drill, were dismissed. Since they had no way to get home, they were probably waiting for him outside.

The group leader for Edward's settlement was Sharon, and she led them through the discussion. Everything was not well. Edward, she pointed out, had not registered, even though he was here in the gym. Explain that. Did he have trouble finding them? Was something wrong with Edward? Was he perhaps injured or confused? A check at the medical tent and then personal observation had confirmed that Edward was fine. Edward didn't register with his settlement because he'd brought outsiders with him, and these outsiders had turned out to be a serious liability.

"It's as though we've never discussed anything. It's as though this workshop never happened," said Sharon. "We fought the interests of the group. In real life this might have turned unthinkable."

"I hardly think . . ." Edward started.

"Hold up, Eddie," warned Thom. "You don't talk during your critique."

"What's a possible consequence for Edward?" said Marni.

Geoff jumped in. "I think we should do something humiliating to his parents. That's much more disturbing, because he'd have to see them get hurt. I think that's a good punishment. The punishment doesn't fit the crime; it is the crime. I mean, I don't want his parents to be seriously harmed, necessarily, but there's nothing worse than watching your parents, who are defenseless, get hurt in some way."

Everyone laughed. Everyone except Sharon, who glared at Edward.

"Okay, guys, I get it," said Edward. "If there's ever a real crisis, I'll be sure only to look out for myself. Don't worry, I've learned my lesson."

"Unfortunately, Edward, this is not about you learning a lesson," said Sharon. "I'm glad your colleagues think it's funny, but this is about deterring others from suddenly deciding they can bring friends with them on an evacuation."

"My parents aren't my *friends*," he said. "They're my *parents*. I thought they'd gotten a call, too. I didn't realize some people didn't get called. Who here with parents still alive wouldn't have done the same thing?"

Some hands went up.

"Yes, Liz?" said Sharon.

"Me," said Liz, putting her arm down. "My parents are at home right now. It would never have occurred to me to bring them along."

It wouldn't have even *occurred* to her, Edward thought? How do you get to that place? He didn't even like his parents, but he brought them along. Was that kind of thinking out of date? Had everyone evolved?

A few people echoed this. They'd left their parents behind.

Good for you, Edward thought. This could easily have been

the real thing. Wasn't that the point, that you never knew? You murderous fucks.

"Does anyone think it's strange," Edward ventured, "that our parents weren't called tonight?"

"Honestly, Edward," said Thom. "This is the second time you've spoken during your critique. We shouldn't have to warn you about this. You can't learn from what happened tonight unless you're completely silent now."

"I thought that what I learn doesn't matter," Edward snapped. "Isn't this about you learning not to be like me?"

"No chance of that," said a young woman on the opposite side of the circle, who stared at Edward so defiantly that he looked away.

On Edward's way out, Frederick broke from a mob of admirers and grabbed his arm.

"Edward, a word."

He'd never stood so close to Frederick, never had a private audience with him. As much as he disliked him, he couldn't deny how compelling Frederick was. Impossibly handsome, confident, with the figure of a small gymnast. This was a person for the future.

"What you did tonight was arguably brave. You demonstrated a priority for love and loyalty. You protected two fragile people who had no other savior, even though technically they were not in danger and would have been much safer at home. Technically, we may have decided that they were a danger to *you*, and yet you went to them anyway, endangering everyone else. You made a choice, and on the individual level, that choice was courageous and selfless, even if at the level of the group you risked our entire operation. If those had been my parents, may they rest in peace, and I didn't have my years of training, and I also didn't have sophisticated instincts and survival habits, it's possible I would have done the exact same thing. In other words, if I were *you*, and knew *next to nothing* about how to keep people alive today, tomorrow, and the next day, I might have brought my parents here tonight as well. It is completely possible. It's precisely because I can relate, however abstractly, to what you did that you won't see any lenience from me. Not a trace. On the contrary, you will meet great resistance from me, and if you do anything like that again, I promise I will hurt you. But I want you to know, face-to-face, how much I admire you."

When he got outside, his mother was asleep in the car, his father leaning on the door.

"I bet you're expecting an apology from me," said his father.

Edward was tired. He said that he wasn't, that he only wanted to get home. He had a big day tomorrow.

"Because I didn't do anything wrong," his father continued.

"I know that, Dad."

"It doesn't really seem like you know it."

"I do. I would like to go home now, that's all."

"Okay, go. You're the one who screwed up, anyway. We don't need your help. You should be ashamed of yourself. Go straight home. Your mother and I will walk."

"You're not going to walk."

"Katherine! Katherine!" his father shouted into the car, banging on the window. "Wake up! We have to walk home. Eddie refuses to drive us."

"Dad, get in. Please. I'm driving you home. Don't worry."

"Because we wouldn't want to put you out."


They waited in the line of cars revving to leave the high school parking lot. Some people took these evening drills—hellish and deeply pointless as they were—as valuable social encounters. So Edward and his parents sat in traffic—his mother asleep, his father grinding his teeth—while athletically attired settlement leaders strolled up to cars and leaned against drivers' windows, chatting it out. Running the drill backward, doing the blow by blow, reliving the night because the crisis protocol training was all they damn well had in their lives.

Edward didn't dare honk. These glad-handing semiprofessional tragedy consumers would turn on him, attack the car, eat his face. Or, worse, they'd stare at him and start to hate him slightly more, if that were possible.

His father, on the other hand, hadn't noticed that they weren't moving.

"That Hannah is a Nazi cunt," his father said.

"Dad, you can't say things like that about people."

"She's a Nazi cunt with a tiny cock."

"Okay, Dad."

"What, you don't agree? You don't like her, either. Tell me you don't agree."

"I don't agree. She's in a tough position. She's just doing her job."

That set him off.

"Just doing her job! Gandhi was just doing his job."

"Gandhi?"

"Not Gandhi, that other one. That other one!"

His father was in a rage.

"Which other one? Hitler?"

"The one with the stick. With the blowtorch that reaches across fields down into bunkers. The one who had that huge set of keys! Like a thousand keys on that goddamn monstrous key chain. The one with the small gun they have in the museum in D.C."

"Mussolini?" he guessed.

"Fuck you!" his father yelled. "Goddamn amateur!"

Edward locked the doors of the car.

"I'm not sure I know who you're talking about," Edward responded carefully, "but I know what you mean. You really don't like Hannah. I get it."

"Bullshit. You know exactly who I'm talking about. You learned about him in school. I remember you coming home one day saying you wanted to be this motherfucker, this dictator, for Halloween. Imagine how your mother reacted to that."

His mother. If this had really happened, how would she have reacted? She probably would have cheerfully gone along with it, fitting little Eddie with a large key ring and a blowtorch, sending him off into the neighborhood to gather candy. At the moment, though, his mother had the right idea. She was snoring softly in the backseat.

At Edward's office the next day, a receptionist fell from her chair and died. The paramedics set up a perimeter around her desk while colleagues from the office looked on, whispering. Edward tried to keep his employees calm. He ran a modest shipping firm where nothing like this ever happened. Why wouldn't the paramedics touch her, even if it was clear she was dead? Their fear did not bode well. What was the protocol? One of them squinted through a monocle at her body. The others pushed back her cubicle partition. They took pictures and air samples and questioned the coworkers who sat nearby, but they stayed away from her.

The paramedics consulted a radio, then turned to question Edward and his employees.

Had anyone touched this woman? Her clothing? Her hair? Her skin?

No one answered, but of course they had touched her. Edward

had still been in his office when she collapsed, but he understood that they'd tried to revive her. They'd loosened her clothing, breathed into her mouth, pounded on her chest. The usual hopeless tricks, taught by sad specialists at adult education centers. And, one year ago, at this very office, for a reasonable discount. Were you not supposed to touch someone who died?

A few hands went up, and these people were escorted to a private office.

"What's going on?" someone yelled. "Where are you taking them? What are you going to do?"

"Calm down, they'll be fine," someone else answered, and this set things off.

"How do you know? You don't know anything. You have no idea what's going on."

The paramedics announced that the office would need to be cleared. Everyone out, quickly and safely, and this quieted people down. They were to please follow their evacuation drill. Employees could wait across the street in the park. They wanted to be able to see everyone from the window.

For what? Edward wondered to himself. So they can take aim?

It would be a little while before this was resolved, the paramedics explained, so people were free to get coffees if they wanted to. Edward hung back until most of his employees had filed out. It was really not appropriate for a paramedic, or anyone, for that matter, to tell his employees to take a coffee break. But he would let it go.

He introduced himself as the boss and asked what was going on, what did they think?

They stared at him.

"Because we thought it was an aneurysm," he went on. "Except she's so young. A stroke, maybe? At any rate, it's horrible. Was it a heart attack? Probably not. What do you guys think?"

When they didn't answer he continued to theorize out loud,

naming ailments. They were leaving him stranded. He couldn't handle this conversation by himself.

"Sir," said a paramedic, "we'll have to ask you to leave with the others."

"Okay," Edward said. "But do you know how long this will be? I need to know what to tell my employees. We have kind of a crazy day ahead."

It was true. Edward had five job candidates to interview after lunch, and he had been planning to spend the morning in preparation.

The paramedics shook their heads and stared at him again, as if they were baffled that Edward expected them to stoop to a conversation with someone like him.

Edward wasn't finished. This was his office, and they were sprawled out in his chairs, and they'd moved and probably broken office equipment he'd paid for, while completely ignoring him. Or, at the very least, failing to take him seriously.

"It's Kristina," he said.

Again they looked at him in their odd way, like doctors standing around at a morgue.

"Kristina is her name," Edward said, gesturing at the dead woman. "She's from Ditmars. I hired her about six months ago. She went to college . . . I forget where. She was a terrific employee. Here's her emergency contact information, if you want it. But maybe you don't want it. Maybe you guys don't care. Maybe this is simply too boring for you and that's why you can't speak. You're bored. Well, her name is Kristina. Show some fucking respect."

One of the paramedics stood up.

"Sir," he said, gesturing at an officer holding a cell phone. "This is Deputy Arnold Sjogren. His sister was a close friend of Kristina's. We know exactly who she is, we grieve her passing, and now we are doing our jobs. The longer you stand here yelling at us, without any facts, the greater risk you place yourself in. I can't speak for my colleagues, but I personally do not require a lesson in respect. We are risking our lives today, and you are not. Who should be showing respect to whom?"

It was cold outside, not yet ten in the morning. Kristina must have only just started work when she died. In truth, Edward reflected, she had been a detached figure in the office, a kind of ghost. When she was trained, including a short session with Edward himself—since he tried to impress upon his new employees the larger aims of the company—she seemed indifferent. He felt obliged to act excited about his life's work, even if it sometimes exhausted him.

Across the street stood his employees, shivering and coatless, holding their arms. Others huddled together, crying.

Edward and his employees—all fifteen of them, or it'd be fourteen now—were not accustomed to being outside together. It was Edward who made them nervous, and he knew it. He shunned the public spaces at work for this very reason, protecting his employees from the destabilizing effect of his presence, keeping to his private office whenever he could. What a kind service to offer, to keep them from having to see him up close. He tried to be nice and cordial, but it was true that in some deep way he had trouble thinking of them as human, with lives outside of the office. Was this bad, especially if he never showed it? He thought of himself as deeply empathic—if mainly toward himself. In theory he held a strong share of empathy in reserve for a stranger he had yet to meet.

His team was standing in the little patch of dirt that passed for a park. When Edward approached they fell silent. A broad swing set creaked on the other side of the square. As the boss, it seemed that he should speak. He should sum up, or lead them in prayer, or say something, perhaps, cheerful. Maybe it was too soon for that?

"Well, poor thing," said Edward, finally.

"Did you call her family?" someone asked, and the others nodded, leaning in.

This alarmed him. Was he supposed to do that? How could he call Kristina's family if he didn't know the facts? At any rate he'd left the emergency contact card with the paramedics.

"They're taking care of it," Edward said, nodding up at the building.

But were they? He could feel his employees thinking that this was *his* job. He was supposed to take care of it, not some bland paramedics, inured to calamity. What if one of *them* had died, he imagined them thinking. Would Edward, their supervisor, neglect to call their families, leaving it to some rookie EMT who might not even be able to pronounce their names? What fucking kind of boss was he? Any one of them could have died today. They could die tomorrow, or next week. Could Edward be trusted to call their spouses or roommates or parents—to at least pretend that he cared?

After they stood there looking at their feet, someone volunteered that they'd been discussing how Kristina might have died. They focused on Edward again, and again he hated being in charge.

"Did you learn anything? What did they say?"

Edward shook his head. "I shouldn't really comment," he said, adopting an air of secrecy. "They asked me not to say anything. I'm sorry. I'd better not."

Oh, was he something. For a few moments Edward's employees could—wrongly! wrongly!—see him as a person with exclusive information, entrusted with a secret. An insider. And in exchange, what? What did he get for this lie? Well, for one, Edward would never forget what he'd said here today, how low he'd fallen. That seemed fair. A fair deal. He might as well bask in their awestruck sense of his power. Why not enjoy it for a while?

People started to drift off. Jonathan took a sandwich order, but when it grew too complicated someone suggested that they all go, and they looked at Edward expectantly. This was going to take a while. He sent them off with his blessing—explaining that he should really stay here in case they needed him—and he was left alone in the park, staring up at the window to his office, where, for some reason, the shade had been drawn.

The first job candidate showed up right on time, minutes after the hazmat truck and the mayor's motorcade pulled away. Edward and his employees had only just been cleared to return to the building. The candidate, Elise Mortensen, was announced when Edward returned to his office, where he discovered that his documents had been disturbed. His filing cabinets were open. On his shelves the books had been tossed around. Did they think he was hiding something? A smell ran through the room, too, something floral that he hadn't noticed in the outer offices. He didn't have time to take stock of what had changed or to wonder what they were looking for in his office, so far from where Kristina died, when Elise Mortensen came in, adopting an exaggerated tiptoe, as if she were disturbing him, which she kind of fucking was, and asked where to sit.

Edward fumbled through the interview. He started with the dreaded opener *Tell me about yourself,* so he could collect his thoughts. Elise Mortensen seemed to have been waiting her whole life to answer this question and she went for it. She delivered a droning memoir that kept rising in tone, which assured Edward that it might not end until she died. He kept his eyes fixed on hers and established a pattern of interested nods, then withdrew his attention to the place where it rightly belonged. On himself.

Edward tried to piece together the morning's events. What interest would the *mayor* have in Kristina's death, and why would

Frederick from the workshop be part of the mayor's entourage? This was arguably the worst part of the morning, standing across the street watching the mayor exit his car, followed by business-suited staff whispering into their phones, and then, what the fuck, Frederick from the workshop, almost like a government official now, wearing his jumpsuit, carrying a duffel bag.

At that point Edward figured it was okay to bring his employees across the street so they could wait at the entrance. In truth it offered Edward another chance to discuss the situation with officials, perhaps reestablish his authority. This was his office! He paid rent here, and the death had happened during working hours at his business. And he, not that he wanted to broadcast this, was liable for what happened. But of course he was rebuffed at the door by a police officer, even while his employees looked on, knowing—how could they not know?—that Edward had no influence. No role to play. He was a bystander just like they were.

When the mayor came out, Frederick pointed at Edward in the crowd.

"There he is!" yelled Frederick, and the mayor's entire entourage peered into the crowd, as if a rare animal had been sighted.

Edward froze.

"That's the man!"

Next to Edward stood Philip, who returned Frederick's greeting, said things were fine, considering, and what the hell, a tragedy, right, to which Frederick shrugged, pointing at the mayor with a knowing look. This wasn't about him. Edward lowered his hand and stepped behind Philip, where it was warm and safe, waiting for the motorcade to leave.


There was a final interview that afternoon, and then he could go home. Edward thought he would die. At times like this, when he didn't want to be seen by anyone in the office, and with the bath-room so conspicuous at the other end of the office, the entire staff watching him go in and come out, Edward peed in a jar that he kept in his drawer. He was sealing the lid when the last candidate was announced: Hannah Glazer. Oh dear God. The same Hannah, the settlement leader, who'd turned away his parents.

On his desk was her résumé, which he couldn't focus on, but he willed himself into the conversation. As ever, it was difficult to look at her and be reminded of an enormous segment of life—the segment in which you were naked with a stunning person and she was not repulsed by you—that was not available to him. She wore tailored black clothes, her eyes clear and mean, and her hair was arranged in one of those old-fashioned styles, pasted to her head at the top and then curled out at the bottom. Quite lovely.

"What interests you about the position?" Edward started.

"You're kidding, right?" Hannah said, glaring at him.

So he would have found no viable candidates today. A recep-tionist had died, and he'd have to interview for her replacement, and now he'd need to schedule another day of interviews for this position as well.

He had to hold up appearances, or else his appearances would turn deranged. "I'm not kidding, no." Maybe they could keep this short.

"Are we going to be pretending today?" Hannah asked.

"Pretending what?"

Edward looked longingly at his window, wondering if he could get up enough speed for it to shatter if he threw himself against the glass.

Hannah stood. She spoke calmly, but she was seething. "I seri-ously question your ability to be fair here, given what happened. Last night I did my job. I did my job. And today when I very much need this position, a position I am ridiculously qualified for, here you are, mister fucking policy dodger, ready to dole out a punishment because I followed instructions in a difficult situation."

"I'm sorry," said Edward. "What punishment have I doled out?"

"Not hiring me," she said. "I saw your eyes when you knew it was me. You knew you weren't going to hire me."

"That's not true."

It was, for the most part, true.

"I wonder if I could interview with someone else. Is there someone else on the hiring committee so I could be assured a fair shake?"

"Well, it's only me. There's no committee. This is my company. If I recuse myself from the interview, for my intense bias, my inability to evaluate your suitability for a position in the company that I created from nothing, a company I understand better than anyone else in the world, you'll be in this room alone. Shall we do that?"

Hannah didn't laugh. "I'd like to continue this interview under protest," she said.

Was that a real thing? Was there a form you could fill out?

"Listen," said Edward. "I would understand completely if you didn't feel comfortable going forward, if you maybe wanted to try somewhere else." Please, please, try somewhere else.

"You sound like Frederick now. Get the person to believe her rejection is actually her own idea. Classic Frederick. Old school. I bet you've been told that before."

"Never."

"I guess it's no secret about me and him," Hannah said, grinning.

Edward stared at her.

"That we're involved. I mean, everyone must know at this point."

He wished he didn't. That was knowledge he'd very much

rather not have. He picked up her résumé, waving it at her. "Shall we?" he said. "An actual interview, and to hell with the past?"


Hannah Glazer was right. She was qualified for the position. Edward was crestfallen. She was smart, articulate, preposterously experienced, and when he challenged her with difficult production scenarios—bottlenecks on the front or back end, human error, acts of nature—she produced a staggering arsenal of troubleshooting strategies, more sophisticated than any he'd ever heard, which she rattled off casually, as if they were too simple to be of interest anymore.

"You know," she said, "Frederick is good at this sort of thing, too."

This sort of thing? Was his job just a hobby to her, something to perfect in the off-hours?

"But of course he's more of a manager/leader/boss type. As you might imagine."

"Of course," said Edward, even though what did he know about Frederick and his life outside the workshop?

"So . . ." said Hannah. "I mean, if you ever thought of taking a leave of absence, or retiring or something like that—not that you're that age yet—Frederick could be a really ideal person to take over."

He could only stare at her.

"I mean, of course, only if, you know, that sort of thing has been on your mind. Taking a break. Succession. Lineage. You know. Just don't forget about him. About Frederick. He could really do your job, and still have time left over for his other work."

On her way out Hannah looked at his couch. "Is that where you do it?" she asked.

"Do what?"

"Fuck them."

"What?"

"All of the desperate people who come looking for work. Is that your casting couch?"

"This isn't like that. It's just a couch."

"You didn't think, when I walked in, that within twenty minutes, if everything went well, you'd have me down on it?"

Edward couldn't answer. Was that an option that he'd somehow missed? Two minutes into the interview she was yelling at him about his bias. Was that some deeply veiled flirtation?

"So you've fucked no one there? I'm curious."

She didn't seem curious. She was yawning.

He looked at the brown couch and thought back, and back, and back. The tally, indeed, on that particular activity, in that particular location—or, in fact, on any couch ever—was, indeed, zero.


His phone rang that night and this time he wasn't going to screw it up. He grabbed his bag and headed over to the high school, alone.

The roads were quiet, streetlights shining so fiercely the neighborhoods were bright as day. A siren issued into the night, deep and low. He'd never heard this before. The closer he got to the high school, the more the sound became like an engine rather than a siren, rumbling beneath the ground. When he reached the turnoff, he came upon a sea of abandoned cars, doors jacked open, hazards flashing.

Edward stopped fast. The cars racing behind him closed in, trapping him there. He could do nothing but leave his car and walk, as the others must have done. When the drill was over, it would be one hell of a mess driving out of here, but for now he had to get inside.

He was one of the first to check in with Sharon, and it seemed she almost smiled at him. She looked strange and excited, her face glazed. Maybe he could show her that last night was a fluke.

From across the gymnasium he watched Hannah's settlement grow, waiting for a sign of his parents. Now that he had checked in, he wasn't supposed to leave, and since this was a drill, since it didn't matter, he resolved not to care. Probably his parents hadn't been called. This was some new thing they were doing, a test of loyalty he would fail no matter how he responded. Anyway, he'd long ago given up trying to understand the methods of the workshop. Even if his parents had been called, the phone was broken, and how would they know? It couldn't matter. But Edward kept looking over to Hannah, even as the gymnasium filled with bundled-up people, and children, and, of all things, animals—smooth, golden dogs—a few of them wandering sleepily across the hardwood floor, moaning. He'd never seen it so crowded. The generator roared over the chaos—something felt different tonight.

To be fair, he'd had that feeling before. Maybe he always had that feeling. They were good at making you believe that this was the real thing, at last. No matter how false and strange things were, Edward always thought it was smarter, in the end, to believe they were real. You'd better not get caught thinking something was only make-believe.

Finally, Edward spotted his father joining Hannah's settlement. He was alone. Hannah waved him in and he vanished into the crowd. The gymnasium lights never switched on and Frederick never appeared to praise and chastise them, to bark strange phrases about a future none of them could imagine. Instead the settlements headed outside to get in line for buses, which were departing from the back field of the school.

The siren was so loud that when Edward tried to speak nothing came out. Some terrible noise cancellation was at work. Was this intentional, a trick of Frederick's to keep them from understanding each other? Edward looked at Thom—who was terminally available for eye contact, lying in wait for it—and Thom smiled, giving a thumbs-up. Thom was excited. He'd wanted to leave for years. He was ready to roll. He had no parents, no wife, and it was as if he was waiting to start a new life somewhere else where they weren't drilling for escape day and night. Unless in their new location, too, wherever in the world that ended up being, they'd have to pretend to leave all the time, just as they'd done here.

Only one other time had the drill run this long. To Edward, that night seemed like years ago, when the workshop began, when it was just a few worried citizens finally admitting to each other how little they knew of the future. But probably it was only last winter. It was a viciously cold night and they'd waited in this very spot while the buses warmed up. He'd been so scared! But then Frederick's girlish voice had rung out through a megaphone and everyone had hurried back for their critiques.

So there was still time. Frederick could call this off and get them back inside.

As the settlements gathered behind him, headed to separate buses, Edward waited and waited and waited, until finally Hannah approached, and, behind her, her settlement, mostly old-timers from Wellery Heights. He had only a moment for this, but he had to do it. There was nothing in the protocol about it, anyway. The protocol hadn't been written this far. It was a blank chapter. They'd spoken so much about how after a certain point nothing could be known, and they were right. Edward grabbed his father, who looked startled, and then the two of them opened their mouths soundlessly at each other. They couldn't hear anything. It was his mother Edward needed to know about. His mother. He shrugged *where* and he mimed other things, things to indicate his mother, which anyone else from any country in the world, during any kind of crisis, would understand, but it was no use, it was stupid. Or his father was stupid, because he either did not get it or did not want to, smiling dumbly at Edward, reflecting the mime back at him as if it was a game. Finally Edward grabbed his father's left hand, isolating the ring finger, and held it up to him, tapping on the ring.

Do you get it now, you stupid old man? Where is she?

Edward's father smiled, put his palms together, closed his eyes, and leaned his head against his hands. A universal sign. His mother was home sleeping. His father had left her there asleep, and don't worry, she was doing fine.

His mother was asleep, alone, at home. In a city that might soon be empty. She was fine.

The buses traveled south. Frederick had been wrong about the highway. It was not an ugly variable. It didn't even present a problem. Was something supposed to shoot out at them from the trees? He was no longer sure what, exactly, he was supposed to fear. In a caravan the buses climbed the on-ramp, entering a freeway that seemed reserved for them alone. They drove for hours. The driver was in radio communication, but otherwise the bus was quiet. Edward sat by himself in a rear seat, staring from the window. At this point, he reasoned, the drill should have been called. They'd done it. They'd proven they could leave quickly, if necessary. But now what? They'd never rehearsed this far, so what on earth could they be testing? Wasn't it a pain in the ass now that they were so far from home, and how exactly were they going to get back? The buses, of course, could be ordered to turn around. But as the sun started to rise, and as muffins wrapped in brown paper were sent back, along with juice boxes and clear packs of vitamin pills, that didn't seem so likely.

During the second day of driving, after he'd slept and woken and then slept a little bit more, he heard a commotion at the front of the bus and the bus steamed and seized and buckled as it started to slow down and pull off the highway.

Thom slid into the seat next to him.

"Holy fuck, right?"

"What happened?" asked Edward, still waking up.

"Sharon."

As the bus lurched to a stop, Edward tried to look, but there were too many people mobbed together.

"Is she okay?" he asked.

Thom shook his head. "I don't think so. She fell out of her seat. All of a sudden. I only got a quick look. But, fuck, man, I think she's dead."

It was a pretty sight. Ten—or was it more—glittering yellow buses pulled over on the side of the highway. Edward's was the only bus that had discharged its passengers, and this was spoiling a lovely image: ragged, tired travelers wandering up and down the embankment while the passengers from the other buses, from behind darkened glass, looked on. Edward found a soft, dry place to sit. What a drill this was! Something for the record books. In a strange way he was excited for the critique. How would you begin to pick this apart? He wondered, surveying the fleet, which of the buses carried his father. Sharon had been removed, conveyed on a stretcher by some younger fellows, who'd hiked her into the woods and returned already. Without Sharon. Without even the stretcher. They were sharing a thermos down in the grass. One of them sang something. Edward wasn't sure what the holdup was now, even while Frederick and some others, including the mayor, huddled in conference down in the shadow of the last bus.

It wasn't long before a signal was given and the buses revved up again. Edward stood and joined the orderly line his settlement had formed to board their bus, but the door didn't open and their driver never appeared. Where was he, and who was supposed to drive them now?

Frederick and his crew had already boarded their buses. One by one the other buses wheezed into motion, crawling from the side of the road to join the highway. His neighbors reacted differently to the situation that dawned on them, but Edward stood out on the shoulder to watch. Of course the windows of the buses were dark, so he couldn't see, but in one of them, perhaps pressed against the glass, perhaps waving at him this very moment, waving hello and, of course, good-bye, was his father. So Edward, just in case, raised his own hand, too. Raised it and waved—thinking, *Good-bye, Dad, at least for now*—as the other buses built up speed down the highway and disappeared from sight, leaving the rest of them alone in the grass by the side of the road.

4

# The Father Costume

My father's costumes were gray and long and of the finest pile, sometimes clear enough for us to see through, though there was no reason to look too closely at that man's body. He preferred not to move. He was not one for excursions. My brother and I accomplished most of the required motion for him: we collected and described the daily food, oiled the Costume Gun, gathered yarn each morning after a storm, and donated any leftover swatches of fabric into our mother's kill hole out on the back platform.

My father threw handfuls of our mother's fabrics in the morning and studied how they fell, diagrams in cloth that could have meant anything. His body was hunched and foreign. He grimaced with each gesture, his face often decorated with cotton bracings. When the disarray proved baffling to him, he brought in my brother for consultations. I sat on the bench and watched them crouch at their work. I could not read fabric. I had a language problem. My brother spoke a language called Forecast. It consisted of sounds he barked into a stippled leather box. When my father wrapped my brother's hands in cotton waffling, my brother could tap out a low-altitude language on the floor, short thuds of speech that my father held his listening jar to. On those evenings when the sky was stretched too tight and the birds struck against it like pebbles on our roof, my brother slept off his Forecast expulsions in a sling hanging from our door. He cried softly inside his mesh bag while I dotted our windowsills with listening utensils, in case a message came in the night.

.  .  .

It would be so nice to think that a boat was not involved, that instead we lugged our things overland in wagons. At least overland we might have been sighted from the air. We would at least have not encountered so many empty platforms, floating alone at sea. My father might have been less tempted to perform so many jettisons.

If I could choose, I would picture my family stopping for small circles of bread in a safe location by a lake. Trapdoors would be carved into the soil there. We would spread our blankets and curtsy down to the food. I would send my father out on a scouting mission while my brother and I ate our bread. He would return to us with a bag of sharp utensils, his mouth sore and bleeding. He would report of mountains in the distance, a possible road. If I could control the outcome, we would not have believed him as he stood there telling his story. We would have remained near the safety of the lake, performing elaborate superstitions under cloth. My brother and I would have attacked my father with chopping motions until he had been silenced. Keeping maybe some of his hair, just in case. Keeping his costume, should we need to become him one day. When the time came. When my father's space was hollow enough for another body, possibly one of our own, to fit into it.

I wish I could say it was not a house we lived in, but admitting to the house is crucial. It gives a certain picture that will be required, in the end, when we are dead: my father, brother, and me, ducking under bags of sharp salt suspended from the rafters to keep the indoor birds sufficiently wounded, too tired to fly away. A house where birds performed a required orbit that affected how a man aged. A house where the flight of a bird might keep your costume young. Our windows fashioned of lens material for the sun to photograph us.

It is a necessary picture, the three of us walking in a crouch, our faces sometimes cut. It will be fine to be remembered that way. I prefer a picture to a written report. A written report would be sure to fail my family. If the sun has witnessed our behavior, perhaps one day we will reappear on some horizon, and we will again walk the earth and inhale some of the world's harder wind, to keep it off the bodies of those people not yet born.

The day in question was not much of a day. The sun paused at the horizon until a cluster of hard, black birds burst from the woods. They tore a path into the sky that the sun could fill, and the sun then commenced to stretch the space around it until something passing for daylight occurred. A smarter family would not have been fooled. A smarter family would have pursued a longer concealment within a cloth camouflage. But it was an accurate enough form of light; it showed the smallest, softest version of my father I had ever seen.

My father woke early and opened four jars in the doorway. He tuned the radio dial to Englishville and we heard a series of recent horizon songs made with a slow, old-fashioned breathing style. In between the music, one of the more famous years was being described by a girl whose voice had to project through a wooden mouth. Her mother apparently had designed the mouth of an old man, so the girl could not be recognized. The antenna of our radio had been soaking in honey overnight. After wiping down the tip, my father pushed it through the ceiling until the music became louder.

The three of us crouched down at the writing hole in the center of the room. It was moist that morning, rimmed with foaming soil, so my father fitted the mouth with scraps of linen and then reached his arm deep into the hole. We each took our turn. Above us the sky sounded like a waterfall. My brother held his breath and smiled when his arm went in the hole, as if he could stay like that forever. The radio would not keep still, buzzing on the countertop as if an animal were trapped inside it. Some other family must have died that day, because our house had too much electricity. If too many people died, there would be lightning in our room. If the men on our road stopped breathing, we would be blinded. We would not be able to honor the kill hole. A fine spray of crumbs blew from the speaker until the air in the room seemed filled with insects.

We packed our things into clear burlap sacks. Father took down the wind sock and inhaled the last remnants of yesterday's air for strength. He passed the sock to my brother, who lazily wiped his face with it before fitting it onto an unused portion of his costume. He spoke three Forecast sentences into his scarf before kissing it and wrapping it around his neck. The language made me drowsy. The three of us rolled our bodies in the Costume Smoother and checked ourselves for wind drag. Father unplugged the four corners of the house and kicked at the baseboards to set the decay timer. He coordinated his kicks with the Bird Metronome until the room became recalibrated and silent, more hushed than I had ever heard it, which made me want to stay there and hold my breath, to take a silence bath, to rub my sleeves and groom myself clean in that brand-new air.

There was nothing for us to do then but wait. I watched my father greasing our windows with oil, drawing pictures of us against the glass with precise, thin lines. In the picture, from what I could decipher, my father was standing in full costume, tearing a piece of bread in half for my brother and me, who were crouched on our heels with our hands raised. It would be a long time before someone looking into the house with a Cloth Diviner could determine that we had left the premises, that the picture of these three men exchanging bread was merely a decoy, erasable, made of oil. With the right manipulations of the hand, those three men could be made to do anything. By then we would be far off on the water.

I wish I could say my father's name. I do not know the grammatical tense that could properly remark on my father. There is a portion of time that my own language cannot reach. A limitation, probably, in my mouth. In this portion of time is where my father is hidden. If I learn a new language, my father might come true. If I reach deep into my mouth and scoop out a larger cave. If I make do with less of myself, so that he might be more.

It would be easier to hold a magnifying glass to the scrap of my father's shirt that still remains. To focus a hot cone of sunlight through the glass onto the fabric that once concealed him. Then the last of him could be burned, and in the sound of the flame a small message might be heard. I wish that his name occurred in nature. I could point to the sky and my gesture would indicate him better than any of my own noises ever could. I wish that there was a new man who looked like my father. I could grab hold of him if he rowed by. I could enter his clothes so that he would never float. Hide in the extra space between his body and the cloth. Drag him down into the water, the two of us sinking double-time, down to where the people are waiting, their reaching hands just beyond my sight now as I stare into the water.

When the boat appeared, my father pulled it in with his rope and loaded our parcels down below. He attached long bronze wires onto the stern that fluttered in our wake, creating the turbulence of a much larger boat, a decoy trail for any Cloth Monitors watching us escape. We would produce a commotion of foam. An attack would be less likely. I was asked to spray the south-facing wall of our house with writing, a script to poison travelers if they ever became stranded at our house, to prevent them from living the way we had, to keep ourselves from becoming repeated. I used one of the safer, mouth-borne languages for the project, restricting myself to words that indicated only those things that could be concealed with burlap. When I was finished, and the wall of our house was like a language trap, I still had some writing left over, which I smeared out carefully over the sides of our boat until it had spread into a translucent glue.

My brother and I held hands in the low morning wind while my father fitted the Travel Costume onto us, adjusting the straps so that my bigger, softer body would not bulge from the fabric. We kissed before saying good-bye to each other, even though our bodies would be staying close. We would share an outfit, which meant that we had to alternate moving about the boat. Only one of us could be in charge of a costume. A bird or man might think my father had only one son on board. I went fully limp first, and issued small motion commands to my brother, who had stronger legs, a stronger back, and better eyes.

The day was mostly a crude alphabet of sounds, like one of the Southern languages recited through a gauze filter. It made my father cross. He rowed crudely, chopping at the water as if it were ice, and we slid away from our home in jerking strides. Animals may have been responsible for the noises we heard, but I saw little that was living, only clean geometries of clouds above a rigid tree line, and a shore that receded the more you stared at it. We sailed the narrow waterway until the houses grew small and pale, whitish blurs on the horizon, and the water thickened beneath us.

For hours we saw only my father's back, tilting against the long oars. On the shore were long descriptions scrolling in the tree line, sentences indecipherable without the proper cloth filter. We had only so much burlap to spare, and the messages did not seem crucial. We were always choosing what we needed to know, yet I had trouble leaving those sentences unread. I thought they might have been placed there for us. My brother moved our costume to keep me from seeing the shore. I saw only the wake behind us, a trail of foam that produced a language of bubbles so intimate I was ashamed to decipher it.

When the sun was directly above us and our shadows were deep inside our own bodies, my father produced the first parcel. There was a cheese that we had been saving. There was a bread. The bread was wrapped in a stiff sheet of wool. It was given to me to undress it. First I held my hands in the water. If I closed my eyes, the water felt as loose and grainy as soil, with bits that broke gently against my touch. My hands were smooth and glistening when I removed them, and the bread unraveled easily. We kept the items of the parcel near our persons, in contact always with our costumes, in case witnesses from the far shore had been employed. In case, my father said, someone was given a reason to come out there after us. We used the cheese and bread without much motion. Someone watching could easily have assumed that we were sleeping. After we ate, I shot a thin piece of wool into the water as an offering.

I have a photo of my brother that is simply a picture of an empty field. I am collecting empty spaces for him that he might like, spaces safe enough for entry. There is a scratchy yellow grass growing wild, a dried white mud, nothing much alive in the air. Trees with shriveled limbs corkscrew over the field, providing a cage of wooden protection. No people there, least of all my brother, least of all even an artifact of his several costumes. There is no clothing. I could throw this photo into water, to feed the image enough for my brother to grow in it. It seems a safe enough place for him to enter, a place with none of the warning signs that in the end kept my brother from going anywhere. He could live in this field, if only I could make him grow there.

We rowed on because my father told us to. Words were exchanged that I could not use. My brother had spent his ration of bread to brace his mouth for brand-new utterances that hurt me to listen to. My father had an angry body that he kept turned away from us. I held my head low and watched the water flowing around us. Signs posted in the channel told of families that had come and gone. Cursive script on wooden placards, counterweighted with buoys, like simple billboards on a road. Short, orbular lights mounted on the signs cast oily images of the various fathers on the water, spotlights of men's faces as if projected from the bellies of birds. The current was troubled enough to dissolve these fathers' faces as it pulled us along, until we were sailing directly over wavy versions of these men as we tried not to read of what had happened to them, who they were, what they did, why they failed.

The signs, in the end, gave way simply to sticks and platforms as we gained the ocean, weeds coiling up out of the water around them. We saw no more writing for hours. My head became blank and I remembered an old song a woman used to sing. It was a song built of pauses and breath, with notes that were just the words a person might use to procure food, yet once I remembered it, it seemed crucial to my own breathing, and I worried that if I forgot to keep time with the song, to hum it always, I might fail to breathe, I might lose my own time for good.

It was early afternoon by the time my father showed his full face to me. I did not care to see it. It was too big. Anyone could have been inside it. He required me to see him there in our boat on the water, and I obliged as much as I could. My brother, I suspect, did his best to look away. I felt the costume pulling at me, tight as a muscle.

The second parcel in my father's bag contained a metronome, with a hollow darning needle that served as the wand. He placed it near my brother, adjusted the dial to Suffocate, and caused my brother, after several spasms of resistance, to stop breathing. Our boat felt lighter immediately, and we began to pick up speed, slicing swiftly through a water channel that suddenly seemed as light as air.

If it were up to me, I would dress my father in a long, clear sleep costume. I would knit linens from my mother's abandoned luggage and spray them from the Costume Gun onto my father. I would weight my hands with heavy blocks of wool, which I would toss in the water to create a retention current, to keep my father from rowing away. A set of spirals in the water that would prove inescapable to him. If it were up to me, I would soak my father's hands in milk, then fit them with gloves of hemp. I would use the leftover milk to make a writing. My father I would fix to a platform on the water until the animals came for him. If I ever saw my father again, I would let the animals come for him, even if I had to costume the animals myself with special attack clothing—father-hunting shirts, father-killing hats, father-chasing corsets—even if I had to teach them how to swim after someone as fast, as expertly clothed, as my father. I would teach them. If my father would not be disrobed, I would wait on my platform until animals came to help. It would be simply a matter of time.

The metronome produced an English sound. My father had stopped rowing. He was collecting small writing samples from the water. I was sharing a costume with a boy who could not breathe.

It was like having a body that was partly cold and numb, a part of my person being now just furniture I carried with me. My brother's head was dry. I could hear it scratching against the facial cloak on his side of the costume, the sound a dog might make if it was buried alive. I tried to adjust some zippers and buttons, but the change only hastened my own breathing, until I worried I might hyperventilate and be thrown from the costume, which could only tolerate a certain number of breaths per minute. During each expression of the metronome, I beckoned to my brother using special, waterproof sounds, which I was careful to conceal from my father. He was busy fitting vials of a possible fluid into the compartments on his vest. A fluid filled with writing. I had seen him wear glass only once before. During one of the famous years, when children operated the electricity console in our town, he had lined his chest with glass and set about to alter the kill hole. We watched him from the window, his body stretched thin and long behind his special outfit. This time, his glass costume consisted of short, stubby bullets filled with fluid. As much as I squinted at him, I could see nothing behind it.

The two of us would never be more at sea. I was my father's only son. Some town registry should acknowledge the change. Looking around me, I thought I could produce a drowning, with a little effort. We exchanged one sector of nowhere for another. Travel seemed exclusively contrived to make houses disappear. There was nothing out there but water. At the most, I saw the empty platforms, like lily pads, scattered throughout the waves. But no land anywhere.

We were going to row until evening. I was wearing clothing enough for two, but there was just one of us now. In tribute, my father broadcast audiotapes of my brother for us to listen to, mostly weeping sounds from when he was younger. He hooked the small speakers of the machine to the outside of the boat and aimed the sound of my brother directly into the water, using a volume mechanism derived from my mother's old sewing kit. A loose, circular current reflected the sound, leaving frothing pools in the water as we sailed through. Other boats might later trigger these sorrow vectors of my brother's, sailing through his weeping pools. He would cry for them, if they could find the right patch of water. If they could sail into it.

Sadness could be stored in an area, sealed in a small spot of water. Water could be the costume for what my brother felt.

I spoke to my father's back with my hands, shielding my speech with a canvas visor. My hands cast the wrong sorts of shadows on the bottom of the boat, a set of lines so precise that they could have been simple English sentences asking for help. It worried me to think my father might misunderstand me. I stroked the empty part of my clothing and scanned the vast, blank water for land. There was nothing anywhere, just the water rippling beneath our boat, which made a low, smooth Spanish sound.

If he heard or saw my speech he did not acknowledge it. He had opened the third parcel, a collection of lenses, which he braced below our sails with a system of rigging I could not comprehend. As I looked up, I saw through the distortion of the lenses a sky and sun that were grotesquely oversized, magnified beyond repair, swollen and bloated and not possible to regard for long. My only thought then was that if the above and beyond were rendered so large, if he had dilated those items of our world that were already massive, and his lenses worked their exaggerations in reverse, how small indeed would the two of us look sailing below in our boat? Had we become tiny enough to no longer be seen? Was my father, with his third parcel, creating a disappearance? Was it a new costume of nothing?

. . .

If it were up to me, I would not come from a place where fathers leave their houses by boat. Where fathers kill a costume and leave heaps of cloth like grave sites in their wake. I would choose a world of straight grass roads, with only famous years, with only days of actual light, where a metronome might be silenced by the right kind of sunlight. I would choose a house free of kill holes where a mother still stood upright and walked the rooms, using a soothing medical voice entirely free of cloth. There would be pieces of time produced through the furnace of the house, and the word *memory* would have an angry meaning. People would have memories to turn red, to fume, to produce a special smoke. If it were up to me, a father's costume could be filled with special English air and set afloat outside a house. This air-filled costume could be fed with chunks of hardened time so that the family inside would not die. The costume would be called a Day Eater. Growing old would be its sacrifice. The Bird Metronome would keep the costume clean. If the chunks became depleted, the costume could feed on the father himself, who would still be located somewhere deep inside the costume, far from sight, in the recesses of a sleeve, for instance, where a specialized darkness might cover the father's body in a thick, gray film.

By sunset, my brother was cast into the water. A hole blown in our costume, his body dragging behind us like a raft. My father would only hand me the needle and thread. I did not know where to start stitching. I could not perform a mending on my own back, on parts I could hardly see or touch. Nearly everything on that boat could have been sewn up. Cold air was striking the new vacancy in my costume. My father adjusted the metronome to Sleep, a rhythmic shushing, but I sat in the back and watched my brother bob in the waves as we lurched away from him.

There was only one small sight hole not covered by a lens, a window that would not translate the world behind it. It was here that my father started passing items through, buttons and photos mostly, some keys, and tiny colorless rags. They glistened and rolled in our wake like old jewels, the key objects of our home donated now to the ocean. Some of them he handed to me first. As I touched every small thing from our old house, I felt a hard drowsiness, as if these objects themselves were drugged and could produce a stupor in me if I so much as looked at them. I handed them out of the boat as fast as I could.

We slept on and off that way, protected by the canopy of lenses. Beneath them we must have looked like nothing at all, an empty boat adrift at sea. We were not bothered. Even the natural sounds of the sea were repelled by our contraption.

In the morning I began sewing a eulogy for my brother out of some white thread we had saved. I made the eulogy as thin as typing on a page, crinkled letters stitched together as if the words of a book could be tweezered in a thread as long as a man's body. I did not know what I wrote. My hands carried all of my feeling, if there was any, but they moved confusingly with the needle and thread, and I preferred not to watch them at work on something I could never describe. I knew that this stretch of water that held us deserved a writing, and that the writing should record the life of maybe the last speaker of Forecast, a person who was quieted by a family metronome and buried at sea. I made a writing of thread to honor my brother and dipped the thread in the water. My father took only a mild interest, stopping briefly from his rowing to hold some of the sentences inside his big work gloves. His visor was down over his face, either as a reading filter or to hide himself from me, I was not sure. I let him hold the writing like that and did not trouble him with a direct gaze. But as our boat began to list and creak, he attached some of the sentences to his belt, sprayed them fast with a hot jet from the Costume Gun, and got back down to his work.

I wish I could say that my father had a steady size, a stable shape. Something finite to his person. That he did not grow larger when the lens allowed it, a ballooning man at the bow of a long boat. Who used his size as a sign that time had passed. A body not to be touched, to be seen only through glass. I would prefer, if I could choose, to remark on a man such as my father receding from sight instead, going small, losing color and voice and power, as if one could achieve his disappearance through squinting alone, through the scratching of glass, the melting of a costume. Using equipment such as Father Disappearing Goggles. As if not looking at him meant that he could not be looked at.

I wish I did not have to say the word *lens* again. Or *boat,* or *water.* I would prefer an ocean scenario where certain words were restricted, due to conditions of climate. Where whole grammars were off-limits, due to cloth shortages. A scenario where the mouth operated under quota. Where there was a quota of water as well, to keep it from repeating, from never ending.

Deep in that next night on the water I heard noises scraping away nearby. The sound of a partition being built. A father at work. The old-fashioned sound of glass being stretched through the middle of a boat. I used the hem of my own garment as a divining lens, but it only enriched the darkness, silenced the clatter, and I decided to wait for a moment of accurate sunlight, if one would come to such a remote zone of ocean—where even the small platforms for men went unoccupied—to discover the operation my father seemed to have set for himself after I had gone to sleep. In the meantime, I chewed on a piece of sweet rope to calm myself.

It was a small night. Many people must have died for lack of space. The weather was tuned to a Shrink setting. The air was swollen. Beneath us, waves slapped at the hull in a plain, repetitive code. If I squinted, I could make out small, sharp words in the code, English words as if formed by a man with a beak for a mouth, singing through a cotton screen. He was another man I did not want to know. I found it was better not to listen. They were not words I very much cared to hear. But as I slid around inside my oversized costume, the world grew quiet again and soon I could sleep, a darkness over my body as thick and final as one of the very first wools.

I awoke hard and wrong, beams of heat around me, air that felt suspiciously like my own breath circling my face.

In the space between us, my father's nighttime work was revealed. He had erected a new skin of lenses, rendering himself, and everything, a distortion on the other side of the glass. It was not clear which of us was costumed in it. I saw only smudges and blurs, the glass clearly bent in such a way as to translate the objects beyond me out of recognizability. I was encased in lens. A Translation Costume my father had snuck up on me while I slept. A coercive suit of clothing that blinded me. Shadows, at the most, roved the skin of my new suit.

As much as I carved into the soft glass with a darning needle that my father must have left for me, I could not break the surface. As much as I pressed my face into the soft glass, I could see only smudges of him, a painting of a man melting in the distance. At my feet was a pile of things, among them my brother's stippled leather box, containing his Forecast sounds, and a sweaty old Costume Gun. I fired a mild jet from the gun at the lens but achieved only a vague pain in my chest, a cramping. I aimed the gun at myself to no effect.

There is a certain jostling stability beneath me now, though it could be a trick of the costume. I may indeed have been jettisoned to my own platform. It is possible that I can detect certain swells of ocean, a system of waves at work on some task I'll never understand.

Or I am meant to detect this, I am meant to feel this.

There may be a father operating on the other side of the glass. I sometimes imagine him there as a small man chiseling into a solid block of cotton. Carving a head, maybe.

I do not imagine him often.

Most days I am content to hold my brother's leather box. I open it occasionally, releasing its Forecast sounds, which slide into my climate like my brother's very own breath, as if we still shared a costume. And though I do not understand the words, I enjoy their defeat of silence. I can picture the costume the words would make, as big as a family, with soft exits, filled with writing, allergic to glass. A costume you would not know you were wearing. So subtle. So soft. Beyond clear. Made only of his little words.

Although I do not understand my brother's words, I know them to be the right ones, the ones that someone had to say. I am happy that they are mine now.

There are so many words I won't say again. I will not say "brother." I will not say "house," or "kill hole." Many of the statements I could make could be smothered by the proper combination of cloths. Silence is simply a condition of clothing. My father has seen to a final deaf costume.

There is little to do now but regard the patches of water, which may really be clouds. Despite their color, despite their size, despite the voice inside them. Clouds which may really be him, my father, moving around out there beyond me, outside of my clothing, where apparently a world still operates. However dim. However feebly.

5

# First Love

could not sleep until I had labored through a regular lust application performed with motion, gesture, and languageflower. There was no script or dance step to the discipline. I administered it to her whether she was home in the head or away, no matter the score between her heart and the world, whether she swooned or cringed when I held her, or if she gazed into space or feigned sleep.

She received my application with short, gasping tones she made with her own breath. The tones could have been stolen from a song. Every sound she made was borrowed from what was once known as music. It was not clear whether I should have responded with sounds of my own, which I had once used to draw people closer to my body, or any noise I could make to harmonize her noise into something passing for speech, which might then tell us what to do. Her sounds emerged most forcefully when the motion of my lust was pistonlike, an event that often featured my person volleying above hers, as if flying in place, she pinned beneath me, wilting in my shadow; or me behind her, as though driving a chariot, while she carved a location for herself into the bedclothes.

When we pursued the discipline, we fought toward the seizure known as nighttime. Nighttime promised a better statistic of invisibility. It was our primary collaboration, to arrive where we wouldn't be seen. We fantasized about a place where we could be wet and boneless, where no one would dare attribute a feeling to us. The safest thing to say about water is that it has no bones, unless a person has been trapped in it.

She would announce her seizure some seconds before it occurred. She used American sounds known as phrases. She said: Here I come; and: Good lord. I imagine the sounds she made once passed for words. When I announced my seizure, often by reciting her name, she held my hand. The sun was briefly refuted and I achieved a dark area. At such times I could see the two of us walking through a garden, looking at the world as though for the first time, believing that the flaring, bright obstacles that kept us from seeing deep into the earth were actually only called flowers.

In daylight she wore motion-limiting weights called shoes. She had a wet mistake buried in her chest. It should never have been put there. Someone had concealed a weapon, which helped her manifest a wound. She tried to sweat it free by performing a function called crying. The five knives of her hand were once called fingers. She stabbed her face every time she tried to eat; the cuts released small blasts of clear air that made the day feel cool. The flag of sadness that concealed her arms was known as a sleeve. The flag flew the colors of her body, which there is no longer another name for. The word *body* used to refer to the evidence left behind that someone had died.

The first time you meet a potential partner presents an opportunity that will never come your way again, the chance to handle them freely, to smell their parts, to disrobe or possibly dismantle them, to mount their hind, to bark at them, to pull back their hair or grip at their scruff and whinny, to rope them to a post, to insert a wire into their back and control them through radio, to scull or tack in their perimeter, to kiss them gently, to hold their face and kiss their cheeks and shelter them from the wind with your wide, hard body.

Your appearance and behavioral strategy play a part in gaining this access to someone new, so it is imperative to keep your person clean and keep his tank and limbs filled with the appropriate fluid, seasonally correct and rich in emotion, to be sure his shoes are hard on top and solid for the long haul, to mind that your own person is posture perfect and can aim his body true, accounting for the possible refractions of light that occur between the people of today, also known as the new wolves.

The shovels we use to cleave the air in two—and possibly reveal a person we might fail against—were once abbreviated as hands. This was when we had two shovels each, and we apparently used them to scoop up objects we thought we needed, or to toss away those that did not please us. When we faced off with a person, the sound of our four shovels colliding produced a shield of silent, wind-free air known as home. This was when there were only two choices how to behave, on or off. We would apparently put some objects into our mistake tunnel, which was still the main opening in the face, and the tunnel was able to convulse around them and propel them deep into the body's grave, which was then called, I think, a belly. The tunnel often became wet, but it had dry sticks in front known as teeth, to provide a final reflection of every object we buried in our bodies. Those people who wanted to consume us could then take an inventory of our assets simply by staring us in the mouth or, more obviously, putting their mouths over ours in an investigation known as kissing. Whenever she kissed me, she was prying for secrets.

My secret was my lucky bone, worn behind my face for good luck. It was an excellent protection against sorrow. Now seldom seen, at least in the daytime, this bone was once worn as an amulet above the neck to ensure a human appearance. Without it, a person might be considered an accident of light. It is a bone that grows in time with the body and achieves a round shape to best support the face. Some cultures call it a "head" and decorate it with paint and stones, or cover it with veils, gels, masks, and helmets.

In America the head sprouts either soft or coarse hair, features small apologies called eyes, and has a round mistake tunnel known as a mouth. The mouth asks for help by carving wind into short breaks in silence called languageflower. During escape tactics such as walking, the head precedes the person and falsely advertises his mood and what he might say. One of its functions is a decoy event called a smile. The head is better known as a flare for trouble. Some areas called cities feature millions of these flares hovering at eye level, and the effect is blinding. The Spanish word for this is *crowd*. In America there is a phrase—Bury your Head—which originates from the Dutch and translates, roughly, as: to marry.

In some parts of America the little bone above a man's neck is considered to possess skills such as pain storage and escape strategies; the bone is suspended above the man as a charm against other people, who would otherwise seize his body and pour themselves into it, a self-camouflaging sacrifice known as a relationship. But other people also use the little bone as a buoy that one should not approach, because someone will die in the space it covers. If you get too close to the buoy, you will be trapped as a mourner. Circling the head is referred to as courtship. It is like chalk around a body before that body has died. It hovers in place and appears attached to the fear spout that was once called a neck. In truth, every man's body is an announcement of a future disappearance. Just by being in the room with her, I was foreshadowing our separation. My head was simply the point where that disappearance would occur. If we ever need to know what will go away, we need only to look at a person. Anyone.

Sometimes the disappearance can be traced. We conceal a part of the world and it's called swallowing. Many of the best objects, including the world's first engine, a fault called the heart, are hidden in the body. It is a competition to hide as much as we can, a form of ballooning that is believed, in some languages, to make us more attractive. We say we love someone, which means we covet the hoard they might be storing in their bodies. While they sleep we reach at their hoard with our hands, an excavation better known as caressing. That is why lovers often say things to each other like: X marks the spot, Come and get me, I have a secret. Having a secret means: I have swallowed part of you and that is why you feel incomplete. Massaging the skin is another way to feel for a secret entry. It is unfortunate that most people do not come equipped with a map and some cutting tools. So much time would be saved. Instead of saying, "Pleased to meet you," we might make a small incision in the chest, wide enough for us to slip inside if the air will no longer tolerate our presence, if the population in the room is just asking for our omission.

In the current era, the male treasure hoarder uses someone else as storage space for his spoils, in case his own body is looted while he sleeps, a violation certain Americans still refer to as dreaming. There will then be bodies that carry his assets after he has been found out. This grouping was once known as a family. People produced families to disperse the treasure and keep the sniper, who was once mistaken for a bird, guessing. In some American dialects, the word *family* means "scatter." Having a family increases the number of targets, cuts down on the father's risk. With more people for the sniper to shoot at, the father has a better chance of getting out alive. His wife and children function as his bodyguards. This is also probably why relationships are referred to as "bulletproof vests."

I had been advised by the Authority that a ritual at the outset of our union would create a relationship, which was then seen as a preferable condition. So I sent her some of the water I had blessed for the dedication of our relationship, telling her to have some of it to drink and to apply some as a lotion to the place she least wanted me to discover, so long as this place occurred on or near her own body. The water might protect her, even if I repeatedly touched her or looked at her, which was admittedly going to be my early plan. But if she spilled the water on her father, there would be a chance that I would kill him. It was a favor to warn her against my worst intentions. I wanted to show her my unsatisfiable side, to get the worst part out of the way, but it turned out that it wasn't just a side, but my entire body, and even the space around it that was unsatisfiable. Wherever I put my body, I left behind areas that could not be fixed. In a relationship every person gives a gift, usually by leaving something out. The best and most cherished gift is to give her the first clue as to why she should begin plotting her escape.

There are men blessed by water, whom women cannot see. This is the only favor water can grant, to cloak our mistakes by adding a layer of reflection to our skin, which helps other people take more responsibility for us, once they see how horrible they can look when we reflect them. We have bodies of water, known also as failures of land, to show us where mistakes are made, because water gathers near error, to magnify it and make everyone feel responsible. This quite natural atmospheric process was once understood as guilt. The apologetic men are laid out flat, ashamed to have ended up a mirror to other men. Dry men have made no mistakes. To look at water is to admit the possibility of error. Some men are still shy around water.

It was her belief that water, taken in drink form, would provide the necessary ballast for her to remain with me. But Americans believe it is unlucky to drink water, because those who do so will live. The body will thrive and grow; and growth, particularly in English, implies movement away from others. The first word for it was escape.

Commitment, on the other hand, is an abbreviation for an inability to move, which is why couples often become heavy together, stiff and slow-moving, eating pounds of food to ensure each other's immobility. Feeding a lover is like making her swallow an anchor. This is why getting married is described as swallowing iron. Marrying is never referred to as "casting off," although sometimes the phrase "taking on a passenger" is used.

Relationships fail when the mouth is too small or refuses food. Touching one's own mouth is the first gesture of masturbation, because it explicitly advertises self-sufficiency. Men grow mustaches and beards to become less attractive to themselves, to decrease the chances of making their partners obsolete. Cultures that eat with their hands are boasting about their lovemaking abilities.

I hoped to find the place she wanted to hide, and I suspected her place was hidden on another woman's body, someone who sulked in her shadow and answered to a different name. Thus an investigation occurred that featured me, in full color, sounding various skins for her secret place, an action more technically known as intercourse, because the man uses his entire body to listen against the skin of another. Often I was obliged to make lust applications to those host bodies that were possibly storing her mystery. Because I was intent on making the future come true, I looked for examples of her everywhere. The bodies that hosted my intercourse often overlapped with the bodies of the people she called friends. They made altogether different sounds and words, and none of us could produce the sound that, in America, had come to pass for her name.

She sent back some of the water she had swallowed and it was clear that she had related to the water by letting it down her throat. This was water that had trafficked through her person to a place I had not been allowed to see. It had more access. I was jealous of everything she ate and drank. The water she sent back to me came in the form of rain. This was when changes in the air were known as weather, when low-flying bullets were still called friends, and periods of suffering were broken up into intervals called days. Back then, the sun still honored the world's objects by letting them contribute the occasional shadow to the surface of the world. Every day something fell on me and my temperature changed. Temperature was another way to remind you that you weren't dying quickly enough; it let you feel too viciously alive. These changes of temperatures were called moods and they had interesting foreign names, but I no longer recall them. I have no memory for anything that happens outside of my body.

I cannot recall the precise words for the phrase: "I'm sorry."

When I learn these words again, I will never stop saying them.

# Fear the Morning

His name had been scratched off his documents years ago. There had been little reason since then to refer to himself, and his rigorous daily schedule kept him from thinking what he might be called if someone addressed him.

In the morning he would make a plate of eggs and dot it with hard cheese. He ate until he was tired, then put his plate in the sink, combed his dry, curly hair until his scalp hurt, then put on his long coat and went out for his tour. Every day the tour followed a different track away from his house, sometimes climbing a hill, other times descending one. He did not wish to see the same people. Their faces troubled him. Any one of them might be the very person waiting to replace him. If he could not avoid a greeting, he said "Hello," and breathed down at his feet while he walked, listening for their departing steps behind him.

Under the coat was a naked body that he fussed at with a special lotion. He thought of it as his own body. A pocket of the coat was torn through at the bottom, allowing his hand to spread lotion while he walked. If he saw a person, his feeling faded, no matter how fast his hands moved. People were no good for his feeling, but he could not have the feeling alone at home, either, so he risked sighting them at large in the world around his home. He preferred to see trees, but forests were no good. Too many trees suggested too much possibility, and his feeling faded. He had to be moving along at a swift pace, with trees looming in his periphery but not surrounding him, clusters of green growth like clouds of algae bursting in the air. Then he could massage his area until his stomach steamed with friction and he became hungry for lunch.

He took his meals in the center of town. Ham was his preferred dish, especially in the winter, when it was shaved transparently thin and rolled inside flavored paper straws. Usually he washed it down with a steeped citrus drink, depending on the season. He liked berry drinks, but his town rarely produced berries, and if a berry-flavored water was ever made, it was bitter and gritty in his mouth. Mostly his town sold long hollows of bread lathered in fruit. The meat was flown in from the north. He ate a meat that had traveled high in the air.

After lunch, he walked home for his appointment in front of the television, where he watched a daily show that concerned people who fought to board a very small boat. Once aboard, they had to row themselves to a pre-agreed target, often an island, but sometimes a town that fronted a river. He had his favorite characters, usually the redheads, because they were seaworthy and never backed down from a fight. But he was more interested in the water and how the water made everybody on the show look sleepy. He liked to see people bursting out of it, scrambling onto the lip of the boat, having their hands beaten by the passengers who had already secured a berth, then slipping back into the water. Sometimes the people said things just as their heads entered the water, so the words were partially muffled, and he tried to give his words that same kind of sound. When he filled his mouth with bread, he could sound like one of the strong redheads slipping underwater after a struggle.

In the unspoken-for hours in his afternoons, he delivered phone calls from a hard, gray phone that had been carved into his wall. There was a code he could press into his phone that changed his behavior when he talked. If he prefaced the person's number with this code, he could speak smoothly and at length from a set of feelings that were not his own. He never wanted to forget these three numbers, so he wrote them on a little white sticker and stuck it to his phone. The numbers he dialed were from a special phone book purchased at a store outside of town. He believed it gave him access to more extraordinary people than the ones he had to see on his morning tours. When someone answered on the other line, he opened the conversation by apologizing to them, using their name and a special, sorrowful voice, which often led them to believe he was someone else. His phone book seemed to have many numbers of people who were waiting by their phones for a man to call and apologize to them. In the afternoons, before his special dinners, he was often this man. Minutes would go by before the people discovered he was someone else, and even if this made the people angry, he often learned about who he had been, and he felt like someone else for a little while, which was so hard to feel for very long, and always made him a little bit hungry.

He had to signal for his dinner with a special light he pointed from his window. Then there might be a crackling knock at the door, as if someone had stepped on a small bird. Sometimes the knock on the door came before he signaled with the light, but he knew at least not to eat his dinner until he flashed his signal.

Dinner was never much other than a plate of potatoes run under a broiler until it blistered with heat. The woman who brought his food stood near him and touched his cheek, and he would endure this gesture until she had left the plate on the table and closed his door behind her.

Once he ate his potatoes, he knew that very little could happen, and that, with some special effort, and much thought, he could arrange things so that even less might happen, until possibly nothing would, a circumstance he might very well be rewarded for. It was a matter of skill. He would perfect this skill until he had arranged for a situation that would go on for as long as he wanted it to, in which absolutely nothing occurred. Even if people defied his wish, and walked the streets and roads in greatcoats spreading lotions over the territory, he knew that no one would see them, or, if they did, they would never remember it. The disruption would seem dreamlike, with artificial colors. The people would be made of bark.

His bedtime came when the potatoes still sat high in his stomach but he could not keep his eyes open. He unrolled a flannel sleep shirt. He ran a toothbrush through his mouth. He coughed his special words into the speech hole in his bedroom.

Last came the only ritual that might help him disappear. If he pressed the three-digit code into the phone again, he could, with any luck, become someone else before he went to sleep, which meant he could give the gift of rest to his other person, the one that he secretly oiled with his hands while out touring, the one he was seducing into taking his place in the great world. He could give his other person a chance to dream and sleep and wake up and toss and turn in the sheets. Then maybe there was a better likelihood that, instead of himself, it would be the other person who would wake up, and something different might happen, something that had not happened yet. He would know what to call himself then. His name would sound very much like an engine does. The other person would be in charge now, and he'd have a very different idea of how things should be done. In this way, he, the first person, the one who had started this, and kept it going day after day with almost no help from anyone else in the world, with the small exception of the woman who brought his dinner, could take a break himself, and hide out close to the new man's skin, right there on his body, under the long coat that moved near the world's trees, where the lotion was smooth and soft, and no light could get in. This was where he wanted to be. This was why he entered a code into the phone and slid deep into his soft, clean bed, waiting for morning.

# Origins of the Family

A man and woman sometimes gather in the evening to discuss their future projects together, a conversation that takes place in a hushed, bone-free room. They tap the walls and call out some of the more popular names for people, to make sure they are alone. The names they recite are shaped inside a bone hollow called a mouth. Their conversation most often freely circles the shame zone that hovers over the table. They take turns arranging the net of bones their skin is concealing so their bodies appear to move. She lifts a small bone resembling a finger, he slides a long, heavy one into place over a chair and expels hot temperature called breath. When they discuss children, they are trying to discover if they can create a new set of bones together. Their difficulties are architectural: can the house support the bones, or will structural changes be required? They submit sketches across the table, editing each other's ideas about the new person. When they rehearse the names they might call it, and illustrate their visions of its ultimate shape and color, each of them listens privately for a vibration in their bones, pressing their fingers into their flesh to determine what they might feel.

Bones prevent the heart from beating so loudly it would deafen the person. They were first called listening sticks, because they absorbed the body's sounds and allowed men and women to hear their own voices during intricate skirmishes in the home. This is why settlers erected mothers-of-bone in loud rooms such as the kitchen. Only later did people bag and animate the mothers so that they might move from room to room, accomplishing broader functions within the family. Boneless people did and said little. They were not capable of fighting. They could hide inside each other's bodies. Without bones, a person, upon entering a room, would deafen the people stationed there. He would have to throw blankets in advance of his body, to baffle the sound he was bring-ing, an application of fabric that amounted to laying a heavy rug in a room, but sharp-bodied girls could be smothered in this way. Sometimes instead of blankets he would throw another person into the room ahead of him, which was referred to as "turning on the light." These people were said to have a blinding effect, par-ticularly if they arrived unannounced and appeared to be strang-ers. Loud people have thin, hollow bones. They can be broken in half and discarded into a pit. They snap as easily as children do, but they will not burn as long in a fire. If a loud person tries to store his voice in a jar, he will not be able to, unless the jar is a mouth worn on the face of someone in his family, which he must prize open with his fingers while shouting deep into the hole there.

One year, people stacked bones outside their houses to absorb the sound of the police, who were talking loudly and pounding on the door. If no bones were available, an entire person was used, who would be escorted away and locked in a room. Every family kept a young person for this purpose. Often they sent him out on thiev-ing missions smeared with a special scent, to attract the police's attention. Now the police are required to carry a small bone in a polished black toy bucket called a holster. If they wish to be heard, they must hurl the bone away from themselves into a field, creating a current of deafness in the air that passes for weather so mild, even birds can fly in it. When birds actually manage to lift off without instantly listing into the colder turbulence that circles a house, where they might crack open over a roof, it indicates the looming presence of the law, and many family conversations grow nervous at the first sign of birds, with fathers sticking their hands out into the air, to test it for sound. When men cough or talk into their hands, they are praying to their own bones, hoping to change their minds about something. The police ride velvet-covered bone cages called horses. Horses are sad because they hear their own bodies sloshing and cracking. They produce an aggressive, highly pitched physical weeping known as galloping, and in this way spread their feeling across large fields of grass.

People have bones so insects won't flood their limbs and inflate their bodies to normal size. A person who is insect-controlled often sits and drinks tea, though an insect fluid called blood flows quickly beneath her skin. She has an accurate walking style and can converse in one or more languages. She sleeps lying down, and uses a filter called hair to attract her mates. The small people in her house call her "Mom," and she answers them by collapsing the tension in her face, a surrendering of control that passes for listening. When she pursues an upper-level-difficulty slalom run of housekeeping throughout her house, she has most likely failed to seal her bones from escape with fixatives called clothing. Her actions become commanded for the good of something larger, such as a naked man who resembles her father, although he might be younger and smaller and weaker, as if playing the part of her husband, though not convincingly. Her motion is voice-activated. When he addresses her, she stands on her toes and lets her arms raise up at her sides. She does a forward bend in the morning to be sure her blood pools at the top of her head. If you sliced her arm open, you would hear a faint buzzing. She has one pair of eyes, and they are often tired and red. When she uses her arms to prop up a document of regret known as a book, her bones form an ancient shape, and a brief, flashing signal is sent out through the window into the fields beyond her house, where the hive is.

If you possess the long, white tubing implements meant to prevent people from squeezing through small holes and disappearing, you have boning material, and you can begin to secure people to your team, insuring them against sudden departure. Bones of this sort were devised by Father so his children could not hide from him. They would no longer be able to collapse their dimensions and defy the restrictions he had built into his house. He had grown tired of a pocket-sized person devoid of shape who could not be broken. He wanted a guarantee, a chance to break something he could not fix. "Having a talk" with Father meant submitting oneself to the insertion of these bones, no matter how much it tingled.

When children fall into a well after being yelled at, it is not the power of their father's voice that has sent them there, but their desire to enter a long, hollow bone in the earth and become cleansed of sound. They would prefer to hide within their own bodies. When children are yelled at by Father, their skin tightens into a grimace over their faces because their bones have grown swollen with his voice. Most facial expressions result when the bones of the head respond to the difficult sounds produced in the outside world. Churches were originally built of bone as an answer to hard noises that troubled people, but the small fathers and mothers who were envious of the unused space around their own bodies entered the churches with hammers and cups. They positioned themselves near the walls and took stones from them, attempting to grow taller, wider, bigger. When you pray with your hands against your face, you are trying to add bone mass to your head, which has most likely become weak and crack-able, thinning out over time. When a priest lays his hands over his congregation, he presses his thumb into the soft part of a person's pudding until the person weeps his full share.

Bodies are hidden in the earth after they have finished breathing so that our towns will appear more peopled to the birds that fly over them, scanning for a weakness in our communities. Their vision does not tell them who is living or dead. They only see the depth of our ranks, namely, how many persons deep we are, what type of hard, white scaffold supports the town, whether our underground people have an organized or chaotic shape. The more buried bodies, the better. The dead, if buried together, create the illusion of an army. A latticework structure is offered for those who still stand aboveground, who must walk over the bones of former people with no guarantee that the earth will not collapse beneath them.

At certain moments, men, women, and children fall to the ground, breathing weakly, clutching their throats. Sometimes these moments are predicted and planned for, which means a hole is prepared in advance and a report is written. After a person dies, his bones still function. Although bones become dry, and the marrow can be scooped from them, and they can be broken in half even by children, a person who was once built of them, however tired and still he might seem, can at least drape a skin over himself and block the important doorways of the major houses in the town from the approaches of nearly anyone, including the people who live there.

# Against Attachment

was fortunate to find a person who would solve my solitude. She would use her hands on my person until it was soothed. She would chop at my husk, then spoon out my sorrow and be its keeper. I located her at a castle. My intention had not been to find her, for I had been busy being lonely with someone else. It was a tangled area of preening people, mostly diaper free, with real feet and hands, and each was traveling alone. You could ask about the weather there, and people would answer you in English.

The great Horace, childhood lover to Homer the Blind, when asked of love and its effects by the town council, who were conducting their Survey of the Mysteries, gathered his robes, stood up, left the auditorium, and never spoke again.

The time was technical summer, a season that had been achieved by nature so many times that a clotted arrangement of birds created splotches of ink called shadows, and whole days passed without gunfire. Shadows were blind spots that everyone shared. Graves were called homes, and apologies known as writing were carved in their surface. Rotten bags were called people. Milk was never sprayed from a fire hose at children until they skittered over the pavement like weevils, but the children wore shields of clothing regardless, and the people who guarded them were often trembling.

.  .  .

There was a chance, however remote, that we—among all the others who also famously walked the earth—would not breathe again, however much our mouths looked wet and ready for action. If we pictured ourselves in the future, we were forced to imagine our coffins shifting on a loosely soiled terrain, slipping into holes.

In short, it was necessary to establish a romantic alliance and to publish the results inside each other's bodies. When we referred to our fear as "tomorrow," our only solution was to seek aerial sensations with each other. Although we pretended to choose whom we would destroy in the name of a relationship, we were instead forced at each other, feigning admiration for the way our bodies lacked fat, hair, and color.

Together we conceived of solitude as a math problem, such like the ancients must have encountered when they saw two different suns in the sky: a daytime sun that was hot and burned out the eyes, and an evening sun that was cool, pale, and white. Each would soon have its own name, but for the time being the suns were anonymous, and they careened to a complex logic, and they were frequently misunderstood. People often died of heartbreak because of them. Maps of the dead called snowdrifts gathered in the mountains. An obituary water called rain fell everywhere, and the ancients—desperate, scared, vain—turned the hammered surface of their faces into it, so that none of it could reach the ground.

Questions we did not ask, because Ovid already asked them so well: In what way would commitment to each other differ from a commitment against our own solitude? In what way would our daily compromises, the shifts against our own nature, build into bulldogs of resentment that we would soon unleash upon each other? In what way would our displays of affection toward each other differ from advertisements of what we most wanted done to ourselves?

A relationship between us—two average-sized people who could not be mistaken for chess pieces, however much our faces looked chiseled and wooden and mishandled—would be a chance to mutually seek solutions to the dilemma of solitude. Other people, we discovered, had a plus or minus charge, similar to those colored beads called electrons. To be around the minus people was to have one's solitude erased, whereas the plus people seemed only to add to the solitude, which had a limitless growth potential, a way of swelling inside the skin, creating an aroma called disgust. If one of us experienced a deepening solitude in a crowd, a so-called Spanish Moment, we might conclude that a majority of the crowd was plus capacity, so overflowing with their own solitude that they could do nothing but share it with whoever entered their sphere. These people hated mud. They did not wish to be killed.

We were partners in a puzzle, then. The difficulty level was 9, or 9.3. There were no clues. We would have to wait until we parted from each other to discover whether we had won or lost. This was incentive enough to over-explore each other's eccentricities, to enter a race toward bored familiarity.

This took place in an area known as the world, where people cannot fly. Cocoons called nightgowns adorn the bodies there. When the cocoons are lifted, an investigation occurs, and the result is often moist, a smearing on of fluids. In this country, we breathe into each other's genitals with a periscope called a straw. We blow on them. We make a fan out of notebook paper and wave it over the area, using the age-old excuse that we simply love to read, and what better narrative than the one inscribed upon the genitals of our familiars? We play pipe organ music out of a stereo that looks like an old wooden shoe. Sex is not an event that someone is invited to, however much we sit by the phone anyway, waiting. There has been so much moisture between the people that streets have been built to collect the runoff.

We met inside the clear globules of fat known as air. There was no milk in the room. Swimming skills were not required. There were no weapons. A pocket-sized emissary named "Joe" introduced us. I did not love myself.

Afraid of the predictability of my attraction, I started a project called "I don't like you." It was intercut with other popular projects, such as "I am tired and scared" and "You are so beautiful that I am afraid to have sex with you." Her project revolved around the "Everything's fine" model. She held her cookie up high, and I jumped and touched my cheek to it. Through several mutual misunderstandings, we grew to need each other, a need that could be charted on a calendar. The parchment was signed with an evidence stick. Many children clapped.

It was agreed. She would chop at my husk, and I would begin publishing my name inside her mouth.

. . .

Courtship is based on hatred, according to one of the great thinkers, Robert Montgomery, a man who ate a series of meals, fell down a well, and then died. Hatred was a tactic the Phoenicians used when they met an enemy, and it has been the reigning wartime model ever since, however plain, however obvious. She and I, my solitude defeater, were no more enemies than any ancient man and woman bagged in cheap skin and fading hair, yet a battle was afoot, employing weaponry such as indifference and laughter, kissing and ambivalence, rubbing upon each other's bottoms with a bath brush, and waiting to see who would have the honor of starting the first argument. The goal was not to admit that we each suspected a future dependence upon the other. We commenced a theater of attractive indifference in order to seal our obligation to each other. We engaged in a strenuous denial of need. A holiday might one day be made out of this behavior. It would be called "Monday."

It was not illegal to know each other. It was just difficult. We used different cities as launching pads, when cities were linked by layers of chuff called roads and roads were not called devil carpets.

The ancients were so disloyal that they died and never thought of their loved ones again. Homer called dead people "traitors." The greatest loves were simply forgotten, and the bodies of leaders and slaves alike began to melt. The love between two people has never been stored in a vial and sold in a shop, yet sometimes she and I, the two of us, on the threshold of no longer caring for each other, a precipice called the Waking Moment, lay together in the bed shaking at each other's bodies as though we only had water inside us that could be easily poured away. We used a wringing technique called a hug and squeezed at each other with great force, hoping that somewhere on a floor beneath us there was a drain big enough to take the water part of this stranger we had been loving and wash them away, quite far from us, and then further still, until we could only hear the faintest sound, which we might mistake for a river.

# Leaving the Sea

t was before I discovered I could survive on potatoes and salted water, before my wife started going for long walks into the thicket, before our house started leaning, started hissing when the wind came up after sunset, a house no different from a gut-shot animal listing into the woods, a woods no different from a spray of wire bursting through the earth, an earth no different from a leaking sack of water, soft in the middle and made of mush, when my children used their spoons to make a noise if I spoke to them, clashed their spoons in my face when I spoke, stood small before me using their utensils like swords, whether my words were hummed or sung or shouted, whether I was kind or cold of voice, which was before I felt the cold finger hanging between my legs, a bit of ice high on my inner thigh, a patch of clammy cool-ness, instead of a hot and ample limb that could dilate if I so much as smelled her, when smell was a theft of wind, when wind was a clear blood leaking from trees, before my mother began saying it was *so difficult* whenever she tried to navigate so much as some stairs, a sidewalk, the doorway to a home, before I likened waking up to a car crash, equated walking to a free fall, working in the yard to grave digging, cooking food for the family to slathering glue on the walls, dotting the glue with beads, with jewels, when I likened weeping to camouflage, opening mail to defusing a bomb, when my wife began to say "Only if you really want to," before I developed the habit of pretending I wasn't looking at her, when the eye was an apology hole, when the face was a piece of wood under the couch, when the couch kept the body from crashing through the floor and beyond, when *beyond* was something I had yet to think about at night, when unspeakable movies played through my head, before I went to such lengths in town meeting situations to cheat my face to show my good side to whomever might be caring to look, to anyone even accidentally looking my way, believing that if only my face was viewed from certain angles then I would win something and something would come true for me and the words that broke the seal of saliva between my lips might mean something to someone and be actually useable, the way a shirt is useable as a barrier, the way a piece of wood is useable as a weapon, before I realized that my good side was competing fearsomely to duplicate my bad side, matching and maybe surpassing it, so that the bad side of my profile appeared to be on the advance, folding over the border presented by my nose and mouth and brow, rising up my head like a tide, when a tide did not refer to the advance of water, when most words had yet to wither, when their meaning was simply not known, before I flexed my arms if my wife happened to pay out the hug I sometimes still suffered to ask for when we encountered each other in the hallway, and then noticed that she noticed me flexing my arms, yet hoped anyway that I could harden myself under her grasp and impress her with my constant readiness, when I tensed my stomach if she gestured to touch it, in case her fingers sank into me as though I were a dough, so that if she was ever near me I would contract, clutch, convulse, at first deliberately, then later out of habit, a set of twitches triggered first by her presence, then her smell, then just evidence of her person: shirts, purse, keys, photos, her name, seizure-inducing, threats to my body, when I had yet to conceal the terrible territory known as my bottom to anyone who might see it, including the children and adults and dogs of this world, whom I pitied by wearing big pants, even to bed, letting my shirts drape over my waistline to serve as a curtain for the area, when clothing served as a medical tent, an emergency service, before the phone started ringing one time only, the doorbell chiming off-key in the morning to reveal no one standing at the door, mail appearing with empty pages inside, little stones clicking against the window, footsteps fading on the lawn, scuffling sounds, rustlings in the hedge, all of us always at the table, in our beds, our rooms, at the door, somewhere, unfortunately always locatable, lost-proof, when there was never any going below the radar or keeping off the map, every person and noise accounted for, before I could hear everybody swallowing the food that I made, could hear the corpse sounds their mouths made, as though everyone were eating a microphone, the food going into their bodies and dropping there in the dark like stones, when I planted objects inside these people who were supposed to be my family, who had conspired to look enough like me to serve as a critique of my appearance, and these objects were not being digested, rather they were eavesdropping, spying for me as I positioned myself elsewhere, sitting on the couch with cookbooks or catalogs or magazines or books, when reading was the same as posing for a picture, modeling yourself for the book so that you will be seen as you wish to appear, when looking at pictures was the same as swimming underwater, before I discovered the flaw with my teeth that I confirmed every time a mirror was near, checked as often with my tongue, whenever I needed a reminder that my chew pattern looked like footprints, discovered others checking it, their eyes never on my eyes but always cast down at my mouth, confirming the flaws of my face, the vein in my nose that looked penciled in, the unfortunate curve to my fingers that blunted my hands and promised no hope that they could ever again keep hold of a cup, a bowl, a plate, some money, some hair, before my private limb was diagnosed as crooked, before I ever, as a regular practice, got down on my hands and knees, took myself out of the world of the stand-ing people, surrendered my altitude, dropped down into table position, burying toys and letters in the yard, chipping at asphalt with a spoon, cleaning the hidden parts of the toilet, chasing my children on all fours outside in games where Daddy is a bear or dog, so that they could jump on me and ride on me and kick into the place where I would have gills if I were something better that had never tried to leave the sea, something more beautiful that could glide underwater and breathe easily, on my hands and knees at work looking for files or papers or reports, on my hands and knees crawling up to my wife in the bath, on my hands and knees in the closet, in the kitchen, in places like home where the action seems best viewed from ground level, where the action has ceased and a person can retire from view, right where the dirt starts and the air ends, the last stop for falling things, where things come to rest and get lost, on all fours as a strategy against vertigo, to be someone who has already toppled and can fall no further, is already down, low, at sea level, but not yet underwater, so that someone could come up to me and accurately say, "Man down!" before it was safer to be a person, one who had to go by automobile to view the people known as his parents, before viewing times were established with respect to his parents, days of the week with cer-tain times and restrictions, such as when the two of them would be sleeping, or priming their bodies for sleep, or dragging them-selves out of bed for the purpose of sitting there on their couch on display to my children, who could arrive at the location that contained my parents and examine them, a procedure that passed for a conversation, for play, for affection, a deep examination of these old people who were somehow, and dubiously, affiliated to them, which was well before the man came, before the man came, before the man came, knocking at the door one night, a tight report against the wood, letting himself in, sitting with us at the dinner table in the fashion of family, the man a smiler with a better face than mine, getting down from the cupboard a plate for him-self, extracting his own place setting from the drawer, which was the first drawer he tried, walking right to it, so familiar, sitting with the kids, talking to the kids, whispering to the kids until they put down their spoons and laughed and used their faces for the man, before he brought his arm up under my jaw one night when I fumbled out of bed to pee, leaving me not even on my hands and knees but on my back, not gasping or hurt or scared, just disap-pointed, to be on my back in my own house, so that nights there-after when I groped over to the bathroom to pee even a drop, or stand there with closed eyes and wait until I discovered I had no muscle for the peeing my body was telling me I needed to do, I would keep my arms up to keep from being struck, walked with my guard up, averting my head, waiting to be felled, when even in the daytime around the house I was ready with my arms to block what was coming at me, before I discovered him in my place in bed one evening upon returning from the bathroom, a successor where my body had been, holding on to my sleeping wife, when sleeping refined your argument against your spouse, and looking at me from a face that once might have been mine, still well before our house felt thin, not windproof or lightproof or people-proof, but a removable thing that we could not weigh down enough, because, as the man said, we were hollow, though I might not have heard him, since this was still before I heard the airplane, before everything overhead sounded like an airplane, even when I could locate no airplane, just the most booming sound overhead, which stopped getting louder or quieter, as though an airplane were cir-cling, but doing so invisibly, when invisibility indicated objects so close you felt them to be part of your own body, before I started hearing the big sound in the house when I turned on the faucet, the radio, the lights, when I opened doors or windows or jars of sauce to shush the white and gluey food I was offering everybody, and there came the sound, when everything I did seemed to invite more sound in, my motion itself a kind of volume knob, my body a dial, which if I used it would effect a loudness in the house that made life unsuitable, myself unsuitable, the world too loud to walk through, tasks such as walking, a loudness, washing, a loudness, speaking, a certain loudness produced by the machinery of the mouth, dressing for bed, a loudness like preparing for war, lying in bed, an earsplitting, terrible loudness, the noise of waiting for sleep, asking the children to be quiet, itself too much of a hypocritical loudness, my breathing itself, only my breathing, a loudness I could no longer bear, my breathing, my breathing, too loud for me to keep doing it. I was going to deafen myself if I kept doing it, breathing was going to render my head too packed with hard sound, it was too altogether terribly loud. Something very much permanent needed quickly to be done. A new sort of quiet was required. A kind of final cessation of breathing. A stifling. To be accomplished, no doubt, with those often out-of-reach weapons called the hands.

6

# The Moors

At work today, Thomas the Dead, as he had privately named himself, made a grave miscalculation by using baby talk with a colleague. He had not previously stooped, even with his own child, to baby talk. Why give the boy another reason to look at him in that cold, queer way of his? Nor had Thomas indulged in the sweet-toned animal coos that his colleagues babbled at one another when they banked and crashed around the lab on their foolish errands. Thomas preferred last words, the sort of speech to be discharged on one's deathbed. He guessed that some unpleasant number of decades ago, as a teenager, when he wore a thin beard and sported a tie with his short-sleeved dress shirts, he must have sounded old and tired and bitterly impatient, a youth who had already drawn firm conclusions on the key issues of the day, back when certainty was a young man's best chance at securing a mate and avoiding a life of hellish solitude, not that this had worked so neatly for him. Thomas was one for whom speech, the bursting, songlike kind that showed the world what an imbecile you were, was an annoyance that also happened to sour his body like a toxin.

Thomas and the colleague had been refilling their coffees at the same time because he had failed to calibrate his advance on the self-service beverage cart. Thomas's mistake, like most of the behavior he leaked into the world, had been avoidable: to join another human being in a situation that virtually demanded unscripted, spontaneous conversation, and thus to risk total moral and emotional dissolution. Death by conversation, and all that. Entirely avoidable. After all, he had seen the colleague approaching, a hand-painted mug dangling from her finger. Thus the peril of a bald, unpoliced encounter with her could not have been more glaringly clear, and the blame was squarely in his corner. Possibly it was the way the colleague glided shamelessly past Thomas's desk. What is it called, he wondered, when you provoke feelings of inferiority and general shittiness in others simply by the way you walk? When your mode of personal locomotion, in its devil-may-care mastery, serves as a scold to everyone fat and moist and ingloriously failed, sitting in their chairs, tired, swollen, and angry?

The warnings didn't matter. The colleague flew past his desk, flaunting how alive she was. He could smell her superiority and sheer you'll-never-have-me-ness, the bottled freshness that had shrouded her in a twister of perfume. Can one copulate against such a column of wind, he wondered? Are there handholds? And Thomas, triggered by scent and irritated lust, swallowing a powerful urge to dry heave, sprang after her as if she was a vehicle he suddenly needed to board, despite knowing (or not knowing vividly enough) that he'd only have to wait behind her at the coffee cart and worry the air with his oversized body.

Anyway, Thomas couldn't fathom how a person who hoped to live through the day could subscribe to such a Lego-strewn fantasy of worker relations the word *colleague* implied: as if a group of people whose heads were darkened by the very same hovering ass—something he decidedly never learned in night school was the term for how the human voice sounded when the mouth was smothered by an oily slab of buttock—would ever link arms, sing songs, and be massively productive together, just because they peed against the same wall or starched themselves into a stupor on the salted Breadkins from the vending machine every day. *Colleague* was a dressed-up word for the coworkers who would feast on his chest if they ever found him unconscious in the bathroom, yet she was his colleague, or coworker, or peer, or, well, enemy, and Thomas couldn't help thinking of England. Really he pictured an old, sodden map of England, which, even as it molted in his undisciplined imagination, he knew could not be prodded for even the most glancing accuracy (who policed, he wondered, just how badly people imagined things to themselves?). It wasn't so very far away, this England, with its bearded men who fought to the death over Plato, who politely disrobed and entered the sexual transaction without a break in their conversational patter, as if it would be the highest rudeness to gasp or cede rhetorical ground at the moment of penetration, even with a half-ready British piece of genitalia that reeked of potatoes.

The colleague walked gaily down the hallway, while Thomas, drafting in her tunnel of merriment, took up the somber rear. The two of them in procession—like a dashing mom with her slob kid in tow, thought Thomas (a kid who was noticeably *older* than his mother)—past the outlying desks and mail bins and various lab doors that were fitted with, instead of doorknobs, the long chrome lever arms that one normally saw on walk-in freezers. Thomas may as well have called after her: *Mommy, wait,* and he felt a sudden urge to gurgle, fall to the floor, and rub himself for comfort. Chalk that up to another *entirely appropriate response* he would never indulge. If only he had a dead body, or was it money, for all of these, uh, unpursued urges.

They were not exactly friends, Thomas and the colleague, but the two of them coffined up in the same stinking diesel elevator enough times—trespassing each other's borders with wartime regularity and altogether too little overt treachery—that didn't it, he thought, merit some kind of default marriage in the end? Was there a better working definition of marriage than a weapon-free battle between exhausted adults, with an agreement to gaze above each other's heads, icing each other out with indifference? Cold War would be the way Ramsey, in equipment, would dismiss it to Thomas, Ramsey who delivered transmissions on married and fathered life whenever Thomas had to sign out gear—a beaker, a tray, and an allergen-percolating tool the office referred to as the Bird's Face—and who frequently reported the sickeningly early hour he was wrenched awake to monitor his paper-eating, tantrum-spurting kid, a youngster who by eight thirty in the morning was at least four hours deep into his terrible day, according to Ramsey, battle-scarred and as strung out as a torture victim, which, come to think of it, was a pretty adequate description of Ramsey himself. In fact, whenever Thomas tried to picture Ramsey's boy, he pictured another Ramsey, and saw two red-faced Ramseys chasing each other around an oatmeal-splattered room. Big Ramsey and Little Ramsey, trying to kill each other. A classic story of father and son.

Thomas guessed that at times, maybe in the elevator, the colleague could smell how little he had slept, while in retaliation he could see the sauce stain on her back, or the rumpled tidings of underwear advancing over her waistline. That was a fair piece of intimacy, in the end. Shouldn't they, by now, have already trucked past the romantic swells and decadent fits of sharing indulged by the other middle-aged marrieds, toward a brisker season of restraint and theatrical indifference regarding each other's mild but steady pain? If they knew each other at all, that is.

For Thomas there was only one outlet for a journey down this hallway—the coffee cart—since he lacked clearance to any of these rooms or freezers or whatever they were. On bright-lettered signs the doors might have cautioned: *Carcass inside. Turn back!* But turning back would draw too much notice, and he doubted he could rear up and reverse course without some kind of verbal narrative support of his decision—*I'm turning back now because I'm scared!*—and the thought of such a strange and conspicuous outburst, even one more finely stated, made him feel vaguely sick. What kind of idiot does things, then says why?

So off he trotted after her, drugged with regret and adrenaline and the sort of fear that felt like a boring old friend. He had no mug of his own. He'd have to work that out later. And there was an issue with his, uh, pants. Ahem. But for now he was up and at large and he did his best to gather his face and body into an expression of deep purpose, even if there was none he could rightly claim.

The colleague was a long woman, medically attractive, perhaps intensely attractive. But when Thomas, as was his habit, called up in his mind the nude and indeed the coital prospect with her, simply to work out the mental visualization side of things, in place of vaginal goods Thomas could only conjure a charcoal sketch of the area, just a shabby pencil drawing of something he was supposed to want to bury his face in and weep with relief into. This bothered Thomas because although he could not draw, he could imagine all sorts of drawings, an encyclopedic catalog of, uh, *especially rich imagery,* which turned out to be an entirely useless ability.

It wasn't the specific armature of nudity that he longed for, anyway (the canals and curves and rough red patches bursting with boiling hair), but something dutiful in him—as if his erotic strategy was being assessed through surveillance by specialists— bowed to an elementary form of sexual speculation, and he customarily launched this material on his inner slide show for their sake. Perhaps these specialists would see that Thomas could hew to the national erotic standard. But, if anything, he was fair-minded about his crotch pictures, courteously rendering them from the hips of nearly everyone he passed. The result was a kind of gallery, the mug shots, he called them, and it calmed him to realize that his central-most imaginative act, the vision work he was called to most consistently and which occupied him more than any other creative task, was to flesh out in his mind the sexual organs of everyone he saw and to catalog this data for later use. Mostly the genitage that colored his gallery was rendered from some distillation of a person's face, that is, if the face had been squeezed like a sponge or crushed underfoot. The aesthetics here—what Thomas thought of as his functioning design paradigm, because he had read in one of June's *All About People!* folios that we create our private images out of a deep sense of order, logic, beauty, and inevitability, whether we like it or not—involved the notion that a dog (or spouse or child or anything we care for and, in particular, feed) comes to look like its provider. Or something from the stronger, more powerful face is sprayed over the weaker face, rendering it nearly identical. There was a funny-sounding scientific rule to be invoked here, whatever it was called. An old biological trick, which makes us think, Thomas guessed, that we are really caring for and feeding ourselves. One's crotch stuff should in some way invoke the face, tell a story about it, Thomas felt, or, rather, one's face should, in its lines and swollen crags, map the sexual *terroir*. Someone more poetically afflicted could charge up better metaphors about that one. Or maybe it meant that his imagination was severely limited, deriving its ideas from the face. He guessed that artists would laugh at how obviously sourced his material was. Or maybe they'd just be bored. In any case, Thomas was confident that if he saw someone's face, he could tell exactly what their genitals looked like. *Exactly.*

Once they arrived for their coffees, Thomas would have to try to drum up some chitchat with the colleague that would not, when it was analyzed for content and style and delivery, by just whoever gave a shit, get him committed to a home, or tossed in a closet that someone somewhere must keep warm for the miserable and lonely and disturbed. Which is what these people did, wasn't it? They spoke in cold chunks of wordage and no one ever wept or seized or died. The nearly sexual urge Thomas had to destroy himself through difficult encounters, encounters like these with women who surpassed him in every measurable way, would provide the sweet subject matter for days of mistake analysis, the richest pastime. Now I know what I'm doing this weekend, he thought. It was as though he'd been programmed to do exactly the wrong thing, and not for the first time he pictured a keypad on his back that anyone could access, a sweaty keypad that he couldn't very well clean without one of those curved brushes. This would be another part of his body that itched and hurt and broke and sometimes bled. Add it to the list. Fat Men with Itchy Backs would be the support group he would join. *Let's go program Thomas,* the kids might say, and he would lift his shirt so they could have their fun, tucking forward until his belly bulged over his legs. Whose idea was it, this body of his? Do we need yet more reasons to feel disgusting? Or if not a keypad, maybe an embossed alphabet over the rib cage—if you can find my ribs, he thought—raised up in scarred topologies like a cattle brand, so pedestrians and God knows who else could effortlessly dispatch him into crisis and shame *simply by coding him,* even as he spent nights at home trying to fashion a utensil that would allow him to take control of the area, or at least to shield it from typing strangers.

Protection was what Thomas wanted, from people, their words, their bodies, and the storms they kicked up when they came anywhere near him. Couldn't the office supply a saltwater receptacle for him to hide away and brine in when there was no actual work on his desk? A casket—upright, transparent, so the others could see him suspended in saline—to keep him from harm?

It wouldn't matter. He'd sniff out the surplus misery anyway and grind his face in it until the itch stopped, but pretty fat chance of that.

It had been a day of no apparent weather, with gray cars hushing by like silent tracers and air so swaddled and wet it seemed filled with foam. Last week a streak of birds had been sent forth to pop and burst against the office window. Thomas figured it to be some pageantry tossed off by the city to stuff the sky with color, but the official word from the listserv was that a new time-keeping system was being tested. He hadn't bothered to calibrate his watch to it, even as, hourly, birds smeared through the air, struck the office window, and dropped from sight after the impact. A neat poof, a bright cloud of dust, and the bald white clock on the wall clicked off another hour.

No one in the office, so far as he could tell, had even blinked, as if, *oh,* this kind of slaughter was just a matter of course. And if Thomas never actually saw a pile of birds rotting in the court-yard, such a pile was inferred, wasn't it, which was quite enough of a worry to nurse until the office lights were browned down at sunset and the employees were released into the streets so they could stagger home, hump their wooden comfort dolls, and moan into their blankets all night. Or whatever Thomas imagined them doing when they weren't construing allergic thresholds, putting the beaker to a theory, or tearing into sandwiches with a single, angry finger.

That was history now, sucked into some brownish whatever. There was no one else on their feet now except Thomas and the colleague. Thomas looked back into the cluster and saw necks and heads, fat red arms. It was error sampling time, at least in his

unit, and it was nervous, spastic work. So much lab work resem-
bled one's early attempts at masturbation. There were angry little
bursts of typing, and the group of employees seemed to wheeze
as a single beast with one faulty lung. He was careful to silence
himself while he walked after the colleague, to guard his breath
and keep his pants legs from shooshing. But just because no one
was looking at him didn't mean his pursuit was going, uh, unnoticed. Thomas kept his head steady but stole his eyes toward the
greasy surveillance camera, a lens jammed badly into some mottled Sheetrock, behind which Sully in the security room would
be fastidiously ignoring them. Thomas guessed that Sully's pants
would be shucked and he'd be wrapping a slice of soft white bread
around his penis while the security monitors revealed in blue light
the morons who walked and slept and stood and self-groomed
around Crawford Labs.

This was the easy part. A straightaway down the lab's hallway
that would allow him to get himself together. Big goddamn ha, ha
to that. He pulled his shirt as he walked, dug his thumbs between
his belt and pants, deep into his gummy sides. *You can't very well
hang on to yourself!* The wise old maxim of someone important
who was now rotting in a hole, a phrase lost to needlepoint and
coffee mugs. He licked a finger on each hand and worked dry
spit over his eyebrows. Such pointless grooming. If only he could
shed a limb, or reach inside his face and reshape it so he looked,
maybe, a small bit less Thomas-y. *Let's do a little work on that face,
how about?* As it was, his face looked as though someone had *tried*
to reshape it and failed.

The colleague, in her cloud of superiority, had done her prep
in private, no doubt. *She was born prepped,* Thomas thought, and he
pictured her in adult form being birthed in a clean bright room
somewhere to a team of scientists, who wiped her off, hosed her
down, and fitted her in specialized gear so she could go out and

make other people feel bad. She actually, probably, looked forward to such workplace sojourns like this, so she could flaunt her shit here and there and take everyone down a notch.

But was there a lower notch? Thomas wondered. *Let's invent a new notch, underground, and let's get you nice and cozy there.* He'd find out pretty soon, at the beverage cart, where the basic transaction of drink retrieval, the animal quest for hot, black fluid that Thomas rigorously pursued *alone* so as not to ever, and that would mean never, have to enter a discussion, would be precisely too long to undertake without some kind of conversational exchange.

The problem was that the beverage cart was lodged alone in an arena-sized space referred to by the laboratory staff—by pretty much anyone who worked and drank and ate and felt pain at Crawford Labs—as the Moors. The Moors was so misconceived architecturally that none of the so-called founders of Crawford could do anything except stash the coffee cart in it, stain it with some Germanic decorations that seemed spritzed from a hose—a hose with different ethnic tips—and hope not to die. Somewhere there were architects rubbing their hands together, laughing at the idiots who were daily demoralized in the spaces they designed. Demoralized, crushed, belittled, and then, for fun, desexed in the most complete possible way. Genitals flicked off neatly at the base. Holes smoothed over with one of those Photoshop tools. Bottoms filled in with putty.

The Moors may as well have had a genital-removal station you visited on your way out. Water-fountain height, retractable into the wall. Tilt in your hips and come back clean. And the egghead architects laughing and pointing, maybe even rubbing themselves into states of ecstasy. Their brains probably sat outside of their heads, simmering in jars of cola. It was a pornographic pleasure, no doubt, to watch people killed in buildings, killed slowly, brought near death and held in suspension simply by precalculated dimensions, by room design. Someone had already thought of this, he knew, the killing power of buildings, so, who cares, another great idea he could not claim as his own. Buildings were coffins, of course, but that came later. First they were killing machines. Did it matter to anyone how mixed that metaphor was, and where had he read that, anyway? It was probably one of those chapbooks that had been ribboned together as a wedding present for him and June, someone's younger brother's dissertation. *Best wishes, here's my brother's piece of obscure scholarship. We love you guys!* He didn't remember ticking that off on the registry at the fucking Shoe Hole, or wherever he and Juney had listed the material bill of goods that would transform their ordinary marriage into a super-powered alliance.

No doubt there were cool loaves of data on a server some-where devoted to the subject of architectural annihilation, and the theory was clearly *infallible,* Thomas thought, lumbering after the colleague, who was bouncing out of sight at the end of the hall-way. Yet anyone who likened a building to a coffin, anyone who went public with what every known human in the world already totally accepted to be true, was officially considered an asshole.

Of course, the Moors must have been built to enable the kind of productivity that architects fantasized about while at work in their hoteliers—whatever those studios were called—where their young assistants, wearing T-shirts and no pants, rendered drawings, bound by contract, by the apprentice's promise, to *relieve impediments* to their masters' creativity. The Moors was probably meant to be a place where people would be thinking and performing at their best, why not, a blueprint premised on the belief that the actual people who would seize this space for their displays of high-performance creativity would not be defeated, tired, unattractive, and sad. *Excepting our friend the colleague, of course. Immune to space. Sad-proofed.* The Moors was designed for people who couldn't be

bothered to die on time. Architects don't make buildings for people who are a bloody mess, just soup, really, because then there'd
be no buildings, just tureens. Had there been a dissertation on
that? Whose fat brother wanted to take that one on? *Tenure fucking
awaits.* Vats would be trucked in from the factories, into which the
people would be poured. Architects have somehow gotten away
with thinking that people are not already technically dead, dead
beyond repair, according to the accepted measurements, while
really they are sloshing inside their clothing, walking spills. It is
their first mistake, Thomas thought: believing they are not building coffins. Why weren't architects simply called coffin makers?

This week there had so far been no birds, but birds would
have seemed a mercy compared to the unknowable bundle of
something breakable that had replaced them. Instead, the civic
timekeeping strategy this week seemed to be a sickly wet thud
that shook the entire building, bringing down a sudden hush on
the analysis suite at Crawford Labs each time, as though a sack of
something, *something capable of feeling great pain,* Thomas was certain, had plunged down outside, landing badly with what sounded
like a sharp moan of grief. Each time he looked to the window
today he saw nothing and heard nothing, and if his colleagues
met his glance when he sought some kind of communion over
this, uh, he wasn't sure *what* to call it, they dragged their faces
toward him with theatrical fatigue, as if he were a janitor coming
to remove their trash: guilt, gratitude, and disgust smoking from
their heads. He had taken a night course once and in the minor
educational residue that remained he knew there was a word for
when a group of people collectively ignored someone's pain. A
very fine word. Even the bland, bread-shaped people in his office,
remarkably, had the higher functions of cruelty available to them
and could serve up chilling displays of indifference. But whatever that term was for such a moral crime, it was fuzzed out now.
Not that having the name for it would really help.

Thomas walked into the bright flat space, just steps after the colleague, and put his hand to his mouth. There was always this terrible adjustment. The smell was not of coffee so much as a burnt
limb. Who knew what got cooked and killed here every night.
Somewhere, no doubt, there was footage. This, then, was the
Moors, a death space stained in beige, with a lone coffee cart, like
a Tudor spacecraft, stuck into the floor. Windows, no sir. Doors, no
sir. Octagonal space, check. Or, actually, maybe some other number of walls, one of them, if this was possible, slightly *lower* than
the others: It wasn't a four-sided room, that was for sure. He had
done his romantic time in trick rooms; it was one of his favorite
dates with June long ago, but this one fell short of the kind of
optical illusions that gave you mild diarrhea or freaked you out or,
for some reason, brought out the horn dog. The distorted low wall
in the Moors felt more like a mistake, after the fact, and maybe
now the Moors was only a trick room for people like him, with
overfed faces and eyes so tired that everything they saw seemed
crushed, shrunken, and slightly moist. *Every room is a fun house if
your face is broken.*

He uncovered his mouth and cautiously sampled the air,
expecting for a moment to pass out. Ahead of him the colleague
slowed, and Thomas nursed the doorway, sipping little breaths
with the spazzy orbit of an insect. He was wary of thresholds—
some ungodly number of people got their shit handed to them in
thresholds—and certainly he had not hovered about at the foot of
the Moors like this before, because he had his ways of determin-
ing the area was empty before committing himself to the journey
(what idiot didn't?).

Thomas looked at the fine-suited shoulders of the colleague
and wanted to write RIP on her back. It was clear that the design-
ers of the Moors hoped its occupants would die spectacular deaths,

and Thomas marveled that the colleague had somehow not spent her good cheer already and been roundly undone by the room. Generally, the people who returned from their adventure to the coffee cart, fitted with beverages, looked gray and dry and past all feeling, even if they had entered the area with a sexual glow, with good ambulation and overly publicized happiness. The most rigorous denial, not that he partook, was brought to its knees in this place. Let's see the colleague not die a thousand little deaths, starting right now. Thomas found that if he had fountain or specimen work he could sit and watch his colleagues coming out of the Moors, and the experience felt similar to watching a chain of prisoners of war, the kind who had been sucked clean of life and now just shuffled in ill-fitting skin, beyond even any kind of animating pain.

The colleague, however, seemed shielded from the preordained defeat of the Moors. She swung her mug, and in her carriage was the simplistic bliss of a feeder before the great table of some famous god. She seemed to be indulging a moment of choice, and deep sighs of pleasure gusted from her chest, which from behind seemed to Thomas as though a soft wall was breathing. A soft wall swollen with something almost unbearably luscious underneath. Was that an okay thought to have? *Hello, soft wall,* he wanted to say. *I love you.*

This mug had been waved in his face before, too, and there was perhaps no other piece of pottery in the region used to draw so much rebuke from its witnesses. The colleague whirled it in such loops it seemed she was winding up to hurl it against the wall. And perhaps that would be fitting. Someone's child had been wrongfully praised for making this mug, and now someone was rigorously putting it to use at work, *actually drinking from it,* to prove that taste, style, fashion, sense, and even logic itself—the holy quinitude of scrutiny—could be easily dismissed when it came to the astonishing achievements of children.

Thomas took in the baked, lumpy mess of it as it swung back and forth. What kind of monster couldn't outright love a mug like that, love it without conditions, love it fully, and maybe, who knows, ejaculate on it out of joy? Are you that despicable? he asked himself silently in a booming voice his father might have adopted when he played the barrister in one of his cringing bouts of summer stage (a reminder arose that he should like to issue to everyone: Never watch your father perform in a play), that you must actually assess this mug with your full adult faculties as if you were a critic? Is there a power surge available to you when you cut down a child? Fine to be a gatekeeper of the fabricated objects of the world produced by lady and gentleman artisans, a mediator of value, as such, but this is a mug shaped by a child, for God's sake, and what exactly is proven by its dismissal other than high and selfish pettiness, a deep insecurity, and a compulsive desire to alienate anyone in your blast radius?

The rhetoric flowed easily as Thomas silently attacked himself on the colleague's behalf, and it was not entirely unpleasant to take on such an easy target, to hector from such a fixed moral point, even as he gazed at the grotesque mug swinging in front of him, rimed with lip junk and who knows what else. *Chuff and bilge from the mouth. Speech powder.* He puffed and tilted and half wished the colleague would turn around and notice him already, since there was something gallant flooding up. Thomas the Brave, defender of children, appearing now in the Moors, ladies and gentleman. Wouldn't she, in some way, have to admire this, his sticking up for her kid? If only she knew my thoughts she would take her pants off. *My thoughts should count for something.*

She did not turn around. Willing it with his mind only seemed to make him tired. Thomas surveyed the brown wool length of her as she surveyed the coffee cart, and there was something sorrowful in how undefended she was, at least from this angle. People do not prepare for how they'll be seen from behind, he thought, and it seemed decidedly unfair, if fairness still had any currency, that anyone could gain such a supreme advantage simply by taking up the rear and looking at a bodily territory that had in no way been readied for this sort of discerning view. *Hello, my name is Thomas and I have seen you from behind. I have been granted the lion's share of what there is to be known here.* The colleague had no doubt poured vast resources into the project of her appearance—she was a prim and sharp little project of a person—but had spectacularly failed to engineer a posterior perspective.

To some degree, there was something inhuman about her from this angle, the Thomas angle. But when he thought about it, the term *inhuman* seemed wrong, however enjoyable it was to use. *I stood at the Moors with the inhuman colleague.* That sounded rather fine. *It was evening, and I carried the inhuman colleague up the stairs to my rooms.* In truth, this vantage, revealing the colleague's disheveled back body, showed Thomas a part of the human that he must admit he felt no particular fondness for: the weak, sad, unnoticed part—keep your sadness under a rock, you sweet-boned colleague!—that could not be properly shielded by clothing. The great failing of the fashion industry. *Clothiers, where are your geniuses of disguise?* Posturally the colleague showed no sign (this wasn't a poker face she had so much as a *poker body*) that she knew some kind of serious assessment of her was under way, but indifference was a subterfuge, of course, and what could she gain, Thomas wondered, by revealing her worry? What did one ever gain? People prep themselves, if they prep themselves at all, in the front and, at most, glance over their shoulders at the mirror to see the grotesque calamity of their backsides, which become pulled long, pulled so terribly long, from the contortion. Should not a person of the colleague's rank and stature have in her employ an assistant, a perspective manager (bring back the architect's apprentice!), who might engineer many different views of her, so that her power and

clout would not be so easily undermined if someone happened to
see her out in the open like this, unprotected, completely vulnerable and, well—Thomas paused and looked around the Moors,
wishing someone could appreciate the dramatic pause—killable?
He spilled an ugly little laugh at the colleague and swiped at the
air as if to erase it. I will be your backside witness, he wanted
to whisper. I will see the sorrowful view. Send me, Thomas, first
into the sad space. Because what good was the colleague's power
if she could not hide how desolate, nomadic, and freshly assaulted
she looked from behind?

But there was no hiding in the Moors, and didn't he know it.
The sole bit of shelter was the beverage cart itself, fashioned to
look like a house—a Tudor with chalk-plaster walls and splintered
beams painted even darker to appear waterlogged, or possibly to
suggest a more authentic species of wood, with predrilled worm-
holes and hand-painted knots and other calibrated imperfections
that someone, somewhere had labored over—a chalk outline of a
dead person appeared in Thomas's mind. As fussy as the cart was,
Thomas had never seen it tended to, filled or emptied, adjusted.
And the design strategy—a Tudor house pumping coffee by the
barrel—always did something sour to his mood. *Depressed* seemed
too strong a word—he was saving this word for something really
special—and yet something awful did well up in him when he
visited the Tudor, even alone, when it was safe, and not being
poisoned by a colleague. Because since when was a Tudor house
a place to retrieve coffee? Precisely what historical narrative was
being trotted out? Would it not be more apt if it was a behead-
ing station, complete with guillotine? Other than the atmosphere
of coziness a Tudor supposedly conveyed, which was predicated
on one's being able to hurl up a foreign language with the red-
faced inhabitants whose hands were boiled and fat and who probably stank of vinegar, the cart had wheels and offered dehydrating

beverages from a stout, flesh-colored spigot punched into its fake wall. If that was one of the mandatory fairy tales barked at the children of his generation—a house is really a sack of hot fluid on wheels, in which a giant, perhaps, swims—then he'd missed it growing up. Shouldn't the coffee cart have skins, or, what were they called: peelable facades? A seasonal surface was needed, to mottle and fade and turn gray, only to slowly fill with blood, to pulse and throb, to maybe even bleed slightly onto your hands when you touched it. That would be a worthy coffee cart. A life-form in the Moors, with a dark leak of coffee. I would drink death water out of that item, thought Thomas. A thousand percent for sure.

It was late morning and the air in the Moors might as well have been brown. Soon there would be seizures of lunching erupting in the soft spots, bursts of solitary and group eaters from Crawford, their faces glazed with fatigue. Chances were that some colleagues would flood the Moors with their wilderness sounds and smells, blocking Thomas's path back to his desk. Which meant that Thomas was pinned down, in military terms, between the Moors and his work space. Hadn't he read that there were always nine ways to escape a trap? Was it nine? Did they all involve death, or was it just most of them? Maybe this had only been in a novel, though. Someone had dreamed this into being—*Nine Ways to Escape Anything*—and now people like Thomas had to suffer by wishing it was true. What good did that do anyone?

Just then the colleague stepped to the cart with a little squeal of pleasure, and Thomas felt nearly sucked into the space she had vacated. Her special noise—colleague noise number nineteen, probably—was the workaday exhaust of a body in search of drink, the kind of natural acoustic shedding that apparently emanates from people when they pursue their biological needs alone. It is only in company—*Look out, shame!*—that we become quiet. Not so the colleague, whose chirping whoop could be, if Thomas only had the technique and speed, rejoined with some equally guttural and possibly joyous chest noise.

Thomas had to wonder if this was how it worked in zoos, when a gang of beasts was suddenly shrieking together, dry humping the scratching post, doing flips around the pen. As a boy, standing in front of the oval domes that held such gorgeous creatures, Thomas always felt that the animals had noticed him and were calling him out, in their berserk fashion, and it didn't seem to be his imagination that the shrieking subsided into hushed tones of relief when he walked away from them. Such power he had. He used to give the matter a lot of thought, because there was time then to worry about how much he sickened those who saw him, and on his most rational days it was clear that his body itself was triggering a frenzy in animals and humans alike, with removal the only solution to hand. *I'm walking away so that you might calm down,* which was something, come to think of it, he often had to say to his own child in present times. But elsewhere, when he indulged the need to argue for his own survival, he had to concede that there was a chance, however slight, that the animals, in shrieking and howling and tearing at their own skins, were, in their special way, approving of him, welcoming him, possibly even inviting him into their midst. Was this another missed opportunity he was supposed to be worrying about now?

No one was waiting behind him in the Moors, so the protocol now was unclear. If he moved forward to fill the colleague's space, advancing in the queue, not that there was legitimately a queue, it would leverage direct pressure on the colleague, encouraging haste and reminding her that *someone else loomed.* He thought of those times in banks when he walked into the lobby and people seemed suspended in place, as though they had forgotten what they were doing. *My friends, the puppets,* he wanted to say. These people were not clearly in a line, though, nor were they distant enough from the line to seem unaffiliated with it. Menacing business. Artists of affiliation, they should be called. It took talent to make everyone around you start to worry and second-guess their most basic goals. (He saw himself—handsomer, thinner, slightly girlish—at a podium, holding an audience of animals in thrall with his lecture: *In my work, I explore the confusion that results when physical-proximity laws are stretched beyond the breaking point. I seek to destabilize normative pedestrian traffic and queuing strategies by engaging unresolved coordinates with my physical form and holding fucking fast until someone wants to kill me. The setting for this work is the bank or the store, our shared spaces, where I will cause people to ask fundamental questions about my coordinates.*) These hovering people required to be questioned on the matter; they were asking to be addressed—*ask me where I stand!*—and Thomas knew that, no matter what, he did not want to be questioned on this or really any other matter. A credo! Fend off inquiry. How much simpler could it be? *One's actions should prevent all approaches.* Why weren't there needlepoint frames for that?

How soon could Thomas move after the colleague moved, and would that not trigger a complaint on her part? *I have the right not to be imitated.* Behavioral goddamn copyright, *right?* Yet he was distant enough from the cart, if he didn't shadow the colleague, and indeed from anything in the Moors, that it might appear to a newcomer—please God forbid there ever be a newcomer—death to the newcomer!—that he was not waiting in line, but loitering in the center of the Moors with some arcane religious purpose in mind. Or not even arcane. This is a man, others might argue, who is about to sacrifice a child on a pyre. Grab him now before he strikes his match.

Unclaimed space might have been making this worse. The Moors had never developed a specific use by the lab, which was funny when you thought of it, since wasn't every cubicle acre everywhere else at Crawford Labs fought over by every spazmodia he worked with? They were like Sooners, or Okies, or . . . Thomas paused as a smile flushed into his face, the sort of smile that required a hand to squeeze down . . . Jews.

He shot a look around the Moors because this was the kind of thought that would seem so, who knows, *detectable*. You don't just think something like that and not show the whole known world what you're made of. These thoughts steam off of your head, they're inhaled by everyone around you. He knew that they weren't Jews, and yet, calling up in his mind the sweaty-headed figurines who passed for his co-employees, the people who might meatily regard him if he ever held the floor (in the contest that had come to be known as Speak Well or Be Killed) and served up a passable, even yeoman performance, he wished he had the sort of acquaintances who would swallow this whole: pretending that the Sooners were Jews and that the Jews had a head start on the Homestead Act, tearing through the dust bowl and planting flags, erecting shtetls, bursting with song as the sun went down on the freaking veld. Was it a veld then, or did velds come later, or from elsewhere?

Standing in the Moors, the whole image—people, his people? stampeding over unclaimed land, a thunder of Jews—turned oily in his head, and it was good riddance. Acquaintances were precisely the people who cold-warred you when you ventured something borderline. This wasn't Jew hating, he protested to no one, this was Jew loving, loving the Jew so heartily that you sent him into the past to accomplish great things and save lives. Go forward, or backward, young Jew! But tell that to the acquaintances. Acquaintances operated a bellows that blew over you a cloud of reeking air. To the Jews he knew, Thomas was not really Jewish, and yet to the non-Jews he sure as hell was as Jewish as it ever could possibly get. He had pegged the needle. What was this zone of belongingness called, other than stage three alienation? In their minds, the non-Jews bearded Thomas and gowned him and maybe also had their disgusting way with him on an old abandoned couch in the desert. How many times had others imagined killing him, he wondered, and was there possibly a critical mass at work, where technical death occurred if your death was dreamed of by enough people? Had this colleague killed Thomas in her mind? Chances were. Or who knew, but couldn't the possibility of his wished-for death account in some way for the unusually cold, blue, rigid way he felt? *You're killing me,* he wanted to say to her. *In your mind, I can feel it.*

The building shuddered and, for a blinding second, the Moors went dark. *Bedtime,* thought Thomas. *Thank God.* A sharp hiss snapped the lights back on and in the strange glare a smell came to him, something far off, like a person being cooked. He blinked into the brightness, rubbed his face, and looked again at the perfectly composed colleague. A bloodbath wouldn't get her attention, and perhaps this was the top secret these people shared: They were dead as stones and the world could pour over their cold bodies, but to hell if they'd ever notice.

It was time to push on. Something wasn't so superfine out there, and the Moors didn't seem like the very best place to be.

Thomas met the newly vacant hole in the Moors—the colleague hole—by invoking the insect strategy of progress. He inched forward, ever so carefully, with small dips in reverse, as if he was apologizing backward while steadily gaining ground, an orbit calculated to look like nothing was being achieved. He entered the colleague's shadow, and even though it was not a real shadow but a dark spill at her feet, as if something awful had flushed from a bag attached to her waist, it was her shadow nonetheless and Thomas was gaining ground. How to get ahead at work: Pretend you're moving backward. How to get fat: Swallow your own laughter. This was how his parents used to dance, shying away from each other as if to say: I'm sorry, I'm sorry, I'm sorry.

So it was that he inched into her shadow, and suddenly the air was cool and clean and he found himself breathing in fast little gulping thrills. Had anything more intensely dramatic happened ever?

*This is real life, folks,* Thomas wanted to say. *Make no mistake, it is on!*

As strategic as Thomas was, the colleague seemed to be choosing that other, uh, unexamined path, and even though she must have smelled and sensed and very nearly goddamn tasted Thomas, she trilled about indifferently and took, if it was possible, even less notice of the ridiculously fine gentleman nearly riding inside her clothing. Do I have to become you, he wanted to ask, for you to notice me? The liberty she took, to effuse in his presence— the simmering pleasure fountain within the colleague that she'd turned up to full—was, what was the word, *problematic.* Because if indeed a person only succumbs to such biological gurglings alone, she clearly did not yet know he was there, or couldn't accord him the status of the present. And yet he was living pretty hard not three feet away from her. Was this kind of omission seriously within her power? Was he meant to actually embrace her in order to prove his existence?

Thomas backed away. This sally would be recalled. Her smell, her climate, the so-called sphere of the colleague was too much. Doesn't one break into pieces in such an atmosphere? There were laws to be invoked, certainly, yet the fuck if he knew what they were. Perhaps that's what anyone's personal smell ultimately was: the residue of the people who had shipwrecked against them. Thomas felt he would get sick on the colleague's past if he stayed too near. This wasn't worth it, he knew, and he looked at the sad space he'd have to crawl through to get back to his desk, without his rotten coffee, the doorway that had never before delivered such unequivocal disease to his person before. Was this doorway number freaking one, and was there any possible glory behind it?

The fundamental difference between Thomas and the colleague, a difference in their mistake management protocol, heh heh, was that the colleague was smiling through this disaster (he could tell this even from the *back* of her head), dipping and dodging and spewing happiness like a strange machine designed to broadcast cheerful moods to people who weren't sure what to feel. *A mood Sherpa.* What would you like to feel today, little sir?

Whereas Thomas, well, he was showing a medium-high capacity for colossal not-so-greatness. He looked around and saw just walls of nothing, smelled the burned body smell, and had to restrain himself from trying to chew his way out of the air. He had to remind himself as he held his ground behind the colleague— wait quietly for your coffee, little sir!—that there was still—thank God—a barrier between his thoughts and the world, and that people could not look at his disheveled, sea-bloated fatitude, his pilled attire that had been washed into sheer roughage, the extra fat mounded on the backs of his hands—in case I have to eat myself someday—and have any blessed idea of his, uh, *special thoughts,* as such. There was, as yet, no tool to read into the clot of his head, and if he grimaced or smirked or grinned or just looked as shit-crazed as he absolutely, in some objective sense, *was,* there was no proof of the inside material, and this was sufficient and soothing negation to the chance that *a disclosure* was occurring without his knowledge.

Things were calming down. This was good. The mistaken shadow invasion, the day the colleague's shadow was breached, was now strictly archival, stored for the crowd who would watch this on video someday. Would it be called *Mishaps at the Moors? The Day My Ship Caved In? I, Colleague?* What a shrill little bit of drama that had been loosed into the labs, but for nothing, and Thomas looked around for someone to blame. This was pretty basic. Things were okay. The colleague would get her coffee. Thomas would wait his turn, like a good little sir. One by one, events in a divine order would bleed into the day. A little seepage of correctitude, that's all. The noon hour would bring its dose of calm. Thomas would nod at the colleague as she passed him, a weary but confident nod like one of thousands he gifted to people every week. Some mastery would be inferred. A vague suggestion that usually someone would have stood the line for Thomas to get a coffee, but today, why not, let's see what the regular people do, let's build empathy. Oh, who knows, maybe Thomas and the colleague would embrace before she departed the Moors. She'd have to find somewhere to put her coffee, though, or else he'd feel that hot mug on his back and their contact would be queered. There'd be too much caution, and what kind of embrace was that? So there were things to work out, details to finalize. But this would be fine.

Perhaps, if he was lucky, if he survived this test, which is certainly what it was, his heart wouldn't blow out of his chest into the Idea Wall that loomed above the beverage cart. Maybe that was the real meaning of the term *redshift,* thrown endlessly over his head during proof-of-concept meetings: a noiseless exit of the heart from the dehydrated and fat body of a man who was ... Why bother finishing the thought. *Poof.* He could hear the sound his heart would make being sucked clean from its cage of bone and fat. Wasn't this the time when *properly prepared* people had some fatherly advice they could squeeze from their pasts to help them fire hose the crisis, so they could roar with laughter, drink a stein of thick foreign beer, and do something unspeakably gratifying in the backwoods to a small animal? Because every so often it feels good to tear a hot warm thing to pieces. The things our parents taught us, those sage lessons from the older set, or something. *Father always said* . . . but nothing came to him. He cast around in his background, in his memories, in the finer sayings his parents had condescended to share with him, but it felt like he was sticking his hand in a tank of rotted fish.

If he nailed his own head to the Idea Wall, precisely what, uh, idea would he be conveying?

Another bag—or whatever the awful thing was—dropped outside, and Thomas realized he wasn't breathing. A sweet shroud of silence had hazed up moments before the thud, or the crunch, or whatever the name was when something made of flesh hit the asphalt with the acoustical resistance of canvas. In hindsight you always knew you heard something falling, it was sort of what you didn't hear, thought Thomas. He wanted to joke about this, but all he could come up with was *hindsight is . . . not funny.* There was a strangled cry after the thud, and he saw too little of the colleague's face to tell if she was registering this, the hurt, the crunch, the goddamn sound track of cruelty that somehow was getting piped into the lab and that was meant to let them know it was noon.

Oh, right, he thought. This was one of those times when only fat men named Thomas were privileged to hear death sounds. Some special access was in play, but it didn't feel exactly, uh, special. Times like these were Punishment Invention times. Thomas saw himself later that night, or as soon as he could square away the details and *complete the domestic schedule* with June and the child, sitting in a chair at home, pounding one of his hands with a mallet until it finally stopped bleeding and became smeared into the upholstery like gum. The goal was to move beyond the obvious and stereotypical pain of such, uh, appendage hammering, into the prolonged sweetness that came when one's very nerve endings were doted on until they saw light and air for the first time. That will teach me, he thought. That will show me not to stand up and do anything or go anywhere. *Next time you'll think twice before being alive!*

The colleague, no doubt, was not a connoisseur of the self-punishment, sad to think. This type of hygiene was foreign to her, no doubt. How did one even fraternize with people who could not entertain vivid scenarios of self-mutilation? How was the sexual act even possible if one's partner could not entertain being crushed under a truck, even as a cathartic exercise?

What important piece of her brain was missing that deprived her of such, well, deeply necessary acts of *physical editing*?

The colleague powered on at the coffee cart, doing God knows what. From behind she appeared like a giant storybook girl at a table of mind-blowing presents. It was amazing how a teaspoon of professional rank authorized people to dance in your face and publish their happiness with such free dispatch. Thomas guessed that this colleague was an associate something or other. If one day you weren't hourly but salaried, suddenly you radiated joy like one of those children about whom it was politely said had yet to *come into their own* in terms of, uh, showing signs of an inner life. Stupid but happy was how he always saw it, as if there was a difference, and why not, since part of their brains had been sucked free with a crazy straw and everyone pretended the obvious imbecility was some kind of prototype maverick behavior not yet ratified by the schools. The goddamn careful language they used about kids who drooled in a puddle on the floor. And then to have an adult, *the superior colleague,* channeling this moronia, a kind of spokesperson for failure to thrive, even inside her smart pantsuit, which could only accomplish so much mitigation of the, the—he wanted to whisper the word out loud, stage-whisper it—so much mitigation of the *retarded.* The word should be spat, he thought, and spat at her, but that wasn't going to quite convey what he was thinking, was it, and her formal attire was confusing things anyway. Pantsuit as softener of cretinism. Perhaps that was the solution to the clods of the world. Dress them up in business attire. Had she studied that behavior at a conservatory?

Thinking this through, watching the colleague attend to her beverage like it was her final act of love, Thomas wished he could say to himself that he'd reached his limit, that it was too much and so and so, and how could he ever, and oh my (the kind of language he loved to hobby with in private, in soliloquies of indignation), but he regularly found himself capable of bearing ever greater insults and grievances, as if he possessed a sort of highly stretchable orifice through which the transgressions of others readily flowed. He marveled at his tolerance for precisely this kind of massacre. He wanted to bow to the power of the colleague, a lady who could stay in character under even the most extreme forms of pressure. There was a fish he recalled with such accommodating features, a blobby kind that simply ate the mistakes of the sea, and yet he knew there was some kind of virtue, ecologically, to what this fish did. Or didn't there have to be something good here?

When a species disfigures itself in order to conceal a conflict from its mate, turning itself inside out and soaking deeply in the toxins of a terrible dilemma, all the while shielding a loved one from a crisis, that's called . . . Oh, who fucking knows?

This would be his role, and all blessings to the clarity that afforded. Thomas, meet Thomas, he wanted to say: You two should make love tonight. He did not enjoy, at least not fully or not without some regret, picturing himself getting bottomly impaled, but he worked these pictures up in any case, and they were among the more vivid of what he called his mule cartoons. Thomas as mule to the competent, confident, attractive overachievers, with a few middling stragglers as well, who might be surprised to learn that they had been cast as, well, as rapists, really, in Thomas's overworked scenario machine, humping him until he wept, breaking him in half, drop-kicking him off a roof. They shucked his pants and stepped up to his area and they repeatedly defiled him. They shot him, they dumped him in the sea, they led him to alleys where they dug holes and sometimes scraped what was left of him into a pit.

There was an oeuvre of material in these mule cartoons, but no clear way to render it down so others could see it. How *did* one share such imaginings? Thinking himself dead was his special skill, he knew, and maybe the antidote was not to feature his own feelings so heavily, to accord them meaning and weight, since they didn't officially matter (now there was a bit of parental advice he could juice: "No one has to know what you're thinking," a chestnut shared once by his mother after Thomas experimented with an afternoon silence project during what he called his *junior year at home*), because in abstract terms what was so wrong with chancing into a coworker at the coffee cart—*Hi there, Colleague!* some finer version of Thomas might say—and, who knows, sharing a pretty intense bit of quickfire, meant to flush the groins with blood, misting a bit of sex into the air? There were worse places to meet, and couldn't the coffee cart be the best location to lay waste to the awkwardness that interfered whenever Thomas began to smell the possibility of the good, craven congress with unhospitalized women the world had yet to fully pay him?

Never mind the logistics that would make such, hmm, congress unlikely. They were at work, they were fully dressed, they did not specifically know each other, they could not exactly go to his house, because even if Juney wouldn't notice, well, the nurse certainly would. Now, if the colleague were hidden in a sack, for instance, and he lugged her into the house, the nurse would have to personally check the sack, which she would not, and Thomas might then wait for her to depart before releasing the colleague from the sack and, if necessary, working to revive her.

None of this would be very, ha ha, *collegial,* though, would it?

The coffee flushed into the colleague's mug with the violence of an industrial toilet, and then she pivoted to the fixings table. It was a nimble move, adorned with a sweet little grace note that impressed Thomas. She was, in her way, sort of elegant, and the gesture suggested that even late in life they could have sex standing up against the closet door. Was there an overture here? A dip of her shoulder and a slight tilt in the hips, like a kind of curtsy. It was customary, of course, to respond to such flirtation. One flirted back. One did not look cross or bothered, and one certainly didn't *pretend not to notice* that a clear message had been sent, because that suggested a *radar-deficient head,* a head rotted out and insensate. *Not me. Not my head.* He would be alive to the possibilities here. These were bridge gestures from the colleague. They resonated with aching desire. Or if they did not, they should, which is what mattered from a legal perspective, and he could now safely argue that *she initiated the intimacy, sir.* Was there a pose he could strike, so he might reflect his desire back to her and perhaps boost the abstract flirtation into actual congress? A conversion tool was needed. Somewhere a book might instruct him how to flip his mood and adapt. How quickly could a person, without having a stroke, shift from a feverish state of vicious resentment to a soft and vulnerable romantic coquetry?

Underfoot was a carpet the color of absolutely nothing, and in any case Thomas too often found that the shoe-gazing posture—staring at your feet and lost in thought—was a glistening invite to be questioned and entreated or otherwise involved in something quite outside the bounds of one's reasonable and well-earned solitude. Hang that shingle and be fucked, he knew. He would not be caught staring at his feet, and the busy nature of the colleague—the weevil show she had chosen to stage—gave him a perfect spectacle to rubberneck. If he was being watched—*if?*—then he could aver to the instincts of that short-haired, single-toothed animal he had read about, whose eyes will follow motion and color, which was bursting in front of him and which he'd be a fool to ignore (not because what the woman was doing was even *remotely interesting,* but because to overlook the frenzy would seem highly suspicious and, to repeat a phrase from the quarterly review of his performance at work, *dangerously insular).*

It was unfortunate that so much could be learned by watching someone refill her coffee, and he wondered how knowing someone was supposed to help with the basic erotic problem. In mere minutes he had developed knowledge about the colleague that was especially, uh, not without issues. For instance, she was afflicted with a tragic longness nearly everywhere: in the arms, the face, and, most dramatically, the torso, which seemed to require something like a cummerbund—women might have another name for this, no doubt, a catalog-friendly product term that upgraded the sexuality of what was essentially a surgical scarf—to conceal the area that a shirt would normally cover. The concern that seized Thomas was that this kind of garmenting could never be emotionally withstood, in terms of sheer human endurance, falling beyond what he felt he could survive without hurling himself off a roof. It was astonishing how alienating it was—a sash!—because Thomas would have to deal with it if he and the colleague ever became involved in a romantic tishy tash, to untie and fold and place it somewhere, or even, fucking hell, to tie it for her after breakfast under the blank and milky eye of her medically dead father who was wheeled in each morning for cereal as she dashed off to a conference, leaving Thomas behind to clean up her disastrous house which . . . Thomas put a halt to that one, deeply outside of any likely reality, a form of inner travel he excelled at and which at times could yield *useful material worth sharing with the public,* and yet he felt a surge of anger at the colleague in any case, as he stood behind her at the beverage cart, drawing up steam in her shadow. Did it actually matter that those things had not, and would not, happen? And by whose expert accounting? There was good mileage in their remote possibility; this fury could not have been wholly invented, and in the end it was her fault that such a thing could even be *thought.* Her fault entirely. Such was the colleague's power to disturb him, and weren't potential mates meant to be soothing in some regard, rather than provoking such terrible worry so quickly?

Not that he would, or ever could, know, and a Theory of the Ideal Mate was too unbearably something something to pursue. At a certain point, any blood-filled mate with the power of speech would do, but the whole thing was a pipe dream anyway. They were getting coffee at the same time and that was it. Years ago, Juney would have said to him, *Thomas, the sun hasn't come up on that idea yet.* And tucked far back into her smile would be the panic that was soon to permanently seize her mouth. As for the colleague, the sheer monolith of courtship had yet to be scaled, and Thomas understood with a shudder that what courtship mostly entailed these days (throughout known history, perhaps) was the grueling scrutiny of an endless parade of her friends—all of them spoiled somehow, if not by outright poison poured over their faces so their flesh appeared melted and stank of fruit, then spoiled internally, rotted out, and primed to hate anyone who meant to cuddle and leak with their friend. No doubt the colleague's friends festered in a world of private jokes, finished one another's sentences, and turned every courtship into a game of . . . He tried to think of a game involving rifles and children and the race to build coffins. If these friends excelled at something, it was at deliriously liking one another despite all good sense. Just as the world gazed coldly at the moronia steaming off these people, they would close ranks and love one another more fiercely. They would test Thomas's sense of humor, his resilience, his irritability quotient—*off the freaking charts, Colleague!*—and his basic endurance for the most, well, for actually any conversation, because to talk to any of them even beyond the brutality of a shared "hello" would feel like, it would feel . . . Thomas was too tired to call up the specific form of torture—and the notion of producing a metaphor for himself seemed suddenly ludicrous—but he finally saw himself crushed under an iron slab, able to breathe just enough to panic and worry and panic and then finally to die of fear. He'd not survive such a gauntlet, and he could think of far better ways to feel like utter shit than to waddle up to a bar and drag his face through a range of *barely acceptable gestures* with a group of her friends, who may as well have worked over his groin with a hammer and saw.

It would not be a good day for such an examination anyway, even if he had time to go home and change after work. That morning, Thomas had risked the pants that showed everything, darted khakis that could siphon a single drop of pee from his weeping, cold appendage and bloom a fist-sized stain on the fabric before he'd even returned to the seat where he could hide his crotch. Perfect wicking material, his pants. The sweetest feature of his cubicle was that it hid what he called his *little horrible* from the medical scrutiny that was the basic sensory currency at his employ. The true meaning of cubicle: No one can see your crotch. He'd

already wadded a parcel of tissue over the offending eye during
one of his fourteen trips to the bathroom, but that, too, had ultimately proxied a haze of dampness that was already bordered—to
anyone who cared to look—in a ring of what appeared to be salt.
A tide line had seized his pants, and it was a puzzling development. Was there salt in urine? Or, more likely, had something in
his urine cocktailed with the laundry detergent used to clean his
khakis? Thomas himself crotch gazed mostly to avoid eye contact,
a type of connection hugely misunderstood and, to his mind, mis-
used. But crotch gazing brought in important evidence, and why
wouldn't the others in the office have their scopes trained on his?
What a time to be at large in the office and waiting for a big-and-
tall woman to beverage up before he could even get his own drink
and vanish.


A salutation with the colleague's name seemed the best move.
But throughout his six years at the lab, Thomas had been told this
woman's name so many times that in its place all he could summon was a dull sound in his head, chuff chuff chuff, like bone
being scraped with a knife. He could recall the circumstances each
time he had been told her name—where he had been standing,
who had told him her name, and how he had summoned his face
into a gesture of interest until it ached with fatigue, an effort that
occupied him so totally that he failed to do the one thing that
mattered during the transaction—commit this woman's name to
memory. What was the name in biology for species that exhibited
reverse, or was it perverse, learning? Thomas couldn't remember.
Something something. A four-legged, hot-bellied creature that
took the wrong cues and constantly impaled itself, raped by bears,
subject to night weeping. Reversely deducing, was some language Thomas remembered about the thing. But the colleague's

name wouldn't come to him now, just the sound of a body being carved to pieces. He thought he could produce this sound with his mouth if she cheated her face his way, cough it at her, now that she was at the fixings table, and she would have to appreciate how he had renamed her abstractly, a pure word that had never been spoken before. But actually the colleague would have to do no such thing except possibly pretend, as politely as she could, that this hovering man, breathing on her—whose penis, she knew (how could she not?), was abnormally cold, was so preposterously cold in the tip—she would have to pretend that he had not lost control of his body in such close proximity to hers. His sound for this colleague would be beautiful, but it would probably only seem to her as though Thomas had failed to sneeze, or had shat, perhaps, a little. And then he would be marked, and her pity and scorn and indifference—the holy trinity!—would take him back to those great old days with June, before she started getting so tired, when romance consisted of a series of stuttered apologies, parsed out over the course of an agonizing day, breaking her down until a sort of exhausted indifference set in that would allow sex, sometimes, to occur.

The colleague smiled to herself as she performed an inscrutable modification to her drink. Sugar, milk, straws, little sticks. Something that looked like a rubber eraser, waved over the drink? Part of the coffee poured out into the sink when the taste caused her mouth to winch. Renewed administrations, careful sips, exaggerated grimaces and frowns. The colleague responded to her own actions with some kind of overstated mouth semaphore— for whose benefit Thomas didn't know, since she had yet to even stand and face him, fat Thomas the sadness machine, Mr. Thomas Last Name with the blankety blank, Thomas Fuckinstein with a cold Mr. Horrible.

Thomas cheated himself into her sight line. Oh it was a neat

little shuffle, icebreaker number 49. He offered up his eye contact, but the colleague still seemed facially averse. She was perhaps
one of those people said to be in dialogue with herself, preoccu-
pied, super-focused, in deep parallel, enjoying her own company
(something only unbearable people are encouraged to do, when
no one else is capable of being near them), smugly demonstrating
that she was a society unto herself and did not need a mottled,
fat, overdressed, pee-soaked coworker like Thomas to chorus with
because the two of them happened to be getting coffee at the same
time. What so stymied Thomas was that the colleague was hoard-
ing the moment, playing his role for him, leaving him to wobble
blandly behind her and pretend that he was not eavesdropping
on—or even aware of—an encounter he had every right to take
part in. The colleague had effectively split in two and Thomas
had become the third wheel. The anthropology on this seemed
doomed to him. Everyone else in the world may as well die, since
I've got this encounter covered. *Ladies and Gentlemen, now playing
the part of Thomas: the Colleague!* Apparently long ago a contract
had been struck (he pictured her proud, bearded father, young and
strong, with one of those oversized European wallets stitched to
his T-shirt) that compelled her to participate facially in the smallest endeavors. He saw her accepting this responsibility without
agony, signing her name, believing that she had this one licked.
Oh my God, the world is so easy! I can so beautifully do that!

Soon Thomas would be getting his own coffee, and he'd probably throw out his back pressing down the lever on the coffee
thermos. He could possibly stage his own performance to demonstrate his parallel version of grotesque self-sufficiency. If the colleague wanted to destroy him with her publicly antic solitude,
he could huddle with himself and confer over a mock issue, to
demonstrate how athletically committed he was to being by himself, since solitude was a sport, at least as the colleague practiced

it. He could weigh a scenario, for instance—this suggested a possible physical expression—shrugging, hunching, balancing the scales—and would show anyone looking at him—Sully!—that he was so absorbed by his own issues—Look at Thomas! He's lost in thought!—that he had unknowingly begun to dramatize the pros and cons of an argument whose details were elusive to outsiders but clearly important.

Except who really did this but a character in a play—*oh you sad fakers,* or that moron—the Shrugger, was he called?—who showed up now and then in one of Thomas's son's cartoons. *Burned into the screen. A fucking television ghost.* This had led the boy—miracle that he even spoke—for a time to say nothing but "I don't know" for weeks, even when you said Good Morning to him and Good Night and I Love You and Please Stay Out of the Road. It was always "I Don't Know" that he responded with, a small lad in food-stained pajamas, and he spoke it quietly and with so much calm certainty that it was hard not to believe him and hard not to think that this small boy had somehow cornered the market on the perfect response.

Careful, William.

*I don't know.*

Good morning, cutey.

*I don't know.*

Thomas finally decided that if you had to settle on a single phrase and broadcast it in the home until the people around you succumbed and cried uncle, or just cried, not that June could really cry, then this one would do fine. His son didn't know, and that made two of them.

The colleague probably knew, he thought, looking at her. Of course she did. She knew and she knew and she knew, and then some. She knew with enough knowing to burn, and God help you if you're not her, because speaking of cornering the market, she's cornered the market on this. What is that like? he wondered. What is it really like? *Can you tell me, Colleague? Can you tell me what you know?*

It was a thousand years later, and it seemed that a terrible snow had fallen and already melted in the Moors. Creatures had been born and flourished and died and now turned to dust, the last traces of which you could *just see* if you squinted at the very fine air that seemed to be slowing down around Thomas, and then the colleague wheeled around with her coffee and walked right at him.

Thomas looked quickly away, to where there might have been trees growing, the branches stretching out and shading him with little splashes of shadow. In the end, what a pretty place this was. He saw a fine path the sun could take as it rose and set, and the people could crawl from their bloody holes right past his feet and drag themselves over to the watering pool, to drink or die there.

The colleague's face—*where had he seen it before?*—looked so fresh and young and her skin was radiant, as if no one had ever beat her in the head until she wept herself to sleep. She had made it through, one of the few, and here she was to rescue him! A little thrill started to bloom in his chest. *Why wouldn't everyone want to be poisoned by this sweet air?* The dust around Thomas was thickening into a swirl, and he was sure glad it wasn't him sauntering over with such speed and purpose toward the scary man waiting in line. Can't go through him, can't go around him, must go over him: the name of a game his father used to play with him. *Oh to be me right now, for a little while longer.* Birds clustered up from everywhere, it seemed, and he marveled that the colleague could still make such a brave show of things.

Thomas braced himself as she approached, but the colleague was all easy smiles and there was no avoiding this one.

"Hi, Thomas, what's up?"

Of course she knew his name. Of course she did. She bent her head into her cup, sipping and looking up at him as if nothing, nothing, nothing.

There was a luscious chemical in this moment; he felt it in his blood like a great seizing itch. A man would die if he felt like this for too long. *A man would die.* He stood his ground and watched the colleague's face start to register him as he failed to speak. *The face can't hide what it knows!* he wanted to say. *For all of your power, your face is showing me what you think!*

It was true. She was struggling desperately to appear relaxed as she stood in front of him and he didn't respond—*while I stand here melting*—but her eyebrows were worrying their way down and she seemed ever so glad that she could shield her mouth in the mug. *That very same mug. No matter what we've been through, it is a mug that I truly love.*

Her whole face should be bottled, studied, sold. This was a fine mix of feelings: concern tweaked too hard, a game attempt—learned perhaps in an acting class—to show concern, since she must know that she was obliged to show concern here—this man was not speaking, and *oh, those trees*—but she had never been so consciously pressed to exhibit such a shattering dose of concern, probably, and how did one really even do that without getting a shit-crazed angelic look going? This was a woman who was scared out of her mind looking at him.

Maybe it was the air of the Moors that had found its way inside him, because he was filling up with a great ballooning warmth, and this dear woman was offering her face to him, such a fine and well-fashioned face. What did one really ever do with faces? Something was required now, something really special. It was too awful to think that he would not be allowed to take this face home for his very own, to hold it up and gaze at it whenever he felt sad or tired. How good it would feel to cuddle up against this woman, to feel the warmth of that skin and maybe the soft, sweet wind from her mouth that could puff some of the terrible dust away from him. *There are small bits of them, those people who have gone before us, blowing over me. Madame, can you help me?* Could she perhaps be invited to assist here, to shield him with the wind that only her mouth could make? Could it truly hurt to ask, and to ask as a creature new to this world, having crawled free of the trees, new and needing everything she alone could provide?

He pushed out his lower lip and opened his eyes wide and sweet for the capture. He would give her his best and most innocent face.

"Tommy wants cah-weeg to hold him."

There, he'd said it.

Her face went big and long and open. It seemed that she was trying to swallow.

"What?" She lifted her cheeks into a question, and Thomas thought it must feel good to want to know something as badly as that. If only he could speak for her now, to say what she was too afraid to say.

*Mommy needs you to answer now, honey. Please tell me what's wrong.*

It was dark and it was cold and the face looking at him so sweetly, glowing at him, had the most splendid mouth. Too many trees, well, this was what happened, wasn't it: The air turned solid and dark and you couldn't see or do much of anything. He liked trees, of course, they had their place in the world, but this didn't seem right. Trees should be a comfort, not a problem. Whose idea was this, really? June would be quite upset, quite upset indeed. He'd need to get to her and be sure she was okay. Had he left her somewhere safe?

He rather knew this woman looking down on him, smiling, and, he thought, with time he could come to love her, and this would be okay. Would she be taking him home, now?

Thomas was on his back now, and the shade of the great trees felt wonderful.

"*Ho* dmee. Pweese," he said to the woman. "Pweese ho dmee."

There was a cup of water on his desk and a damp cloth in Thomas's hand. The cloth was pressed to his head, and his head felt exquisitely nice. The hand holding the cloth was his very own and it was really a fine hand that you could not complain about. Everything was in order. He was sitting. He was safe. He was holding quite a pleasant damp cloth and he couldn't recall his forehead ever feeling better than now, with this nubby wet washcloth pressed against it. *Smuggle it home. Oh, you must.* He had not thought to press a cool cloth to his head all the time, even if it was awkward to hold it there while walking. He had not thought that he could do this, but really he could, why not, what was stopping him? It felt delicious and perfect. Thomas wondered if the others were on to this. What a first-rate discovery, really. It was sad to think this cloth would dry out someday and begin to chafe and disturb his head. But that was dark thinking. No more of that for me, he thought. This is my time, my time to enjoy. These aren't even small pleasures. They are the largest kind there are.

The building thumped, and a hoarse cry—from deep inside a bag, was it?—sounded. He steadied his cup of water. Oh it could have been anything. Offices make sounds, don't they, and what did he even know about the immense workings of a building like this? Someone must have run the chart on this and checked it out. Of course they had. Clearly it was not for him to worry about. Oh for more of this bait not taken. Where would they store it now that he couldn't be fooled?

Thomas would ride the day out. If he heard something he'd say nothing. He'd do only the fair work on his desk. At five he'd shed the Crawford bibbing in the changing room and slip on his coat and hat. A glass of water would be nice. Perhaps some more water to splash on his face and wake him up for his journey. It'd be good to get home. When the doors shooshed open he'd be swept into the street with the rest of them and he'd tuck into the wind, lean hard against it, and start the long walk back. See you, he'd say, to anyone listening.

With luck, his boy will be waiting at the door when he comes home and Thomas will gather him up and take him inside for his dinner and bath. Tonight he'll sit with the boy over food at the low wooden table he'd once built. There'll be the usual chores and the materials to be readied for tomorrow's trip to work. Everything in the house just so, the surfaces sponged clean with soap, and he'll certainly be sure to remember to lock the door tonight.

It will feel especially good to remove his clothes and pull on his night shorts and sleep shirt. They are soft and always clean and this is an outfit he loves to wear.

Off with the lights downstairs and a story read aloud at the foot of the lad's bed. A story about a horse who is lost for such an incredibly long time. The horse grows old and forgets it was ever lost and the girl who has lost the horse becomes a distracted adult, too busy to say anything nice to anyone. Until one day she is reminded of her horse and she weeps and thinks of the wonderful times she had as a girl. On the day the horse dies, thousands of miles away from her, the girl, a young woman now, stirs in her sleep and suffers a terrible dream.

After he reads the story, a last check of the house and a shush and a kiss to the boy before shutting out his light. His son's eyes will shine for a moment in the darkness, and Thomas will, as is his habit, wait there in the silence of the doorway and listen for a softly whispered "Dad."

And even if June is already in bed and plugged into her machine by the nurse when Thomas comes into the bedroom, well, he will still lower the bed guard, lift the wires, and crawl in next to her, if just for a moment.

When the streetlights sizzle out finally and the cries from his son's room grow quiet, he will take the moment for himself, he will take it and hold it and try not to squeeze so hard that he kills everything that is beautiful about it. These are the most perfect seconds ever delivered to the world, aren't they? It is like someone has packaged them in a soft bag that you can unwrap until they flow over you. Quiet, with cold air, and everyone else so wonderfully hushed, when all you can hear is the far-off singing that has always meant everyone around you, every last creature, is doing fine. What a perfect time it is to be alive, a great time to breathe in the sweet air.

He will hold himself perfectly still next to his sleeping wife and listen so hard it hurts, until all sounds but his own breathing are vanished from the air, and then Thomas will sit up and look at his Juney.

"I missed you today," he will say.

And then Thomas will lean over to kiss his wife good night.

# Acknowledgments

My thanks to the editors and early readers of these stories: Heidi Julavits, Denise Shannon, Deborah Treisman, Jordan Pavlin, Andrew Carlson, Andrew Eisenman, Deb Olin Unferth, Matthew Derby, Rob Spillman, Ben Metcalf, Halimah Marcus, Sumanth Prabhaker, Marty Asher, John Freeman, Ellah Allfrey, and Bradford Morrow.

For insight, generosity, and friendship, thank you to Michael Chabon. Thank you to Sam Lipsyte, for everything. Thanks to Matthew Ritchie and Anne MacDonald, Artspace Books and Madras Press. To Yaddo and the MacDowell Colony, thank you for the space and time. Thank you to Chris Doyle and Michael Sheahan for the most ideal space of all.

To Peter Mendelsund: Thank you for your beautiful work.

A NOTE ABOUT THE AUTHOR

Ben Marcus is the author of three books of fiction: *The Age of Wire and String*, *Notable American Women*, and *The Flame Alphabet*, and he is the editor of *The Anchor Book of New American Short Stories*. His stories have appeared in *Harper's*, *The New Yorker*, *Granta*, *Electric Literature*, *The Paris Review*, *McSweeney's*, *Tin House*, and *Conjunctions*. He has received the Berlin Prize, a Guggenheim fellowship, a Whiting Writers' Award, a National Endowment for the Arts Fellowship in fiction, three Pushcart Prizes, and the Morton Dauwen Zabel Award from the American Academy of Arts and Letters. He lives in New York with his wife and children.

A NOTE ON THE TYPE

The text of this book was set in Bembo, a facsimile of a typeface cut by Francesco Griffo for Aldus Manutius, the celebrated Venetian printer, in 1495. The face was named for Pietro Cardinal Bembo, the author of the small treatise entitled *De Aetna* in which it first appeared. Through the research of Stanley Morison, it is now generally acknowledged that all old-style type designs up to the time of William Caslon can be traced to the Bembo cut.

TYPESET BY

Scribe, Philadelphia, Pennsylvania

PRINTED AND BOUND BY

Berryville Graphics, Berryville, Virginia

DESIGNED BY

Iris Weinstein